I0762098

LONG NOSE LEGACY II

LONG NOSE LEGACY II

A Dog's Story of Fame and Jealousy

J. G. EASTMAN

Character Illustrations by
CHANEL "DEZZOI" SCOTT

ART DECO DOG PUBLISHING

LONG NOSE LEGACY II
A Dog's Story of Fame and Jealousy

Character Illustrations by Chanel "Dezzoi" Scott
Book Design and Art Direction by J. G. Eastman

This book is human authored.

J. G. Eastman | Art Deco Dog Publishing
P.O. Box 193
Moss Beach | CA | 94038
artdecodog@gmail.com

Ordering Information:
This book is available for purchase in the U.S. and internationally
through Ingram, Amazon, other online stores, and retailers.

First Edition

Published by Art Deco Dog Publishing

ISBN 978-1-7323827-5-6 Hardcover
ISBN 978-1-7323827-7-0 Paperback
ISBN 978-1-7323827-9-4 eBook

Library of Congress Control Number: 2018906349

Printed in the United States of America

LongNoseLegacy.com | @LongNoseLegacy

LONG NOSE LEGACY II is endorsed by the BORZOI CLUB OF AMERICA

For Sophia and Stephania
and our/their Borzoi,
Annie and Rosie

Contents

Acknowledgements

Imagine you wrote your first novel and before you could officially launch it, you woke up one morning to find it being shared and promoted online by Borzoi fans all over the world. That happened for my first novel, *Long Nose Legacy: A Dog's Story of Royalty and Loyalty.* And I am so grateful. And I continue to be grateful for my readers who share their love of dogs and heartfelt stories with me. I also appreciate the Borzoi Club of America for endorsing both of my books.

I am thrilled that my first novel's Italian publishers, M-House Editrice in Milan, Italy, perfectly recreated my story in Italian for release in Italy and Switzerland. I will forever be grateful to Charlotte Wheeler and Garnett Thompson who introduced me to Borzoi and opened my heart to a new (albeit fickle and haughty) love.

I especially appreciate the friendship and support of my book launch team—Sherri & Dick Khan, Thom Matson & Hank Stuart, and Kathy & Mike McKim, and to Gilbert Lazzari for purchasing generous quantities of my books to donate to a women's and children's shelter.

I would like to gratefully acknowledge Stephen Kearin, my dear friend and creative partner, who can, with the "flip of a switch," embody Carnegie's endearingly bratty spirit. Together, we discovered there was another story to tell for these privileged Borzoi sisters. I owe him for several delightful passages in this novel. My deep appreciation goes to Jo McGinley for being the charmingly wise voice of Madison for our film project.

I'd like to thank animation film director, Wendy Rogers, who provided so much insight into sister relationships.

A very special thank you to Chanel and Ramslee Scott for their brilliant illustrations of my characters for my books and our film project. This talented duo possesses a rare sense of delightful visual humor in their character drawings that cannot be taught.

My deep gratitude to the incomparable Rafe Chase, whose unlimited talent and impeccable taste inspires me every day. *(No, we're not crazy. We just like things a certain way).* His encouragement and support mean everything.

Thank you to Cathy Faustine for proofing my manuscript, advance readers, Beth Medeiros, Sharlene Cardoza, and Arlene Belvini for their enthusiastic support, Clark Kenyon for his book publishing expertise, Tim Orr and Regina Saisi for their comedic inspiration, fiercely creative Laura Hazlett for fond memories of our Shrine Auditorium show (and many others), Shawne Mastronardi and our dear departed friend and concierge, Rob Rowell, for our New York adventures, Sabeth Ireland for being a creative force, Jamie Ina, DVM and Michael Ina, DVM, and the real—and truly extraordinary photographer—Julie Chase.

Most of all, I must thank my parents for gifting me with the love of animals from an early age, my sons, and my husband, best friend, creative partner, and ruthless (but kind) editor, Glen Eastman.

Borzoi

Means "Swift" in Russian

Once known as the Russian Wolfhound,
Borzoi are sighthounds who are
bred to be swift and tough enough to
pursue and bravely pin ferocious wolves
or to completely takeover your furniture
(and your heart).

The Important Non-Person Characters
of
LONG NOSE LEGACY II

"...according to the ultimate authority, who is *definitely* me," *says Carnegie*

Amazing Gracie (Gracie)

Carnegie's and Madison's mom

Carnegie

Madison

Carnegie
Ike

Madison

Little Puppy (L.P.)

"These two only *think* they're important,"
says Carnegie

Glory and Precious

Carnegie's and Madison's Understudies

Madison and Carnegie

CHAPTER ONE

Fateful Phone Call

D*ing!* The luxurious penthouse's private elevator doors parted, and Borzoi sisters, Carnegie and Madison, blasted out as blurs of long white fur. The foyer table with a tall crystal vase spun around, teetered, and righted itself.

They recklessly slid on the polished marble floors and galloped through the chic living room like it was an equestrian course, jumping over chairs and clearing tables.

At a full-out run, Carnegie artfully snatched a cookie off the kitchen counter. Madison grabbed a lemon, made a sour face, and spit it out.

They raced down a long hallway, trying to beat each other to their bedroom. They leaped from the doorway and landed in their huge faux fur beds at the distant end of the room. They circled three times in unison and dropped like lead weights into the plush pillows.

"So nice to relax at home," Carnegie said, rolling on her back and stretching her long front legs over her head.

"Yeah. This place is pretty nice," Madison agreed…and then sighed.

Carnegie flipped upright. *It's always something with this one*, she said to herself. "What now?" she asked.

"I miss our old house," Madison said. "Don't you miss our big yard with all the trees and things?"

"Look out the window, Maddie. We have a big yard with trees just across the street."

"That's New York's Central Park. I don't think we own it."

"I'm pretty sure if we can see it, it's *ours,*" Carnegie said, confidently.

"Well, we can't see Anastasia," Madison said, starting to lick her right front paw out of anxiety. She snuck a look to see if her sister was watching, then tucked her wet paw out of sight. "I like it better when she shares our bedroom with us."

"She's just away at person obedience school. I thought Ana was already good at sit-stay, though," Carnegie said.

"I think they call it college."

"Whatever. She'll come home a lot. She promised."

Carnegie and Madison had recently moved with their family—eighteen-year-old Anastasia and her parents, Spencer and Catherine Braxton—from an historic mansion on five acres in Upstate New York to an Upper East Side penthouse in Manhattan overlooking Central Park in the heart of New York City. The Braxtons hoped that living across the street from the large park would help Carnegie and Madison adapt to city life.

"I read that Borzoi are good apartment dogs," Ana had said. "As long as they get enough exercise, they're happy to just lie around." She looked over at Madison, who was sprawled out on the sofa with Carnegie, who was using her sister's back as a head pillow.

"Yes, they're definitely good at that," her dad said.

"We'll just have to be sure they get that exercise," her mom added. "You'll be away at college, and your dad and I work. We better look into hiring a dog walker."

"Or a dog runner," Ana said. She went to the sofa and moved Carnegie's limp legs in a running motion. "Look! Exercise while you sleep."

"Somebody could get rich with that one," Spencer said.

Moving to Manhattan proved more life changing than they could have imagined. It started out simply enough—with a phone call from Garnett Dixon, Madison's and Carnegie's breeder.

Garnett had taken their snobby, aristocratic Borzoi mother, Amazing Grace, on an international dog show tour originally planned for Madison. As the pick of Gracie's famous American Royalty litter, Madison was chosen to carry on their kennel's legacy of Grand Champions, and she more than lived up to her noble pedigree. But despite Madison's spectacular show dog fame, she only wanted a simple life at home with her family, so being away for international dog shows was out of the question.

Like her mother, Madison was stunningly beautiful—tall and slender, with long, silky white fur and a pretty black mask, tan eyebrows and cheeks, and a graceful plume of a tail that swept the ground. And, of course, she had the elegantly long—very long—Borzoi nose that is their trademark. Madison also had something very special, all her own—a large black heart marking on her left side, which is the side judges see at dog shows.

Carnegie was nearly Madison's identical twin—just a bit bigger and nine pounds heavier than her sister's seventy pounds. Carnegie attributed this slight plumpness *not* to her extra-large appetite but to extra cuddliness. She, too, had a black heart marking, but it was smaller and on her right side, not on the side that the dog show judges see. Carnegie was the definition of what some call "extra." At her puppy show debut, she chased the other dogs around the ring. And later, as an adult, she pranced around so majestically with her tail high in the air like a royal plume, it was almost comical. Her "extra" personality sabotaged her dream of being a famous show dog—in particular, more famous than her sister. While Madison's career soared, Carnegie's never got off the ground.

At the time they moved to Manhattan, Madison had retired from her winning dog show career. And, although Carnegie never had a career to retire from, she nevertheless believed herself to be the *winningest.*

The Borzoi sisters' lives in their new home were uneventful and carefree—until that fateful phone call…

"Catherine? It's Garnett," she said in her sophisticated Southern drawl. "How are y'all doing?"

"Oh hi, Garnett! We're good. It's great being in the City. Ana loves college and is doing well. She's here this weekend. It seems I still do her laundry."

"No one does it like you, Mom," Ana called from the sofa where she was watching TV with Carnegie and Madison. Catherine shot her daughter a look of fake gratitude for the fake compliment and resumed her conversation.

"So good to hear from you. Are you in town?"

"No. Gracie and I are in London for a few more days…but I didn't think this could wait. I got a call from Josephina Trudeau. She's a Broadway show producer—a famous one—and she said she saw someone walking Madison and Carnegie in Central Park the other day…"

"That would be Henry. He's our dog walker."

"Dog runner, Mom," Ana called out.

"Sorry, Garnett, I've been corrected. Dog runner. Did she see something suspicious? We're all worried about the dognappers that are taking dogs and holding them for ransom. Last week, a pair of little Frenchies disappeared from Central Park. We keep telling Henry to be cautious."

"I read about that. So far, it's been small pedigree dogs, but you can't be too careful. No, thankfully, it isn't anything like that. It's just that your Borzoi girls made quite an impression on the show producer."

"They're a beautiful sight walking together. They always turn heads. But why did she call *you*?"

"She traced Madison to me from the dog shows we've done. There's no shortage of press articles and photos. Madison was quite the dog show star. But here's the surprising part. They want *both* Madison and Carnegie to audition to be in a Broadway musical."

"Our dogs? In a musical?" Catherine asked in amazement. "And they would go to an audition?"

"Yes, at a Broadway theater, no less. And if they get the parts, they'll need to sign on with a talent agency, go to rehearsals, a publicity photo shoot, press engagements, not to mention performing six days a week for the run of the show…"

"This is a *lot*, Garnett," Catherine said, sitting down. "Spencer and I are totally tied up with our jobs."

"You're right. It *is* a lot. My Borzoi have been in films, operas, and fashion shows, so I have experience with agents, negotiating contracts, managing the dogs onsite, and that sort of thing. I guess I'm saying I'd be happy to take most of the responsibility off your hands and be their manager—assuming you all agree, of course. The audition is in three weeks, so we have some time to decide."

"Well, it sounds exciting, and I'm sure Ana would love to see them in a Broadway show…but I'm going to have to talk this over with Spencer."

"Of course. I'll call you when I get back in the States. Give Madison and Carnegie a hug from me. Bye-bye for now."

"Travel safe."

As soon as Catherine hung up, Ana was on her.

"What was that about? Are our dogs going to be in a Broadway show? Are they, Mom?!"

Without waiting for an answer, Ana ran back to Madison and Carnegie and lifted their chins, so their long noses looked especially snooty. "You're going to be Broadway stars!"

"Let's not start tossing bouquets onstage yet. Your dad has to agree. And you know, they have to get the parts."

"Details, Mom."

Later on, when they were alone, Carnegie pawed her sister.

"Did you hear what Ana said?" Her eyes were big and bright with excitement. "We're going to be Broadway stars!"

"Uh-huh," Madison said, looking down. It sounded a lot like being a dog show star, and her paw started to twitch.

"Think about it, Maddie. This is why I didn't waste my time in silly dog shows." Carnegie looked off dramatically and put her paw on her beautifully feathered chest. "I was meant for the stage!"

CHAPTER TWO

Serious Smiling

What are you doing with your lips?" Madison asked, watching Carnegie, who was standing in front of Ana's vanity table mirror.

"Smiling…like a person. Mom taught me, remember? She said the persons love it."

"It looked pretty when she did it. Everything she did was pretty. I miss her, don't you?" Madison said with a sigh. She was getting into one of her melancholy moods, and Carnegie didn't want to encourage it.

"Mom's off being a big international dog show star like you were supposed to be."

"I know, but I like it here with you and Ana and everybody."

"We'll see her soon, I'm sure," Carnegie said. She slowly curled back her lips and wrinkled up her nose.

"How's this look?"

"You're scaring me," Madison said with a grimace.

"No…really? I want to have a winning smile onstage."

Madison regarded her sister's snarly face in the mirror. "Maybe don't show your big pointy teeth so much."

"You mean these?" Carnegie asked, pointing to her long canine fangs.

"Yeah, those."

Carnegie tried a number of smiling variations. They didn't look scary but were not quite as endearing as she imagined.

"You try it now, Maddie."

"I don't think I'm in the mood."

"You don't need to be happy to smile. Just do what I do. Curl your lips back real slow like this…and pop your eyes a little. It looks cute."

Madison tried, but she looked buck-toothed and weird.

"Like this?" Madison asked, her voice distorted because of her curled-back lips.

"No. You look insane," Carnegie said. "Maybe just grin a little and leave the serious smiling to me."

CHAPTER THREE

Dog Acting

Garnett received an enthusiastic "go ahead" from the Braxtons, and now she needed the perfect strategy if Madison and Carnegie were going to land those coveted Broadway roles. The musical was named "Hearts Over Broadway."

It doesn't hurt that both of these beautiful Borzoi girls have heart markings, Garnett thought with a smile.

She learned that there were parts for two tall, elegant hounds. One was to play Olivia, the lead dog, and the other, her unnamed sister, whose character was simply referred to as "Olivia's sister."

The dogs needed to follow basic commands like coming when called by Gabriella—the leading lady and their mistress—heeling alongside her, hitting their marks, and staying when sitting, standing, or lying down.

Olivia's role also had some emotional acting where she empathized with Gabriella, who alternated between being head-over-heels in love with Vincente, the leading man, and end-of-the-world lovesick. For these scenes, Olivia's sister accompanied her on and offstage but mostly stayed in the background as a lovely, live set piece.

As with any big theatrical production, there would be bright lights, moving scenery, and curtains to which they had to get accustomed. Add singing and dancing, loud music, and a cheering audience, and it would require tremendous focus and discipline for the dog actors to not get distracted.

Well, we do love a challenge, Garnett said to herself with a laugh.

Why didn't I breed Border Collies?

As Garnett knew all too well, Borzoi are highly intelligent sighthounds but are notorious for not slavishly following directions. Their aristocratic breeding to hunt in pairs, independent of their "owners," makes them feel equal, if not superior. They don't take the human concept of obedience all that seriously.

Madison and Carnegie only had two weeks to learn the dog acting basics. When Garnett arrived at the Braxton's penthouse, she put wildlife shows on the television, played a lively Broadway musical soundtrack, and opened the windows for street sounds. She hoped that rehearsing with background action and noise might help them learn to ignore distractions on the theater stage.

Garnett sat on the sofa's edge and studied the sisters lying on the silk carpet in front of her. Carnegie was staring at her intensely, sensing an opportunity for a treat. She was overly food-motivated and overly enthusiastic about nearly everything—especially if it was all about her.

And then there was naturally perfect Madison, lying in a sphinx position with her head on her paws. She was overly sensitive and shy and couldn't care less about treats or being the center of attention—the total opposite of her showboat sister. Considering their personalities, Garnett sized up Carnegie as most likely to play the lead.

"Okay, girls," Garnett said with an encouraging smile. "You're going to learn to be actors."

She pulled out some dehydrated liver treats that she knew most dogs loved. Carnegie's ears perked up. Madison looked up at her with minimal interest.

"Stand!" she said and stood herself. Carnegie jumped to her feet, but Madison didn't move. "Come on, Madison, you did this for all your dog shows."

Madison reluctantly rose. Garnett awarded them both with treats. Afraid of accidentally biting Garnett, Madison didn't close her mouth, and her treat fell to the floor. Carnegie instantly dove on her sister's treat and devoured it. Garnett sighed and gave Madison another treat, placing it in her mouth.

Carnegie had the makings of a model student, provided the proper treats came her way. She would soon grow bored with the dehydrated liver bits, and Garnett would have to up the treat value to chunks of grilled steak. Madison needed continual coaxing and verbal praise rather than treats.

They already knew how to heel on a leash, so Garnett worked with them healing off-leash, and they did surprisingly well. Of course, there were no squirrels or bunnies in sight that could kick in their prey drive. For a Borzoi, chasing little creatures is irresistible and an absolute priority—a fact some owners don't fully comprehend until their dog, who suddenly took off at thirty-five miles per hour, is nothing but a dot in the distance.

Being highly visual, Carnegie and Madison caught on quickly to the hand signals for the standard commands that would likely be used onstage. For the happy scenes, Garnett taught them to jump for joy. For the sad scenes, to sit and put their paws on her lap and look up sympathetically. As one might guess, Carnegie excelled at the jumping and Madison at the sympathy.

The big challenge was sit-stay—sitting on a marked spot for an extended time. Once Garnett was out of sight, they left their marks to find her. Their conversations went something like this:

"Where'd Garnett go?"

"I don't know. We better go see."

And

"Garnett left with the treats."

"Oh no! We have to find her."

And

"Do you think Garnett went home?"

"How rude. She didn't even say goodbye."

"I guess we're done. Let's go."

It went on like this for days but, finally, there was a breakthrough, and Garnett was happily surprised that after leaving the room for three minutes, she returned to find her dog actor students sitting exactly where she left them.

"Wow! I think you're ready, girls!" Garnett exclaimed. "One last thing…"

As puppies, they had learned from their mother, Gracie, how to do the most charming bow—like a downward dog yoga pose—with their elbows down on the floor and their fluffy rear ends up. Garnett had them face each other, Carnegie on the left, Madison on the right, so when they bowed, both of their heart markings would be visible to the audience. Lastly, she taught them a "V for Victory" hand signal to bow in unison and planned to use it at the end of their audition. "It's our secret weapon," Garnett whispered, winking at them.

After their last practice session with Garnett, the sisters retired to their beds. They circled three times and dropped into the fluffy pillows.

"That acting stuff was pretty difficult," Carnegie said.

"The standing wasn't bad," Madison said. "I'm used to that for dog shows, and she didn't look at my teeth like all those judges did."

"I liked the lying down part best," Carnegie said. "But that sit-stay stuff is super hard to do."

"I know," Madison agreed. "Do you think Ana's college is this hard?"

"No way," Carnegie replied.

CHAPTER FOUR

The Audition

And...from the top...five, six, seven, eight!" the burly show choreographer shouted over the piano and stomping chorus line. "Step, step, step-kick, step-kick, turn, turn! Guy in the hat in the back row—you're late! I need more energy, people!"

Shivering with excitement, Carnegie pawed at the wood stage floor and pulled on her leash, trying to run onstage.

"Settle down, Carnegie," Garnett whispered in her ear. "They're not looking for dancing dogs. We need to wait here in the wings until they call us to audition."

Madison, with her telltale wet paw, leaned against Garnett's legs. Garnett reassuringly petted her head. "You're a showbiz pro, sweetie. This'll be easy."

Madison looked up at her with unsure eyes. I wish I could be confident like Carnegie, she thought. And talented. I bet she could dance if they let her.

The director, a tall, stick-slender woman named Florence Florenti, suddenly stood in the third row of the nearly empty theater. Dressed head-to-toe in black, only her pale face was visible in the darkened house, giving her an unpleasant vampire appearance. She shouted to the exhausted but hopeful chorus dancers, "Thank you! Your agents will hear from us."

Florence turned to the assistant director seated next to her. "Ernesto, let's get the hounds onstage." And then to anyone within earshot, "Where's Ruby? Someone tell her the dogs are up."

Ernesto took the stage with a clipboard and, using it to shade his eyes from the stage lights, addressed Florence, who had resumed sitting in the house. "We've got four each of Afghan Hounds, Saluki, and Borzoi. What order do you want them in?"

"Doesn't really matter," Florence replied. "Go ahead and bring out the Afghans."

Ernesto turned to the wing. "When I call your dogs' names, please form a line onstage with them. Let's see Afghan Hounds Maggie, Misty, Moxie, and Maybelline."

Led by their manager, the huge, long-haired Afghans lightly bounced onto the stage with their thin tails carried in a high curve.

"Let's have the Salukis next," Ernesto called. "Garbo, Gwendolyn, Greta, and Gazelle." The silky, paper-thin Salukis pranced after their manager and lined up next to the Afghans.

"We've got two pairs of Borzoi with different managers," Ernesto called out to Florence, whose pale face nodded in the darkness.

When Ernesto said, "Let's have Madison and Carnegie first," their hearts beat faster hearing their names called out.

"Let's go, girls," Garnett quietly said to them, "This is it!"

Side-by-side, in perfect unison, Madison and Carnegie elegantly glided onstage, led by petite and graceful Garnett, who was an expert at making her Borzoi shine. She thought she heard an appreciative gasp but didn't want to get her hopes up. Standing onstage, the sisters' long, flowing coats glistened in the stage lights—the result of superb genetics and skilled grooming.

Madison looked down the lineup and whispered to Carnegie. "I've seen some of these dogs."

"Where?" Carnegie asked in a too-loud dog voice that came across as a bark.

"*Shh,*" shushed Madison while Garnett shot Carnegie a stern look.

"At the park?" whispered Carnegie.

Madison shook her head. "At dog shows."

"Do you want to go say 'hello?'"

"We're supposed to stay in line. Besides, I doubt they'll recognize me. We were in different groups."

Ernesto referenced his clipboard and called out, "These are the last two Borzoi, Florence." Turning to the wing, "Can we have Glory and Precious onstage?"

Suddenly, Madison put her head down. "Oh no. Don't look!"

Carnegie immediately looked and saw a red and white Borzoi and a cream and white Borzoi following their manager, Randy, to join the lineup. They both glared at her.

"I told you not to look!" Madison whispered.

"I had to see what *not* to look at," Carnegie whispered back. "They don't look very friendly."

"No, I won all the shows we entered. I don't think they like me."

Carnegie couldn't resist looking again and was met with snarls.

"They have pretty white teeth."

"Stop looking!" Madison insisted.

Ernesto lowered his clipboard and addressed the group.

"First of all, if your dogs are standing on this stage—congratulations—you're part of a select group. We started out with photographs of around sixty dogs and narrowed it down to you twelve for this audition. I'm sure you noticed that there are four of each breed. That's because there are two roles and two understudies. We'd like all four dogs to be the same breed, but it's going to come down to their performances and chemistry with our lead actress—so we could do a mix-and-match. We'll just have to see how it goes.

"Before we get started with the auditions, we'd like you to know that we will have a representative from the Animal Humane Society here at all times and at all theater events when animals are involved. Not that any of your dogs have or ever will be mistreated," Ernesto added with a smile.

"You mean like, 'No animals were harmed in the making of this musical?'" Randy asked with a smug laugh.

"Exactly," Ernesto said seriously, staring directly at Randy, who responded with another laugh that sounded more like a snort.

A commotion stage left, where Ruby, the animal acting coach, was making an entrance, took the uncomfortable attention off of Randy.

"Hey, perfect timing," Ernesto greeted her.

Ruby wasn't trying to be theatrical, but with her piled-high cherry Kool-Aid color hair, she made a dramatic entrance wherever she went.

"Hey, kids!" she said, smiling and walking down the line of dogs. "Impressive lineup!"

"Yeah, we think so," Ernesto replied. "Everyone, this is Ruby Taylor. She'll be working closely with our dog actors to teach them their roles. And she'll be the one giving them cues during the rehearsals and performances."

"Sighthounds, huh?" Ruby said with a smirk. "I know you think you're smarter than us humans—and maybe you are—but we're going to learn to work together. And you know what? We're gonna have a *lot* of fun."

She turned to Ernesto. "Let's *only* have the dogs on the stage now, please."

Ernesto instructed the managers to exit the stage and sit in the sixth row, three rows behind Florence. Before leaving, Garnett snuck kisses on Carnegie's and Madison's ears and whispered, "You're on your own now, but don't worry, you'll be perfect! I'll be right out there watching, and there's cookies when we get home."

Suddenly, Moxie broke out of the lineup and bounded after her manager who was leaving the stage, practically knocking him down.

"That's not good," Madison whispered to Carnegie.

"Uh-uh," Carnegie whispered back. "No cookies for that one."

Ruby calmly went after the Afghan, took her leash, and guided her back in line. Moxie stayed in place but whined in a painfully high pitch. Ruby gave her a "look," and she instantly stopped. The dogs were about to learn that Ruby was not like their manager or their mom or dad. She had a quiet but strong authority that dogs instinctively understood.

"Sit," Ruby said, making a hand motion.

The lineup all sat.

She went through all the basic commands using hand signals and then went down the line, handing out treats. When Ruby came to Madison, she was afraid of accidentally biting her, so she barely closed her mouth. Madison's treat fell on the floor in front of Carnegie who started to dive on it.

"Leave it," Ruby said in her quiet, no-nonsense manner. Carnegie froze near mid-air and let Madison's treat lay there.

Oh, but it was turkey jerky! One of the favorites! And it was calling to her!

When Ruby turned her back, Carnegie tried to stealthily reach the treat with her paw. A threatening "*GRRRR!*" came from her right side. She pulled back her paw as Glory lunged out and snatched the treat.

"Drop it!" Ruby abruptly turned around and approached Glory, who guiltily let the half-eaten treat fall from her mouth.

Ruby pointed to the treat on the floor. "See this, everyone? Leave it! At the end of the day, I want to see this turkey jerky still laying there."

Carnegie dared not to look, but she could feel Glory's eyes shooting daggers at her, blaming her for the lost treat and reprimand.

"I don't think she likes you either," Madison whispered.

"No," Carnegie agreed, scooting towards her sister to get further from Glory. "I hope this isn't Ruby's idea of *a lot of fun*."

Ruby continued working with the dogs, this time in pairs, while the others had to stay lying down. Waiting for their turn, Carnegie quietly remarked to Madison, "This is *soooo* boring."

"I'm too nervous to be bored," Madison whispered back.

"Don't be. I'm going to play the lead, and you'll play my sister. You already know how to do that. It'll be easy."

"Are you sure?" asked Madison.

"Of course."

When their turn came, Carnegie and Madison followed Ruby's commands perfectly. Watching from the audience, Garnett couldn't help but admire the pair. I may be biased, she thought, but these girls have star quality.

She wasn't alone in her thinking. In the darkness, she watched Florence and Ernesto, who had resumed his seat three rows ahead of her. Whenever Madison and Carnegie moved on the stage, the two exchanged comments, and Ernesto jotted something down.

After the last pair of hounds took their turn, Ernesto returned to the stage. "Can we have all the managers join their dogs onstage and leash them up, please?"

There was a happy reunion between the managers and their dogs as if a week had passed instead of an hour. Carnegie and Madison both excitedly greeted Garnett and started to bow. She quickly held up her hand. "Let's save that," she said, smiling and winking at them.

"If I call your dog's name, please step forward," said Ernesto, looking down at his clipboard.

"Afghans Maggie, Misty, Moxie, and Maybelline. Salukis Garbo, Gwendolyn, Greta, and Gazelle."

Garnett's shoulders sunk in disappointment at not being called and she petted Madison, who was leaning on her. Madison, in turn, whispered to Carnegie, "I don't think they picked us."

Out of the darkness, Florence stood in the audience. "Front line, your dogs are all lovely, but we're going in a different direction this time. Ernesto has 'thank you' doggie treat bags to take on your way out. Back line, we'll see you tomorrow at nine a.m."

Ruby applauded the remaining four Borzoi and their managers. "Good work, everyone! Gabriella, our lead actress, will be here tomorrow, and she's looking forward to meeting you. Get some rest, and we'll see you back here onstage...bright-eyed and bushy-tailed."

"You did it! We got a callback!" Garnett said to Madison and Carnegie, who wagged their long tails in response to her excitement.

Carnegie looked to see who else would be returning. Glory and Precious narrowed their eyes and snarled at her.

"And we've got company," she whispered to Madison.

"I know," Madison replied, nervously wanting to lick her paw.

As they filed offstage, Carnegie suddenly ran back, nearly jerking Garnett off her feet. "What are you doing, silly girl? It's time to go home for cookies!"

Carnegie rejoined Garnett and Madison and smugly trotted past Glory, licking her lips. And when Ruby checked the stage, the turkey jerky treat was gone.

CHAPTER FIVE

Today, I Become a Star!

Maddie! Maddie! Wake up! Madison! Maddie! MADISON!" Carnegie loudly whispered in her sister's face. Madison slowly opened her eyelids to see a big blurry close-up of Carnegie's wide-open eyes.

"Look! I'm bright-eyed!"

Carnegie jumped back, circled around, and shook her long, fluffy tail at her sister. "And bushy-tailed!"

"*Mm-mmm…*" Madison closed her eyes.

Carnegie shook her sister back and forth with her paw.

"How can you sleep?"

"It seems I can't."

"Madison! Today's the day! The day I'm given the lead role… Olivia! What a lovely name for a star!" She dramatically strutted back and forth in front of Madison's bed.

"You'll be perfect as Olivia, Carnegie."

Carnegie continued her strutting. "I know! And I'll be famous! Way more famous than a silly show dog. Think about it, Maddie… My name in lights!" She sat and waved her paw across an invisible theater marquee in the sky. "STARRING CARNEGIE as Olivia! And Madison as Olivia's sister. You'll be *almost* as famous as me."

"That will be nice," said Madison with a sweet grin.

Carnegie's instinct was partially right. Today was the day that the roles of Olivia and her sister would be cast. The other two dogs would be their understudies. They would learn the roles but only get a chance to perform if the chosen dogs were unable to.

At nine a.m. sharp, Garnett led her aspiring actors onstage. Precious and Glory were already there with Randy. Madison and Carnegie tried to ignore being greeted by Glory snarling and growling at them.

"Someone got up on the wrong side of the bed this morning," Carnegie whispered in an aside to Madison.

Ruby suddenly came to the stage from the audience. She walked over and stood in front of Glory and studied her, then turned to Randy.

"We don't tolerate any aggression."

"S-s-sorry," Randy stammered. "Did I do something wrong?"

"I meant your dog," she replied, giving him a questioning look.

Taking a lighter tone, Ruby addressed both Randy and Garnett. "Good morning. This is an important day. We hope to cast our dog actors in their roles."

Carnegie excitedly whispered into Madison's ear, "See, what did I tell you? Today, I become a star!"

Madison responded with a little grin.

"And to help with our casting," Ruby continued, "I'm pleased to introduce you to Gabriella, our leading lady, played by Broadway superstar Mandi Marin!"

When Mandi walked onstage, she naturally lit it up. Even though she was casually dressed in jeans and a pullover sweater, she had undeniable star power.

Wow, she's so pretty! Madison thought. I hope she likes me.

My co-star! Carnegie said to herself. I hope *I* like *her*.

"Hello, everyone. I'm so happy to meet you all. Like Ruby said, my name is Mandi Marin, but since we don't want our dog actors to get confused, please just call me Gabriella for the run of the show. Now, I'd like to meet these beautiful Borzoi!"

Gabriella walked up to Randy first, who was suddenly starstruck. He fumbled with his dogs' leashes, tangling them up while awkwardly trying to shake her hand.

"Hi, Mandi. I'm Randy McCormick. Hey, funny…our names rhyme," he said with an uncomfortable laugh. "I mean our first names. You know, Randy and Mandi. Sorry. I forgot I'm not supposed to call you Mandi around the dogs. S-sorry, I just did it again. I mean Gabriella. I'm a big, big fan of yours, you know, as Mandi. I don't mean I won't be a fan of Gabriella, uhh…"

Trying to recover his composure, he pointed a shaky finger towards the cream and white Borzoi.

"This is the beautiful Glory. No, sorry, I mean Precious. This one…" He pointed towards the red and white Borzoi. "This is Glory. Precious is the other one I called Glory, but…" his voice trailed off hopelessly.

"Anyway, they're prize-winning *s-s*-show dogs," Randy stammered, ready to collapse from nerves and embarrassment.

"They're both beautiful," Gabriella said with a kindhearted grin, not having a clue who was who. She petted their heads and moved on to Garnett.

"Hello there!" Garnett greeted Gabriella with her signature Southern charm. "I'm Garnett Dixon, and this is Madison and Carnegie from my American Royalty litter. They're…"

"You don't have to tell me," Gabriella interrupted with a smile. "I've watched your famous Madison on televised dog shows, and I've seen her sister, too."

"Girls, say hello to Miss Gabriella," Garnett said.

Madison and Carnegie both sat and raised their right paws to shake hands.

"How sweet!" Gabriella said, reaching out her hand to each of them."

"Looks like we're all acquainted," Ruby called to Ernesto, who was seated in the audience next to Florence.

"Okay, great," Ernesto called out. "Managers, please say goodbye to your dogs for now and take your seats in the audience like yesterday. Thank you."

Garnett leaned over and gave the sisters a quick kiss before leaving and whispered, "Remember our secret weapon. Look for me in the audience when they say you're all done."

Precious and Glory were nearer to center stage, where Gabriella was standing, so Brad, the stage manager, decided they would audition first. Ruby told them to stay and led Carnegie and Madison offstage. She handed their leashes to two enthusiastic young girls, Amelia and Lily, who were theater volunteers assigned to help "wrangle" the dogs when they were not performing.

"This is Carnegie and Madison," Ruby said. "Please keep them here until it's their turn to audition."

"Ooh, we will! They're so pretty!" Lily said.

The girls hugged and petted and kissed the Borzoi sisters, trading between the two because they couldn't decide who was the "most cuddly." A quick comparison of the soft fat padding on their ribcages would have awarded the title to Carnegie, whose obsession with treats gave her a cuddliness edge on Madison.

When Ruby came back onstage, she found Precious standing exactly as she left her, but Glory was now intensely focused on Carnegie and Madison in the wings. "Leave it," she said, diverting her attention back onto the stage.

"Shall we start with Precious?" Ruby asked Florence.

"Yes, that's fine," she responded.

Ruby handed Precious' leash to Gabriella and stood with Glory off to the side where they could watch but not be in the way. The first test was for Precious to heel on leash alongside Gabriella as she joyfully sang and danced around the stage. After that, she advanced to following Gabriella's same routine, but this time, heeling off-leash, which is significantly more difficult. Ruby then exchanged the dogs, and it was Glory's turn to heel on and off-leash. Both performed well, and Randy, who was nervously watching from the edge of his seat, squirmed in delight.

Garnett reached across the seat separating her from Randy and tapped him on the shoulder. He jumped and turned to her in alarm.

"Agh!" he cried out. "Wha-what's happening?!"

"Sorry," she said quietly. "I just wanted to say, 'nicely done.'"

"Oh, okay, thanks," Randy replied, wiping his sweaty palms on his slacks.

In the darkness, three rows ahead of them, Florence called out, "Let's try Gabriella's 'heartbreak' scene."

Two stagehands carried out a velvet chaise lounge and placed it center stage under a dramatically focused light. Gabriella walked into the light, gracefully sat, and gestured for Precious to come to her. Precious was well-behaved but just stared at Gabriella blankly while she lamented about her lost love.

When it was Glory's turn, she got bored and looked around for something more interesting to do…but they both stayed in their places. Watching their disconnected performances, Garnett hoped that the emotional rehearsing they'd done at home would pay off.

"Lights up, please," Florence called from the audience, then addressed the stage.

"Thank you, Glory. Ruby, please bring Precious back." She brought her to center stage and had her stand next to Glory.

"Well done, both of you," said Florence. "They can leave the stage for now, Ruby. Let's have Madison and Carnegie, please."

Gabriella praised Precious and Glory and petted them as Ruby clipped on their leashes, then walked them over to Amelia and Lily.

"Time to say goodbye to your new best friends. We're swapping out the dogs."

"Aww," the girls cried in unison, hugging Carnegie and Madison farewell. Ruby took their leashes and began to lead the sisters on-stage. Madison immediately followed, but Carnegie didn't budge.

"Carnegie, come. Come on!" Ruby coaxed. She tugged again on her leash. Carnegie looked at her with pleading eyes but stayed planted.

"Can we please have Madison and Carnegie onstage?" Florence called out again.

Garnett stood in the audience with concern, hoping they didn't develop stage fright.

Oh no! Is my sister afraid? Madison wondered, starting to feel fearful herself.

"Look!" Lily cried. "Glory is standing on Carnegie's tail!"

"So that's it! Well, their tails are awfully long. You can see how this could happen," Ruby said. "Amelia, lift Glory's foot."

Determined not to move, Glory shifted her entire weight onto her front leg that was pinning Carnegie's tail to the floor.

"She's way too heavy! Help me, Lily!"

"What's going on, Ruby?" Florence called out. Garnett gripped the back of the seat in front of her, feeling anxious and helpless.

"Hurry, girls!" Ruby urged.

Amelia and Lily worked at tilting Glory and finally were able to bend her knee so Carnegie's tail could be released. Several strands of Carnegie's long white tail feathers were left behind in Glory's toenails.

"Let's not let that happen again," Ruby cautioned the girls. "It would be disastrous if any of the dogs missed their cues because of a preventable mistake."

She called out to Florence, "Coming! Just a little mix-up."

Trotting onstage, Carnegie angrily whispered to Madison, "That 'little mix-up' *wasn't* a mistake."

Madison responded with a sympathetic look and whispered, "Sometimes Glory is not very nice."

"*Not very nice?!* I thought she was going to rip my tail off!"

Ruby brought the sisters to center stage where Gabriella was waiting. Carnegie started to smile hugely when Madison nudged her.

"Less big pointy teeth," she whispered. Carnegie tempered her smile into her most charming, non-scary rendition.

"Oh, look! She's smiling at me!" Gabriella cried, happily surprised by Carnegie's greeting. "Madison, can you smile too?"

Madison did her best, which was a cute, distorted grin.

Gabriella clasped her hands in delight. It's fair to say that for this audition, Carnegie and Madison had Gabriella "at hello."

CHAPTER SIX

Horrid Little Moth

Brad, the stage manager, addressed the sisters. "Who wants to audition first?"

Carnegie stepped forward while Madison took a step backward.

"Well, I didn't *really* expect an answer to that question," he said with a laugh. "But clearly, it's Carnegie. Okay, girl, let's see if you can match your mistress' mood."

Ruby handed over Carnegie's leash to Gabriella and moved aside with Madison. Gabriella held Carnegie's leash loosely and looked down at her with a huge smile. "This is a happy scene!"

It wasn't exactly a happy scene in the audience. Garnett had been relieved when the sisters finally came onstage, but now it was *her* turn to sit on the edge of her seat. I'm making *Randy* look calm, she said to herself. Settle down, or Carnegie will sense your anxiety. She took a deep breath, slid back in her seat, and tried to relax.

Moments later, the music started and Gabriella took off singing and dancing. Carnegie followed along, keeping at a good distance. Suddenly, she broke into fancy little steps that almost matched Gabriella's dancing.

She *can* dance! I knew it, Madison said to herself, watching her sister proudly.

Florence and Ernesto exchanged amazed looks. "That's perfect! Make a note to add dance steps to Olivia's choreography," Florence said. "Hopefully, whichever dog gets the part can do something similar."

"Let's see this without the leash," Florence called out.

Gabriella walked them back to the starting position.

"Okay, Carnegie, let's go again."

I thought that went pretty well, Carnegie said to herself, but if my co-star needs another go at it, I suppose we can make a few little improvements.

Carnegie felt her leash be unclipped. That's a good start, she thought. That thing was really hindering my style.

The music restarted, and Gabriella took off singing and dancing again. Initially, Carnegie followed along like when she was on leash, but her fancy little steps quickly escalated to a ridiculous "dance," if one could call it that, with her legs swinging in every direction. Her wild footwork not only upstaged Gabriella, it nearly tripped her several times.

Florence grimaced and looked at Ernesto. "That's a bit much."

"I'll say." He raised his eyebrows and made a notation on his clipboard.

Oh dear! Garnett said to herself, wishing she had a "volume control" for Carnegie's enthusiasm. She felt a tap on her shoulder and turned to see Randy smiling at her smugly. "Nicely done."

Garnett smiled flatly in response, trying to hide her annoyance. She had genuinely complimented his dogs' performances. She had not pegged Randy as being petty. A nervous wreck, yes, but not petty.

"Do you want to see Madison now?" Brad asked Florence from the stage.

"No, let's finish up Carnegie's audition," Florence replied. "Move on to Gabriella's 'heartbreak' scene, please."

The general stage lights dimmed and dramatically focused on the center stage chaise lounge. Gabriella sat and then gestured to Carnegie to join her. She trotted over and sat at Gabriella's knees. Remembering their emotional rehearsing with Garnett, she put her paws in Gabriella's lap and looked up at her.

"That's sweet," Florence commented to Ernesto.

"Yeah," he replied. "Maybe she can redeem herself."

Please, *please*, Carnegie! Garnett silently pleaded. This isn't your strong suit, but you can do it, girl.

Carnegie stayed in position watching Gabriella croon on about her lost love and was on her best behavior. Garnett breathed a sigh of relief, and Florence and Ernesto exchanged looks of approval. Carnegie's performance was picture-perfect…right up until a tiny little moth fluttered down from the overhead lights and landed on the tip of her upturned nose.

I'm not going to share the spotlight with this horrid little thing! she said to herself. Looking down the length of her long nose, she tried reaching the moth with her tongue, but it was out of range. She wiggled her nose to try to shake it off. The moth responded with a tickly and torturous little dance. The more she licked and wiggled, the more the moth irritatingly frolicked.

Abruptly, Gabriella stopped singing and burst out laughing.

"Cut!" Florence called out to the musicians in the orchestra pit, who instantly stopped playing. She addressed Gabriella. "What's going on? Why the laughter?"

"Sorry! I couldn't help it. Carnegie is making the funniest faces at me," Gabriella replied with a huge smile. "Her eyes are crossed, she's sticking out her tongue, and wiggling her nose."

"That's a first," said Florence with an incredulous laugh. "Alright then. I think we've seen enough of Carnegie. Let's give Madison a go."

Garnett could sense Randy sarcastically smiling at her in the darkness. Oh, Carnegie, what on earth…? she lamented to herself with a sigh.

"See you later, funny girl." Gabriella kissed the top of Carnegie's head before releasing her to Ruby, who was upstage with Madison.

Carnegie proudly strutted over and whispered to her sister, "Crushed it!"

Madison didn't know for sure, but she sensed that something

didn't go quite so well with Carnegie's performance.

Ruby told Carnegie to stay. She led Madison over to Gabriella, who greeted her with an encouraging smile and took her leash. "Hello, sweet girl."

Madison looked up at Gabriella in awe. She's so pretty and talented. And suddenly, the pressure of the audition hit her. Garnett is watching me, out there with those people in the dark. And Carnegie. I don't want to let them down, she thought. She made the mistake of looking offstage where Glory and Precious were angrily focused on her. Their snarls stood out in the darkness.

Carnegie was right, Madison thought with a shudder. They *do* have white teeth. Her mind wandered back to her highly competitive dog shows. The thrill of winning and pleasing Garnett. The jealousy and hostility she felt from the other competing dogs and even some of their owners. Her paw twitched, and she longed to lick her anxiety away.

"Madison?" Gabriella's sweet voice snapped her back to the moment. "Are you ready?" She led her to their starting position. "This is one of our happy scenes."

The music started and Gabriella began to joyfully sing and dance. Madison remembered how Carnegie danced alongside her. I can't dance good like my sister, she thought, but I can try.

She watched Gabriella's steps and tried to match her own little footsteps to dance like Carnegie had done. She surprised herself by how natural it felt to move to the music and to replicate Gabriella's joyful mood.

In the audience, Ernesto turned to Florence. "Well, look at that. Dancing talent must run in their family."

"Not quite as elaborate as her sister's dancing," Florence replied. "But, hopefully, not as crazy either." She called out to the stage. "Let's see her off-leash, please."

Madison felt her leash be unclipped and looked up at Gabriella with uncertain eyes. She smiled back with reassurance and said, "Come on, Madison, let's do this again, exactly like the last time."

Garnett held her breath, praying that Madison would not copy Carnegie's wild off-leash dancing. But, to her delight, Madison repeated her performance as if an invisible leash connected her to Gabriella.

"Good girl!" Gabriella petted her head at the end of their dance run.

She's so nice. I *love* her, Madison thought, gently wagging her long tail in response.

Florence called from the audience. "Let's see the 'heartbreak' scene, please."

The general stage lights dimmed, and Gabriella walked to the dramatically-lit chaise lounge at center stage. She seated herself and gestured for Madison to come. Madison loped over and sat at Gabriella's feet, then put her paws on her lap like Garnett taught her and Carnegie had done.

But then something truly magical happened—When Madison and Gabriella looked into each other's eyes, they saw into each other's hearts. As Gabriella sang her sorrowful melody, Madison's soft, dark amber eyes reflected her pain and, suddenly, it felt real. They were no longer on a theater stage, and there was no one watching in the audience. Spotlit and surrounded by darkness, it was just the two of them in the world, deeply connected by love and heartbreak. When tears streamed down Gabriella's cheeks, Madison let out a soft, sympathetic "*AAAWWOOOooo*" howl that almost harmonized with the notes her co-star was singing...and the entire theater was stunned into silence.

Gabriella ended the song by sadly smiling and kissing Madison on the tip of her long nose. In return, Madison stood and kissed Gabriella, licking her tear-streaked cheeks, and everyone—with the exception of Randy—wildly applauded.

"Wow!" Ernesto remarked to Florence in disbelief.

"I know," she replied, rubbing her arms. "I've got goosebumps. I think we're done with the auditions. Would you agree?"

"Absolutely!" Ernesto said.

"Oh…and make a note to add Olivia 'singing' to this scene—and maybe some other ones. It would be spectacular if that's something our lead dog can consistently deliver."

"It'd be a showstopper for sure," Ernesto agreed.

Florence stood and called for the lights to be brought up, then addressed the stage. "Thank you, Madison. Ruby, please bring Carnegie back."

Carnegie pranced to center stage and took her place next to her sister.

"Well done, you two," Florence called out as Garnett quickly stood in the audience and raised her hand as high as she could with the "V for Victory" she taught Carnegie and Madison. Their sharp, sighthound eyes immediately spotted her signal. They quickly moved into position, facing each other with their heart markings toward the audience and, in perfect unison, gracefully and dramatically bowed. Everyone in the theater was charmed and applauded—except Randy, who fidgeted in his seat.

With the auditions over, Ernesto and Florence had a quiet discussion, then came to the stage and invited Randy and Garnett to join them.

In the bright stage lights, Florence's "vampire" styling took on a ghostly appearance.

"Thank you so very much for your time auditioning," she said. "All the dogs did fantastic jobs…but we have made our selections." She paused dramatically and then announced, "The lead role of Olivia goes to…"

Carnegie raised her nose in the air and proudly puffed out her chest, ready to accept her starring role.

"…Madison!" Florence exclaimed. "And the role of Olivia's sister goes to Carnegie!"

Garnett gasped in delight and hugged them.

What? No! That's not right! Carnegie cried to herself in shock. Madison snuck a look at her disappointed sister and sheepishly lowered her head.

Florence continued, "Precious will be Madison's understudy and Glory will be Carnegie's. They'll be expected to step in seamlessly if Madison or Carnegie can't perform. Congratulations everyone! Rehearsals start in two days. Ernesto will schedule meetings to discuss your contracts."

It was an emotionally long drive home to the Braxtons'. Garnett called Catherine and excitedly relayed all of the happy details on speakerphone.

"I wish y'all could've seen them," she said proudly. "They surprised everyone—including me—when they greeted Gabriella with the sweetest smiles. And when they bowed at the end, they brought the house down.

"They're going to need to get an agent, but that won't be a problem. Getting cast in a Broadway musical like this is a big deal. Animal talent agencies will be clamoring to sign them.

"You know, I thought our showy Carnegie would get the lead role of Olivia. I was so surprised when it went to Madison. Carnegie's performance was a little over-the-top, but I think it must have been their 'heartbreak' scene with Gabriella that decided it. Carnegie did the strangest, silly thing. Madison, well, she had us all in tears…"

In the back of Garnett's SUV, Madison lay stone still, trying to make herself small and not lick her paw. Carnegie, who normally used Madison's back as a pillow, had moved to the opposite side of the SUV and was coldly staring out the window, trying to not listen to Garnett's accolades.

Rub it in, Garnett, Carnegie resentfully said to herself. We'll see who's the *real* lead in this family.

That evening, back home and after settling into their beds, Carnegie spoke to Madison for the first time since their audition.

"What was that about?"

"What do you mean?" Madison asked.

"You know. Auditioning like that and stealing my lead role as Olivia. I thought you wanted to play my sister."

"I did," Madison replied. "I do."

"Then what was all that emotional stuff about?"

"You mean with Gabriella?"

"Yes, of course, with Gabriella. You even made her cry."

Madison looked down at her paw. "I didn't mean to. It's just that she was so sad. It made me sad, too."

"Well, you know she was just acting, right?"

"Are you sure? It felt so real."

"That's why she's a famous actor. Like I'm going to be," Carnegie said, closing her eyes and pretending to go to sleep.

CHAPTER SEVEN

Stealing the Spotlight

"Will someone *ple-e-ase* tell me why we're seeing Carnegie's nose in the center stage spotlight?!" Florence loudly called to the stage. "Did her mark get moved? Brad, check it, will you?"

Brad asked the lighting director to turn up the lights and walked upstage where Carnegie should have been sitting.

"The mark's right here where it should be. Ruby, move her back, please."

With each scene run-through, Carnegie had been inching her way out of the darkened background towards the center stage spotlight where Gabriella and Madison were performing their most dramatic scenes. Through trial and error, Carnegie discovered that lowering her body with a combination of sliding her front paws and scooting her rear end forward allowed her to silently move around the stage. As long as she remained in the darkness, no one noticed...that is, until she moved in a touch too far, and her long nose was suddenly brightly lit up.

Ruby slipped her hand under Carnegie's thin, nearly invisible, white collar that they used for rehearsals.

"Come on, girl. You know you don't belong here," Ruby said as she led her back to position. "Sit and stay until you get a signal from me."

What a waste, Carnegie said to herself as she sat on the tape "X" that was adhered to the stage floor. No one can see me all the way back here in the dark. I might as well be a lamp or piece of furniture—which no one can lie on, by the way. What could be more pleasing to the audience than *me* dramatically draped on Gabriella's bed? Did the director think I was just taking a nap? She has absolutely no sense of theatrics. The assistant director and stage manager aren't much better…or Ruby with all her silly signals.

And why do *I* have to share my pathetic little dressing room with that horrible Glory and Precious? But Madison gets a big, luxurious *private* dressing room with luxe furnishings, fresh flowers, and crystal bowls full of gourmet treats, not the paper plates of dry kibble they've been trying to pass off on me. Thank goodness Garnett packs decent meals, or I'd wither away to nothing. Did I mention "Miss Madison" has her name on the dressing room door with a shiny gold star? *Seriously…?* Carnegie was consumed with grumbling and running her internal dissatisfaction monologue when she missed her cue.

"Now, where's Carnegie?" Florence called out. "She's supposed to accompany Gabriella and Olivia offstage!"

Florence turned to Ernesto. "I don't know about her," she confided in a low voice. "When she pays attention to Ruby, she's great, but her performance is so erratic. She looks perfect with Olivia, though. I really don't want to replace her."

"I know what you mean. Well, maybe she'll catch on. Her understudy knows her part, so at least we have that option."

"Yes, we do have Glory…" said Florence with a sigh.

Three rows back, Garnett couldn't make out what Florence and Ernesto were saying, but she got the gist of it—and somehow, the mention of Carnegie's understudy came across all too clearly. Apparently, to Randy as well. Garnett sensed his squinty eyes trained on her, watching for a reaction.

As soon as they got home that evening, Carnegie went straight to her bed. When Madison approached her, she jumped up, circled three and one-half times, and dropped back down, facing the wall.

"What's wrong?" asked Madison to Carnegie's back.

No response.

"Carnegie?...Carnegie!"

She spun around and glared at her sister.

"Like you didn't see what happened today, Maddie? Were you blinded by the bright lights that were *entirely* focused on you and your famous co-star?"

"You mean, when your nose showed up in our sad scene?"

"It wasn't just my nose, Madison! It was *all of me* trying to add some badly needed drama to that scene instead of being stupidly stuck in the background."

"I'd like you to be in *all* the scenes, Carnegie."

"Well, tell that to the director!"

"I can't. You know that," replied Madison, looking down at her paw.

"Never mind. I'll just have to handle this my own way," Carnegie said, turning to face the wall again.

"What does that mean?"

"You'll see. Everyone will."

Later that night, Carnegie listened to be sure Madison was sound asleep, then got up and stood over her in bed. Her sister looked so sweet and innocent, and maybe she was...but it didn't change the fact that Madison had stolen the starring role that was meant for her.

How is this fair? Carnegie thought, looking at Madison's right front paw that was pink from being licked. She doesn't even want to play Olivia. She'd be much happier just being my sister onstage *and* off.

Carnegie went to their bedroom window and looked out over

Manhattan, still brightly lit at three a.m. Although she couldn't see all the way to Broadway, she could "feel" her own name spelled out in lights on the giant theater marquee. And it felt so right. But how to get everyone to realize they made a foolish mistake casting Madison as the lead instead of *her* based on that one silly audition?

Anybody can have an off day, Carnegie said to herself. Like poor Gabriella. She just couldn't catch on to our fancier dance, but I don't blame *her*. She frowned and wrinkled up her nose. I blame that horrid little moth!

And Carnegie's attempts during rehearsals to expand her character's part and show her acting range had *not* been appreciated. Even worse, they were "corrected" by Ruby. Finally, her thwarted nose-in-the-spotlight incident made it painfully clear to her that this shortsighted director and the entire crew were determined to banish her to the background.

Even if I managed to successfully slip into the spotlight, she thought, they'd kick me out before I got a chance to prove what a star I am. The audience—*my* audience—will never see the amazingly talented *me*...unless...

She refocused to her mirrored reflection in the window glass and then grinned with self-satisfaction. "Unless *I* show them," she said out loud.

And just like that, it came to her—the plan. In fact, the *perfect* plan! She checked to see that her talking out loud didn't wake Madison, then continued to ponder her revelation.

Why didn't I think of this before? I'll wait until opening night to unleash all my star power. During a live show, no one can stop me... at least not right away. By the time they realize I'm onstage a LOT, the audience will be hopelessly in love with me...and clamoring for even *more* of...ME!

Then, when the critics are wildly raving about my glowing performance and the show is an instant sold-out success, everyone will *beg* me to play Olivia. Madison will take her place in the background as my sister and be all the happier for it. It's a win-win.

But opening night was still weeks away. Until then, Carnegie intended to strictly follow everyone's directions, as insufferable as that would be. No way was she going to risk being replaced by her dreadful understudy. She shuddered when she thought about Glory, watching her from the wings, white teeth disturbingly on display. Watching and waiting…like a hyena stalker biding its time to pounce on its prey.

And so, with Carnegie's *perfect* plan secretly underway, the rehearsals went seemingly well. There were no longer whispers about Carnegie being replaced by her understudy, which was a relief to everyone except Randy and Glory.

CHAPTER EIGHT

Pucchi Booties

Madison and Carnegie were scheduled to take an offstage break while Ruby worked with their understudies. Lily and Amelia clipped on their leashes and led them backstage to the dressing rooms. They were greeted by an elegantly dressed, extraordinarily good-looking young man standing at Madison's door holding an international shipping box.

"Buongiorno. I am Luca, and I have a special delivery for a Miss Madison," he said in a charming Italian accent. He looked into Lily's blue-green eyes and gracefully held out a delivery form and pen. "Will you sign for it, Signorina?"

Lily stared back into Luca's dark, hypnotically handsome eyes and stared…and stared…and stared…

"Signorina?"

"What? Oh, gosh, sure," Lily said, snapping out of her trance and blushing as she scribbled her signature. "Can you please bring the box inside? You know…like in here…in Madison's dressing room?"

"We kinda have our hands full," added Amelia with a too-loud giggle. She gestured towards Carnegie and Madison on their leashes. "See?" She giggled again.

"Of course," Luca said. "Allow me to open the door for you. Where would you like for me to place it?"

"It?" asked Amelia.

"The box," Luca said.

"Right. The box," Amelia repeated.

"*Umm...uhhhhh...umm.*" Amelia looked around the dressing room for an uncomfortably long time. "How about there?" she finally suggested, pointing to the empty table directly in front of them.

"Certainly, Signorina," he said with an alluring smile.

He set down the box and, with a toss of his long auburn hair, whispered, "Arrivederci" and made his elegant exit.

"Arrivederci!!!" both of the girls loudly called back, then turned to each other. "That means 'goodbye' in Italian, right?" Amelia asked.

"I think so," Lily said, then grabbed Amelia's arm. "Oh my gosh. Can you believe how handsome he was?"

"I know!" Amelia agreed.

"We didn't act weird around him, did we?"

"Not at all," Amelia replied. "We were totally cool."

Carnegie and Madison rushed up and gave the box a thorough sniff inspection. Delightful items, like treats and toys, arrive in these shipping boxes. And there are always interesting smells that tell its history—like where it had been and who it encountered along the way. If the "who" happened to be a dog, now that was news!

Lily excitedly picked up the box. "Should we open it?"

"Well, it's addressed to Madison, and she wants to," Amelia replied. "She was sniffing it like crazy."

"Yeah, okay," said Lily, who didn't need any encouragement. They sat on the floor and placed the box between them.

"Hmm. That's a lot of tape," Amelia said.

"I saw some scissors in Madison's grooming kit," Lily said. "Let me grab them." Lily produced delicate silver shears with gold handles and a pink jewel on the hinge.

"Fancy," Amelia said. "I hope they can cut through all this tape and cardboard. It looks kinda thick."

With some struggling—at the expense of Madison's costly grooming shears—Lily and Amelia managed to cut open the box. Pulling back the flaps, they were delighted to find layers upon layers of beautiful Pucchi designer tissue paper.

"Wow!" Amelia exclaimed. "Whatever this is, it looks expensive!"

Carnegie plunged her head into the mass of tissue paper and rooted around.

"Move, Carnegie," Amelia said, pulling her away. "Give us a chance to see what's inside. Besides, this is for Madison."

Yes, of course, '*for Madison*,' Carnegie said to herself. What was I thinking?

Lily pulled aside the tissue to find eight elegant little boxes, each marked with a gold-embossed Pucchi designer logo. There was an envelope addressed to 'Miss Madison' in refined calligraphy.

"This is for you, Madison," Lily said as she broke open the wax seal on the envelope flap and removed a luxe paper note. "I'll read it to you."

Dear Miss Madison,
May you wear our luxurious Pucchi booties in style and comfort.
With our compliments,
Your fans at the House of Pucchi
Milan, Italy

"Wow! These are from a designer in Italy!" Amelia said. One of the boxes was adorned with a large black velvet bow covered in stunning jewels. "These must be special. The label says *Couture Dog Booties. Handmade in Italy*. Oh, and the style is named 'Madison.' They must have specially designed them for her." Amelia peeled off the bow and tossed it at Lily. "This would look cute on her."

Lily placed the jeweled bow on Madison's head like a tiara. "Aww! She's a pretty princess!"

Really? Being a Broadway star isn't enough? thought Carnegie. Now, she's royalty?

Madison sensed her sister's resentment and tried to look humble.

Amelia removed the box lid and pulled out four exquisite little dog booties. They were expertly fashioned out of an emerald silk with shiny black patent leather soles. An elaborate *'M'* monogram and a sparkly crystal Pucchi logo graced the top of each bootie.

"There are two pairs in the box," Amelia said. "Maybe one pair is for you, Carnegie."

Carnegie perked up…until Amelia had a suddenly obvious realization. "No, wait. She has four feet. It's just one set of shoes."

"Sorry, Carnegie," said Lily, petting her head. "But Madison can't wear all these at once. I'm sure she'll share. Won't you, girl?"

Madison looked at Lily with agreeable eyes.

"Amelia, find some booties for Carnegie, and they can both try them on," Lily suggested.

"Okay!" Amelia pulled out another box and read the label. "Let's see. These are called 'Ruby.'" She removed the lid and gasped. "They're covered in red sequins, you know, like Dorothy's in 'The Wizard of Oz.' Wow! That's something. Okay, moving on to our next booties…'Leopardo.' Maybe Italian for leopard?" She held up the chic tan and black spotted booties. "Yup." Amelia reached for the next box. "These are called 'Silver Screen.'"

"They're *so* glam!" Lily said. "Perfect for Madison on the red carpet."

"I know!" Amelia agreed. "Look, here's 'Leopardo II.' Oh, these are like a snow leopard—mostly white and kind of furry…"

Carnegie turned to Madison and quietly commented, "We already have paws. Why do we need paw paws?"

"And so many?" Madison said. "I hope we don't have to try them all on."

"I'm exhausted just hearing about them," Carnegie replied, "and I don't think they're done."

As if on cue, Amelia continued with the booties unboxing. "And these are named 'Holly'—green beaded leaves with red berries. She can wear these at Christmas time."

"What? No Easter Bunny booties?" Carnegie said out loud.

"*Shh*, they'll hear you," Madison whispered.

"Did you say something, Lily?" Amelia asked.

"No, I thought *you* did."

"Nope, not me," Amelia said, picking up another box. "Oh! Look how sweet…'Rosa.' Think that's Italian for rose?"

"Probably. I love all the little jewel flowers," Lily said.

Amelia dramatically held up the last box. "And…the final booties are 'Balletto'—pale pink with long satin ribbons. Looks like they lace up her legs."

"Aww! Like an adorable ballerina," Lily added.

"I know! So, which ones for Carnegie?" asked Amelia, who was now covered in open boxes of booties and lids.

"I can't decide. They're all so pretty," Lily said. "What were the leopard ones?"

"You mean *Leopardo*?" Amelia said with a silly attempt at an Italian accent.

Lily arched an eyebrow. "Whatever."

"Regular Leopardo or Leopardo II, the snow ones?" asked Amelia, holding up a bootie in each style.

"What if we put them both in leopard—or *Leopardo*—regular and snow? That'd be super cute!" Lily said.

"Totally!" agreed Amelia, handing Lily the box of snow leopard booties. Here, put these on Madison. I'll do Carnegie."

With the Borzoi sisters lying down and cooperating, the booties were slipping on easily. When Lily got to Madison's right front paw, she held it up for Amelia to see.

"Hey, have you ever noticed that one of her paws is pink?"

"Yeah, I heard about that. She licks it sometimes, and that makes her fur pink…so they cover it with white makeup."

"That's funny. Even dogs need concealer," Lily said. "Well, all the more reason to wear Pucchi booties!"

With both dogs bootied up, Amelia and Lily stepped back to admire them.

"*Ohhhh*, how cute!" cried Amelia.

"I know," agreed Lily. "I can't stand it! Let's make some room for them to walk."

"You mean like a runway?" Amelia asked.

"Yes! A catwalk!"

The Borzoi sisters exchanged looks. *Catwalk?*

"Are we expecting a *cat?*" Carnegie whispered to Madison.

"I hope not," Madison whispered back. "They're scary."

"Tell me about it," Carnegie agreed with a shudder.

Their private commiseration was interrupted by the noise of Lily and Amelia frantically shifting furniture around. And in short order, the sisters found themselves at the end of a long, narrow runway.

"Okay, that looks good. Now, how do we get them to walk down it?" Amelia asked.

"What if we lure them with treats?" Lily suggested. "I'll get some turkey jerky."

Amelia and Lily positioned themselves on the distant end of their makeshift catwalk. They both held out treats and called, "Stand!"

Madison and Carnegie stood and then looked down uncertainly at their leopard-bootied paws.

In unison again, Amelia and Lily called, "Come!" and waved the treats enticingly.

Carnegie wanted to get to the turkey jerky first, but the sensation of the booties between her paws and the floor felt so strange, she suddenly forgot how to walk....and froze.

Madison took a few hesitant steps, then lifted her nose in the air and, with the bow tiara still affixed to her head, took off strutting like a high fashion model.

How's Maddie doing that? Carnegie wondered. She's going to get all the turkey jerky!

When Madison reached the end of the runway, she ignored the turkey jerky, turned on a dime, and gracefully glided back to Carnegie.

Lily and Amelia applauded in delight.

"Now you, Carnegie…Come!" called Lily.

In a panic, she whispered to Madison. "Which paw goes first?"

"I don't know," Madison whispered back, "but I left my turkey jerky for you."

Carnegie tentatively stepped out with her right front paw. Unsure of what goes next, she lifted her right rear leg, and her body tilted precariously to the left. That's not working! She shifted to her left-side legs, and that was just as bad in the opposite direction. Her next attempts were no more successful, with her legs randomly flying up and down as if a mischievous puppeteer was yanking at her strings. And for all this effort, she had not advanced one inch down the runway.

Madison watched her sister in bewilderment. "Just walk like normal," she quietly urged.

Normal?! And this advice is coming to me from a dog wearing leopard shoes and a fake bow tiara? Carnegie sarcastically asked herself.

Lily called out to Madison. "You forgot your turkey jerky. Here, girl…before your sister takes it."

Carnegie stopped her struggling and scowled. As if this bootie humiliation isn't enough, now they're pushing Madison to take the turkey jerky she said was mine. Well, that's not happening! She focused on the finish line, took a deep breath, and blasted off with all her might. Like an off-balance propeller spinning out of control, Carnegie became a blur of wobbling limbs…but as fast as her legs were moving, she made little forward progress.

"Oh my goodness…what's Carnegie doing?" Amelia asked.

"Walking...?" Lily replied uncertainly.

As they watched in astonishment, Carnegie's wild wobbling gradually lost momentum like a wind-up toy with an uncoiling spring. When she finally came to a standstill, she looked longingly at the turkey jerky, wavered back and forth, then collapsed in a Pucchi-bootied heap on the catwalk.

"*AWW!*" both girls cried out and rushed to rescue her.

"It's okay, girl," Amelia said sympathetically as she removed Carnegie's front paw booties.

Lily took off her rear booties and said in a pitying voice, "You can't help it if Pucchi booties aren't your style."

Carnegie narrowed her eyes. Not my style? *Just you wait*, she silently vowed. In the meantime, I'll take *all* that turkey jerky, thank you very much.

CHAPTER NINE

Celebrity Stylist

"Rise and shine!" announced Anastasia, bursting through their bedroom door. She tossed her backpack on the bed she rarely slept in since going away to college.

Madison, deeply snuggled in her bed, sleepily lifted her head. Seeing it was Ana, she jumped up and joyfully greeted her favorite girl with a little grin.

"*Aww!* How sweet, Madison! You learned how to smile," Ana said, hugging her.

Carnegie heard Ana but chose not to respond. Doesn't she know it's our day off?

Ana went over to Carnegie and shook her back and forth.

"Wake up, lazy bones!"

Carnegie opened her eyes, smiled a bit too scarily, and then went back to sleep. Ana persisted with the shaking. "You've got to get ready for your photo shoot tomorrow. I'm going to be your celebrity stylist!"

Carnegie's eyes popped open. *Celebrity?*

Garnett had received notice from Madison's and Carnegie's animal talent agent to expect a call from the "Hearts Over Broadway" marketing department about publicity photographs. In place of the next Monday's rehearsal, she was to bring Madison and Carnegie to the renowned Julie Chase Photography Studio in New York's artsy

Chelsea Gallery District. Garnett immediately called Catherine to schedule time for an extra grooming the Sunday before.

"Ana will be on a break from college that week," Catherine had said. "Do you think she could assist you in some way? She's been upset about missing all their theater stuff."

"Sure," Garnett replied. "If she's home on Sunday, she can help groom them and then be with me at the studio on Monday. I can use an assistant."

"Great. I'll ask Ana if she wants to be involved in their photo shoot, but I already know the answer." And Catherine was right.

"Are you kidding, Mom? Of course!" Ana had enthusiastically replied when her mom called. "I can be their celebrity stylist!"

"I don't know about that, Anastasia. I seriously doubt they'll be wearing designer fashions."

"What if they wear their new Pucchi booties? Those are designer fashions."

"I suppose..." Catherine replied, unconvinced.

"Are the booties still at the theater or did you bring them home?"

"We brought them home, but we had to put them in your closet out of sight. They seem to make Carnegie anxious—especially the leopard ones."

"Oh, she's probably just excited about wearing them."

"Didn't seem that way," her mom said, frowning.

"We'll see about that when I get home," Ana said. "Anyway, I think they'd be amazing dog fashion influencers."

"I appreciate your ingenuity, dear daughter, but you know this photo session is entirely about their Broadway show."

"Yeah, I guess. They can wear their own fur paws. They're cute enough," Ana said with a laugh. "But when you think about it, they're *celebrities,* and I'll be *styling* their fur, so technically…"

"Uh-huh," her mom had replied, rolling her eyes. "Just be here early on Sunday to help Garnett bathe and groom them."

With Madison reluctantly resolved to revisiting one of her pre-dog show rituals and Carnegie now overly enthusiastic about being a celebrity, the Sunday grooming-to-absolute-perfection session got underway. Garnett handed Ana a large silver comb.

"Make sure you can comb through Madison's fur," said Garnett. "I'll take Carnegie. For some reason, she's always a tangled mess. They have to be tangle-free before they get a bath. Otherwise, they'll be harder to brush out.

Madison relaxed while Ana easily ran the comb through her long, silky fur. Carnegie, by contrast, was constantly on edge, worrying about her tangled fur being pulled. She shot a warning look at Garnett whenever the comb hit a snag.

Madison was now so delightfully relaxed from Ana's gentle combing that she had fallen asleep.

Everything comes so easy to Maddie, Carnegie resentfully thought. I, on the other hand, have to even endure the indignity of having my very sensitive—and, might I add, very personal—tail feather area tormented. I want *Ana* to celebrity-style me like she said she would! She narrowed her eyes and growled at Garnett.

"NO!" came Garnett's sharp reply.

Carnegie immediately ceased growling and raised her nose to sniff-kiss Garnett's face with her "You-still-love-me,-right?" apology that she used when she pushed things too far. Garnett's reaction softened, and she kissed her on the cheek.

"Alright, girl. You've been pretty patient. Let's get you in the bathtub. You can go first since your sister's asleep."

Ana left Madison sleeping peacefully and led Garnett and Carnegie to the Braxton's master bathroom. The luxe, tastefully decorated room was an expanse of white marble, tall sleek mirrors, and sparkling crystal light fixtures. A massive oval bathtub stood in front of the floor-to-ceiling glass wall that overlooked Central Park.

"My, this is stunning," Garnett remarked, looking around in awe.

"Yeah. Mom says if they ever move again, she's taking the bathroom with her."

It took both Garnett and Ana to lift a reluctant seventy-nine pound Carnegie into the bathtub, but once they did, she practically melted into the warm water. She closed her eyes with pleasure as they shampooed her with her favorite Mango Tango shampoo. After a relaxing sudsy massage, they let out the bath water, rinsed her off with the hand spray, and covered her with a warmed white fluffy towel.

I guess I'm done, Carnegie said to herself. Better dry myself off.

Before they could stop her, she leaped out of the bathtub and landed with a wet *SPLOOSH* on the marble floor next to Ana.

"Ana! Don't let her shake!" Garnett cried out.

"What?"

Too late! Carnegie's typhoon of a wet dog shake sent the now saturated towel she had been wrapped in flying across the room. It hit one of the tall mirrors with a loud *SPLAT*, then slid down, leaving a wet smear. Carnegie's subsequent shakes flung water off her sopping fur in all directions, like an industrial-strength spinning sprinkler had been set off in the room. Garnett and Ana gasped as the water streamed down the marble walls, glass and mirrors, and dripped from the crystal light fixtures.

Ana tried wiping the water from her eyes with the hem of her soaked shirt and groped for another towel off the towel warmer. "These are all wet. I'll get some more." She hurriedly tiptoed through the puddled floor to a cabinet where more towels were stored. She grabbed several and waded back. She threw a towel to Garnett, whose carefully coiffed, chic hairstyle was now a dripping upside-down bowl on her head. Ana used one of the towels to blot her face and wrung out her soggy rope of a ponytail into the bathtub.

Carnegie, who had shaken herself practically bone dry, was now casually sitting and daintily licking some water off her front paw.

Ana looked at her in disbelief. "Seriously, girl?"

They bundled up Carnegie in a beach towel and had her lie down while they wiped down the bathroom and then bathed Madison. With both Borzoi girls squeaky clean, the next phase of the grooming-to-absolute-perfection session commenced.

With minimal coaxing, Carnegie and Madison each jumped onto one of Garnett's portable grooming tables.

"That was easy," Ana said.

"Yes, they know the drill." She handed Ana a blow-dryer, brush, and comb. "Here's the fun part. Their fur has to be completely dry and perfectly styled to match the Borzoi breed standard."

"How do I do that?" Ana asked, then corrected herself. "I mean, I get the styling part, but maybe not exactly what they should look like...you know, specifically."

"Well, their fur grows the right way. Just follow the natural pattern. Ask me if you have any questions which direction to brush. You can do Madison. Her fur dries faster."

"Faster" was relative. To Ana, it was taking forever.

"Ugh! I need a break. My arm hurts," she complained, collapsing into a nearby chair. "I thought you said this was the fun part."

"Did I say that?" Garnett asked with a laugh. "Think of Carnegie and Madison. They have to stand still this whole time. Now, get up. We're almost done."

"Yeah, okay. But this celebrity stylist stuff is harder than it looks."

With Carnegie's and Madison's coats finally dry, brushed out, and glistening, it was time for precision trimming. Garnett reached into her grooming kit and pulled out her professional shears.

"Goodness! Who did this?" she said, examining the damage. The silver scissor blades were hopelessly bent and covered with sticky packing tape residue. "They've only been in Madison's dressing room at the theater. I can't imagine what happened to them. I've got other pairs, but not nearly as fine as these are...or *were*. They're trash now. Unfortunately, my other shears are at home."

"I think Mom might have some haircutting scissors," Ana offered. "She used to trim my bangs—way too short. It was totally embarrassing. I can go check if you want."

"Yes, thank you, dear."

After Ana left, Garnett smiled at Carnegie and Madison. "I don't suppose *you* know who destroyed my good scissors?"

They stared at her blankly.

"Of course not," she said with a laugh. "How could you?"

Anastasia returned with both the scissors and her mom.

"Wow!" Catherine said, admiring the gloriously groomed girls. "Look at these two beauties!"

"I styled Madison," Ana said proudly.

"That must've been a lot of work," Catherine said.

"Not really," Ana replied nonchalantly, with a side glance to Garnett who just smiled.

Catherine approached the grooming tables with her scissors. "Who needs trimming?"

"NO!" Ana screamed, grabbing the scissors out of her mother's hand. "You butchered my bangs!"

"What? Your bangs looked cute. But no need to panic, daughter. I was just going to hand the scissors to Garnett."

Carnegie was so excited about her celebrity photo shoot the next day that it was impossible for her to sleep. She decided to wake Madison but found that her bed was empty. In the darkness, she could make out a furry lump next to Ana on her double bed.

They're all chummy again, she thought. And I'm left out in the dark. Nothing new about that. In fact, it *was* nothing new. Even though Ana always invited Carnegie to sleep on her bed with Madison, she preferred the independence of her own pillow bed—as "shabby" as it is, she added to herself.

When her eyes adjusted to the dim light, she noticed her reflection in Ana's full-length mirror. I'm pretty, she thought, admiring her perfect conformation and long, flowing fur coat. That grooming truly did wonders. Of course, they had a lot of natural beauty to work with, she mused.

She thought about how Madison had transformed into a supermodel when she put on those dreadful Pucchi booties. How did she do that? she again wondered. She tried a number of poses in the mirror—shifting her hips back and forth, crossing and uncrossing her legs, raising one paw, then the other, tail up, tail down. It all looked more silly than super.

At least I have a winning smile, she thought. She moved closer to the mirror and auditioned various types of smiles. Dissatisfied, she frowned at her reflection. As charming as her smiles might be, none were quite *winning* enough for a celebrity. Her smile needed more oomph, more star power. It has to be the *winningest*. She wrinkled up her nose and curled back her lips to reveal her full set of very large, perfectly straight white teeth and rosy-pink gums—a vision drastically beyond what her sister had called "scary." She tilted her head, this way and that, to catch some light on her remarkably long canines. Now, those are impressive! She pictured Madison's goofy little grin. What does she know about smiling anyway? My fangs are *fabulous*!

CHAPTER TEN

Famous Is as Famous Does

At precisely eight o'clock the next morning, the Braxton's penthouse phone rang. Catherine answered and then called to Ana. "That was the front desk. Oscar is on his way up to help you with Madison and Carnegie. Are you ready?"

"Yeah, Mom," Ana replied. "I'm putting their leashes on."

The trio appeared in their foyer just as the elevator arrived. The doors parted, and Oscar, the smartly-uniformed doorman, stepped out.

"Good morning, Anastasia. Good morning, doggies," he said, extending his white-gloved hand.

In response, the sisters stepped forward and sniffed Oscar's glove. Carnegie embellished her sniffing with a mild version of her winning smile.

Oscar jerked his hand back wildly and knocked his doorman's hat off.

"That's just *her* being friendly," Ana said.

Oscar picked up his hat and brushed it off. "If you say so, Miss."

"Yeah, she really likes you." She pointed to two stylish black and white striped bags. "Can you help me with their luggage, please?"

"Your dogs have luggage?"

"Of course. Pucchi designer luggage. We just got it. They have Pucchi booties, too. I think they'd be amazing influencers, but Mom says..."

"What does Mom say?" her dad interrupted.

"G'day, Mr. Braxton," Oscar said.

"Good morning…and, please, call me Spencer," he said with a smile. He was getting ready to leave for work, but he couldn't help stopping to admire how professional his daughter looked. Checking his watch, he asked, "Isn't Garnett waiting?"

"Yeah, we better go," Ana said.

"Break a leg today," Spencer said, pushing the button to call for the elevator.

"I don't think they say that for photo shoots, but thanks, Dad."

When the elevator arrived, he kissed her on the cheek. "Bye, Princess."

Ana followed Oscar into the elevator with Carnegie and Madison, then turned to her dad and mouthed the words: "Don't call me that."

Spencer laughed. "I know. You've outgrown being my princess," he said with a wink as the elevator doors closed.

Their Broadway show office had arranged for their transportation to and from the photography studio—and waiting at the curb was a glistening white stretch limousine. Ana gasped at first but then tried to look unimpressed when the chauffeur opened the door for them.

The Borzoi sisters leaped in and rushed to see Garnett, seated at the opposite end.

"Hi, girls!" she said as they tried to climb on her lap. "You still smell so pretty from your baths!"

Ana asked Oscar to put their luggage on the closest seat and then crawled in and settled beside it. She hadn't been in a limo since her parents surprised her with a special evening on her thirteenth birthday. It was a bittersweet night, she recalled…but that, quite literally, was another story.

"Good morning, Ana," Garnett said. "Our lapdogs are looking beautiful for their photo shoot."

Shaking off her melancholy memory, Ana returned Garnett's greeting and looked around the limousine interior. The long, side seats were stacked with dog show equipment and bins. "Wow, this is a lot of stuff!"

"This is just what didn't fit in the trunk," said Garnett. "We don't travel light."

Ana pointed to Madison's and Carnegie's luggage. "Well, I brought a few accessories too, like their Pucchi booties. You know... just in case."

Garnett responded with a non-committal smile. "I'm sure we have everything they'll need."

It was about four miles from their Upper Eastside building to Julie Chase's studio in the Chelsea Gallery District.

"I think we're getting close," Ana said, looking out the window at the artistically painted buildings. "These murals are amazing!"

There was a reserved parking area for their limo in front of the studio. When they pulled up, Carnegie and Madison rushed to the passenger door window.

Garnett moved to the limo exit and took Carnegie's leash.

"Ana, grab Madison's leash and hold it tightly," Garnett said. "I'll take Carnegie. We can't risk them running loose on city streets."

"Oh, I know!" Ana replied. "And I heard about those dognappers taking valuable dogs. It's super scary!"

Ana wrapped Madison's leash twice around her wrist and nodded to the chauffeur to open the door. Carnegie flew out first, dragging Garnett and practically knocking Ana and Madison onto the curb. Carnegie dashed to the studio's entrance like it was her favorite dog bakery at closing time...but she was stopped short by an ornate black rod iron street gate. Beyond it was a stoop leading up to the studio's double front doors.

"HERF! HERF! HERF!" Carnegie announced their arrival with her demanding brat bark and impatiently pawing at the gate.

"Carnegie, *please...!"* Garnett said, pushing the entry button.

Moments later, Claire, Julie's assistant, opened the studio's front door and street gate. Garnett introduced herself and apologized for Carnegie's rude behavior.

"No...she's adorable!" Claire said, petting her head.

Carnegie smugly looked up at Garnett. *See? I'm adorable!*

"And this is my assistant, Anastasia," Garnett said with a discreet wink to Ana. "That's Madison with her."

"Pretty," Claire said, smiling.

"We've got a ton of stuff in the car," Ana said.

"We'll take care of it for you. Please, come on in."

Although she had no idea where she was going, Carnegie led the way, sashaying up the front steps, swinging her long, fluffy tail.

Julie's studio was undeniably impressive. The three-story historic brownstone exterior gave way to a striking gallery interior with linen-white walls and tall, elegant columns. Sleek lighting dramatically highlighted super-sized black and white prints of Julie's award-winning photographs.

Ana commented to Garnett, "I think I've seen some of these photos in magazines."

"I'm sure you have," Garnett said. "She's quite famous."

Carnegie whispered in Madison's ear. "Did you hear that? Our photographer is famous."

"Uh-huh," Madison replied.

"Famous is as famous does," Carnegie said proudly.

"What does that mean?" Madison asked.

"It means when you're famous, everything you do is famous. It's automatic."

"But we're not taking the photos," Madison said.

Carnegie lifted her long nose snootily in the air and said, "Our photographer is famous *because* she is taking *our* photos."

Madison regarded Carnegie and thought about it for a moment. "I think I get it, sister," she said with a little grin.

CHAPTER ELEVEN

Hard Pass

Claire interrupted Garnett and Ana's photo viewing and said, "If you're ready, I'll show you to your dressing room. Julie will see you as soon as she's free."

"Sure," Garnett replied, then turned to Ana and said in a low voice, "Hold onto Madison until we can get them settled in their crates. I'll try to keep our wild one contained. I don't know what Carnegie thinks is going to happen today. She's out of her mind with excitement."

The dressing room was massive. Mirrors and makeup lights, narrow tables, and cane-back chairs covered the entire length of one wall. Garment racks took up another. There was a seating area with a comfy suede sofa and chairs, stylish tables, and a large flatscreen monitor mounted on the wall. And there was lots of open space to set up Madison's and Carnegie's crates and their large octagon-shaped wire enclosure.

"This will be perfect," Garnett said to Claire.

"It's bigger than my college apartment," Ana said, then caught herself not sounding like a professional assistant and quickly added, "Like it *was*, I mean."

"Great," Claire said. "There's waters and other drinks in your mini fridge. If you're hungry, Craft Services has breakfast set up just down the hall to the right."

"Thanks," Garnett said. "I think we're good for now."

"The crew is unloading the limo, and we'll have your things in here shortly. If you need anything, just text me. All of our numbers are posted on the wall."

"One thing, Claire," Garnett said. "Would you please put a note on our door to keep it closed?" She gestured towards Carnegie, who was pulling on her leash, anxious to run off to who-knows-where.

"Of course," Claire replied with a smile. "We don't want to lose our talent. And our front door and gate are kept closed and locked, so there's no danger of them running out in the street…or worse, being dognapped. Did you read about that?"

"I did, it's terrifying," Garnett said. "We keep these girls on a short leash."

"For sure. They're precious," Claire said.

Precious *and* adorable, in my case, Carnegie thought.

"Well, make yourselves comfortable. I'll see you later," Claire said, carefully closing the door.

After Claire left, Ana, wide-eyed, turned to Garnett. "This is amazing! Are all shoots like this?"

"Just the big-budget studio ones, dear. Next time I go to a lure coursing photo shoot in a freezing cold field, I'll be sure to take you along."

Within minutes, there was a loud knock at the door. Garnett checked to see if Ana was still holding Madison's leash and then called, "Come in!"

The door opened slightly, and an attractive young man with long dreadlocks stuck his head in. "Hello, ladies. I'm Phillip. Our crew's got all your things from the limo. Is now a good time to bring it in?"

"Yes, please," Garnett replied. "You can just stack it over by the garment racks."

Ana tried to look busy tending to Madison and to not gawk at the crew, who looked more like male models than movers.

After they filed out, Garnett handed her an inventory list of what they'd brought to the shoot. "Please make sure everything is here. The limo is parked out front so if anything didn't get brought in, we can easily get it. I can hold onto Madison for you."

"Okay!" Ana went through the stacks of items that had been delivered to their dressing room, read them aloud, and checked them off.

"Pillow beds, wire show crates with pads. They're zebra print. Cute! Blankets, wire exercise enclosure, grooming kit, grooming tables, bowls, cooler with snacks, first aid kit, three supply bins. Oh, and their two Pucchi bags—they're here. Looks like that's everything, Garnett."

"Excellent. Can you set up their crates and enclosure?"

"On it!" Ana unfolded and set up the gold wire show crates and added their zebra-print pads to the bases. She then unfolded their wire enclosure and clipped it together to form a large, freestanding octagon shape. She held up a pillow bed. "Should I put their beds in there?"

"Yes, please," Garnett said. "Put them next to each other opposite the end that opens."

"Done! Anything else?"

"Let's see if they're thirsty, then they can relax in their crates."

Ana got some water from the cooler and poured it into their bowls. Carnegie was too excited to drink, and Madison only took two small licks to satisfy Garnett and Ana.

They led them into their crates and closed the doors. Carnegie immediately began pawing at hers. Garnett softly corrected her. "I know you're excited, but you need a time out. Be a good girl, and you'll get a special cookie." Carnegie's ears perked up at one of her favorite words and, for the moment, calmed down.

Madison was lying against the far end of her crate. "Ana, cover her crate with one of those blankets," Garnett said. "Just leave the front open. She likes that at first when we're somewhere new."

Ana draped Madison's crate, then knelt and looked inside.

"How's our little star?" she asked.

Carnegie barked, "HERF! HERF! HERF!" *I'm over here!*

"I think Carnegie wants that cookie now," Ana said to Garnett.

"Okay…but wait until she is *not* barking to give it to her. They're in the small white bin. Get one for Madison too, although she may not want it now."

Ana looked through the bin and held up an elegant matte black box. "Is this them?"

Garnett nodded.

"They're from that posh dog bakery?" Ana asked.

"They are. I thought having something special for today would be fun," Garnett said.

Ana carefully lifted the hinged lid and parted the gold tissue liner. "*Oooh*, I love the way they're decorated! What do you think, Garnett? Give them a star or Borzoi shape cookie?"

"You pick."

"Okay. I'll give a Borzoi one to Carnegie because it's bigger, and Madison can have a star." Ana slipped the cookies through their crate wire openings.

Of course. Give the *star* to the *star*, Carnegie resentfully said to herself. Nevertheless, she quickly munched down her Borzoi cookie. Madison's star cookie went untouched.

"Ana, are you hungry?" Garnett asked.

"If you mean, do I want a dog cookie? No thanks," Ana said with a laugh.

"Are you sure? At the price, they should rate a Michelin Star," Garnett said, smiling. "No…I think we're in a bit of a wait mode. I'll watch Madison and Carnegie if you want to check out the breakfast buffet."

"Okay, if you're sure. I'll grab a little something and bring it back here. Do you want anything, Garnett?"

"Coffee…black, would be great, thanks."

While Ana was gone, Garnett checked on Madison. She opened her crate door and picked up the star cookie.

"How about if we eat a little something? It's from your favorite bakery."

Madison leaned forward and gently nibbled off one of the points on the star.

"Oh, dear!" Garnett exclaimed when she noticed Madison's wet and pink right front paw. "Have you been licking your paw again?"

Madison looked up at her guiltily and pulled her paw out of sight. Garnett reached in and petted her head. "It's alright, sweetie. We can cover it up…but leave it alone, okay?"

"Knock knock! Can you let me in?" Ana called from the hall. "I've got my hands full!" Garnett closed Madison's crate and opened the door for Ana. She was juggling plates with avocado toast, a breakfast burrito, tropical fruit, a blueberry muffin, and a large cup of coffee.

Garnett reached for her coffee cup. "Here, let me help you with that. Is there anything left on the buffet table?" she asked with a laugh.

"Tons," Ana said. "I didn't touch the scrambled eggs and bacon stuff. And the blueberry muffin is for you in case you change your mind."

"Thank you, dear. Maybe later." Garnett sipped her coffee while Ana savored her outsized breakfast. She smiled inwardly and resisted mentioning to Ana that she never wanted to eat breakfast at home.

Another knock on the door brought Julie Chase herself, which came as something of a surprise to Ana. She wasn't expecting her to be so young with striking blue-gray eyes and a mane of blonde hair. Oh my goodness, Ana thought. Everyone here looks like a model. She quickly checked herself in the nearest makeup mirror and wiped some avocado off her chin.

"I'm sorry for not being here when you arrived. I was finishing up a photo session with some of the other cast members."

Garnett introduced herself and Anastasia as her assistant.

"I love your photography, Ms. Chase," Ana said.

"Thank you…and call me Julie," she said with a smile. "I've been dying to meet your Madison and Carnegie. Is that okay?"

"Sure!" Ana said and then looked to Garnett for approval. Garnett nodded.

"We'll let them out so you can get acquainted," Garnett said, opening Carnegie's crate and gesturing to Ana to open Madison's.

Carnegie stepped out of her crate and stretched into the strangest pose—simultaneously raising her nose in the air, extending her right front leg *forward*, her left back leg *backward*, and curling her tail *upward* into a high plume. It was an unusual position for a Borzoi… or any mammal, for that matter.

Garnett, Ana, and Julie stared, squinted their eyes and tilted their heads, trying to place *what* she looked like—perhaps an enormous exotic bird in flight?

"Dramatic," Julie said, for lack of a better description.

"Yes, this is Carnegie," Garnett said. "*Dramatic* fits her to a T."

Satisfied that her melodramatic move had produced the desired effect, Carnegie politely sat and raised her paw to shake hands.

Delighted, Julie knelt and shook her paw. "Pleased to meet you, Carnegie."

"I'm surprised she didn't smile," Ana said. "That's kind of her thing."

Carnegie silently chastised Ana. *Please*…I'm saving that.

With her sister's unique introduction over, Madison emerged from her crate. She went up to Julie, who was still kneeling, and gently sniffed her face.

"That's a sniff-kiss," Ana said. "She likes you already."

Julie looked into Madison's beautiful dark amber eyes and was equally smitten. "My camera is going to love *you*, Madison."

She stood and petted both Borzoi girls' heads.

"So, here's what's happening today. We're setting up right now for the main cast photo. Both Madison and Carnegie will be in that one. They look perfect as-is, but if you want to brush them a bit more, feel free...but, so you know, it will be a wide shot, and we won't see them up close."

"We'd still like to touch them up," Garnett said. "Should we set up our grooming tables in here?"

"Your Hair and Makeup room is a few doors down from the cast's room—the *human* cast's room—I should say," Julie said, smiling at Madison and Carnegie. "I'll have our crew move your things."

"That would be nice," Garnett said.

"I've got a note here," Julie said, pulling a paper from her slacks pocket. "Madison is to report to Wardrobe after she is groomed and made up. The cast is in full costume, so maybe they have something for her to wear."

"*Just* Madison?" Garnett and Ana asked in unison.

"Looks like it."

Just Madison gets a costume? That sounds right, Carnegie said to herself sarcastically. She narrowed her eyes and looked at Madison, who responded with an innocent grin.

"So, after the main cast photo," Julie continued, "we'll shoot our close-ups—some with Madison alone and some with her and Gabriella. Madison will need a detailed grooming for those. While Madison is back in Hair and Makeup, we'll reset lights, and it would be helpful if Carnegie could stand in for her."

"Sounds good," Garnett said.

Sounds *good?* Carnegie thought. Are you kidding? It sounds *great!* They want *ME* instead of Madison for the standing photos. Of course! She thought back to the night she practiced posing in Ana's full-length mirror and smiled to herself. How spectacular she looked with her long, flowing feathers. I'm the *standing star*.

"How long before their first photo?" Garnett asked.

"About an hour. Claire will keep you informed. If you don't have any other questions…" Julie turned to Carnegie and Madison with a smile, "I'll see you two pretty girls in the studio."

After Julie left, Garnett turned to Ana. "Looks like we've got our marching orders. Let's get Carnegie and Madison in their enclosure so they can stretch their legs and be safely out of the way."

Ana unclipped the opening enclosure section and led the sisters inside. Madison walked directly to her pillow bed and, after circling three times, settled in.

Carnegie stood with her chin resting on the top of the wire enclosure wall, closely watching Garnett and Ana stack the pushcart with their grooming equipment and supplies. There didn't seem to be anything in it for her, so she walked over and dropped into her bed next to Madison.

"You forgot to circle before lying down," Madison whispered.

"Did I? Being a celebrity *and* the standing star is so consuming. I can't do everything. Isn't that Ana's job today—to spin my bed around three times before I lie down?"

Madison looked over at Ana, who was now eating the blueberry muffin she had gotten for Garnett.

"I think she's busy. Did you hear her say she brought our Pucchi booties?"

"No, when?"

"In the limo. I think she wants us to wear them."

Carnegie appeared to consider the prospect, then said, "You know what? I'm gonna stick with the paws God gave me." She held up her paws to make her point. "My God Paws. Hard pass."

Madison thought back to their Pucchi bootie debut in her dressing room at the theater. She had loved the feeling of glamorously gliding along and being applauded by Lily and Amelia. It was exhilarating! But then she remembered her sister lying in a humiliated heap on that same makeshift catwalk, and her heart hurt.

"Yeah," Madison agreed. "Hard pass."

CHAPTER TWELVE

Snow Leopardo

With Carnegie and Madison on leashes, Garnett and Ana walked down the hall to their Hair and Makeup room. As they passed the cast's room, Carnegie quietly remarked to Madison, "I'm glad we have our own Hair and Makeup room. Those persons are so noisy. All that talking and singing and dancing, day after day. It's exhausting."

"You mean the cast persons?" Madison asked. "I'm pretty sure they've been rehearsing for the show."

"Whatever."

"But don't you like Gabriella?" Madison asked. "I *love* her," she added softly.

"She's okay, but the rest of them are just annoying."

Madison and Carnegie's Hair and Makeup room was a small version of their dressing room with black leather styling chairs in front of two makeup stations with brightly-lit mirrors. The crew had set up their grooming tables side-by-side on the opposite end of the room.

Looking around the room, Carnegie whispered to Madison, "So, why are our grooming tables so far from the mirrors?"

"Do we need mirrors? We already know what we look like."

Carnegie responded to her sister with an "Are you crazy?" look.

Suddenly, a short, plump man in overly *large* black frame glasses and an overly *small* white denim jumpsuit appeared in the doorway.

"Hello, darlings. I'm James, but you can call me Jimmy. All my clients do." He went to one of the makeup stations and noisily rifled through his supplies, mumbling. He occasionally paused to look over at Madison and Carnegie, sighed, and then returned to rifling.

"This one, I suppose," he said, picking up an enormous round brush with a rainbow metallic handle. He waved it in the air as he approached Madison and Carnegie.

"I'm doing the hairstyling for the cast," he said to no one in particular, then leaned over and held out Madison's long chest feathers. "But I don't know how I'm supposed to deal with ALL of this..." And then, with a loud exasperated sigh, he picked up Carnegie's tail by the very tip and dangled its plume shape in the air, "...and especially THIS," he added with an air of disgust.

Carnegie whipped her head around at her inelegantly elevated tail. *Excuse me?!* she said to herself indignantly.

"No need, Jimmy," Garnett flatly replied. "We've got it covered."

"Well, if you insist, darling," he said, hastily dropping Carnegie's tail. "Bye-bye." Reversing his entrance, he returned the brush to his station, mumbled something about being expected to perform miracles, and disappeared out the door.

After Jimmy left, Garnett and Ana just looked at each other.

"I think we better get our girls on the grooming tables before Jimmy changes his mind and comes back," Garnett said with a laugh.

The sisters' touch-up grooming was done quickly, and Nora, their makeup artist, arrived shortly thereafter. She was covered head-to-toe in variations of leopard print—with leopard-stenciled hair, leopard-frame glasses, leopard tattoos, leopard-pattern nails, a leopard-print ensemble, and leopard high-top sneakers. When she approached their grooming tables, Carnegie greeted Nora with a modified smile, and Madison slowly wagged her tail.

"Hi, honeys," she said, reaching out to pet them. "Which one of you is our big star?"

Carnegie struggled to keep her smile from turning into a snarl.

I hate her already, she said to herself. She looks like a big Leopardo Pucchi bootie.

Sensing her sister's disdain, Madison lowered her head, stopped wagging her tail, and tucked it between her legs.

Nora pulled back her hand and raised her eyebrows. "Oh…okay. I've heard that Borzoi are aloof."

"Well, they're usually friendly," Ana said, frowning.

"I'm sure they'll warm up," Garnett said. She ran her hand over Madison's long, slender back. "This is Madison. She's playing Olivia." She petted Carnegie's wider back. "And Carnegie, here, is playing her sister. She doesn't require makeup. Madison needs some white makeup on her right front paw. I have some white powder if you don't have anything that will work."

Nora reached for Madison's pink paw. "Let me see, honey."

Madison didn't know if she should surrender her paw to the "hated one." Ignoring Carnegie's glare, she looked to Garnett, who nodded and gave her an encouraging smile.

"She can be a little shy at first," Garnett said. "Shake hands, Madison," which was her cue to extend her right paw.

Madison slowly raised her paw.

Nora adjusted her leopard-frame glasses and took it in her hand. "What a graceful paw, hon. But, yeah, it's a little pink. I think I have some white clown makeup..."

Carnegie looked at Madison and smirked. *Ha! Clown makeup!*

Nora brought over her tall rolling makeup storage trolley. She lifted the lid and pulled out the side compartments and drawers, searching through seemingly endless makeup containers, bottles, and tubes.

"Aha!" Nora held up a small round canister of "Clown White" makeup. She unscrewed the lid, removed the round foam applicator, and swiped it across the creamy white foundation. "This should do the trick."

Garnett leaned in to look at the label. "Is it non-toxic?" she asked.

"She might lick her paw again," Ana added. "That's why her fur's pink."

"I haven't had any clowns drop dead," Nora said with a snorty laugh, "but we'll double-check the ingredients to be sure."

With everyone satisfied Nora's white makeup was clown *and* dog-safe, she applied it to Madison's paw, carefully avoiding her nails and pads.

"If you have your white powder," Nora said to Garnett, "it will help set this foundation.

"Sure," Garnett replied. "Ana, would you get it, please? It's in my dog show tote. It's kind of a flat can and has a powder brush with it."

Ana retrieved and handed over Garnett's powder items. Nora loaded up the brush and vigorously dusted all over Madison's clown makeup, creating a cloud of powder. It drifted up to Carnegie, who was leaning in watching closely—too closely—and it tickled her nose. Carnegie's long Borzoi nose quivered and twitched…and twitched and quivered…until, after a huge inhale that seemed to suck all the oxygen out of the room…*A-a-A-CHOOooo!* she produced such a colossal force sneeze it blew most of the white powder from the can onto Nora's face and glasses, completely covering them.

Oops. Carnegie secretly snickered. She turned to Madison and gaily whispered, "Now, she looks like a *Snow* Leopardo." Madison responded with a little grimace.

Ana tried not to laugh because it was, indeed, funny. "Oh, gosh, sorry!" she exclaimed.

Nora spit out some powder and groped for a tissue to wipe her face and glasses. "It's okay. She probably couldn't help it," she said unconvincingly.

CHAPTER THIRTEEN

The Butterfly

With Madison's paws perfectly matched white, Nora closed up her storage trolley. "I understand Madison will be back here for makeup detailing for her close-ups," she said.

"Yes," Garnett replied. "That's what Julie said."

"Just thinking…it would be better to not bring Carnegie. We wouldn't want her to distract Madison."

"Uh-huh," Garnett said, fully grasping Nora's meaning. "She should still be in the studio. They want her to stand in for Madison."

"Terrific," Nora said. "Oh, and before you go into the studio, please check that their paw pads are clean. I understand there is a light-colored photo backdrop, and they don't want any footprints—or pawprints."

"I think they're clean," Garnett said, "but I've got some grooming wipes to be sure. What about walking to the wardrobe room and the studio? Should we bring more grooming wipes?"

"No. That'll be okay. These floors are pretty spotless. They're mainly concerned about street grime."

After Nora left, Garnett dug around in her dog show tote and found their Mango Tango grooming wipes.

"I'll do it," Ana said, holding up one of Carnegie's front paws.

Garnett pulled out a wipe and handed it to her. "Okay. Just her paw pads, not her fur. When you do Madison's be careful not to wipe off her white makeup."

When their favorite Mango Tango fragrance drifted up to Madison from her sister's paws, she whispered, "You smell nice."

"I know," Carnegie replied.

After a few minutes, Claire stuck her head in the door.

"We'd like Madison in Wardrobe in ten minutes. Will she be ready?"

"Yes!" Ana quickly replied, then caught herself and looked to Garnett for confirmation.

Garnett smiled and nodded, "Yes, of course."

"Perfect," Claire said. "I'll be back in ten to take you. Carnegie can come, too. We'll go to the studio from there."

"Okay, Anastasia, let's get them down off the tables…and grab my dog show tote. Make sure what's left of Madison's paw powder is in there with the powder brush and a grooming brush." And then whispering, "And there should also be some T-R-E-A-Ts."

On hearing a variation of her favorite word, Carnegie's ears shot up. "Oh my goodness," Garnett said. "I think she's learned how to spell."

Like before, Garnett had Ana take Madison because she was easier to control, and she took Carnegie. Claire led them down another hallway to the wardrobe room. She knocked, and after some rustling sounds, Laura, the wardrobe supervisor, opened the door. She had a pair of trousers draped over one arm, a pin cushion on her wrist, and a measuring tape hanging around her neck. Claire introduced them and said she would be back to take them to the studio.

"Which one of you cuties is here for their costume?" Laura asked.

"Madison," Ana said, holding out her leash.

"Okay, come with me, Madison," Laura said, taking her leash. "And it's a little tight in here with all the garment racks, so it would be better if only one of you came inside with her."

Carnegie confidently headed in the door.

"Wait, Carnegie," Garnett said, holding her back. "She didn't mean *you*. Ana, you can go with Madison, and I'll wait out here with Carnegie."

Laura ushered Ana and Madison inside and closed the door behind them. Ana looked around in awe. It was thrilling to see the racks of glamorous costumes, each labeled with their character's name.

Madison went right up to one of Gabriella's gowns and sniffed it.

"*Aww*, she must smell her co-star," Ana said.

"Watch out, Madison!" Laura cried as a clawed paw reached out from behind the gown and swiped at her nose. "June is very protective of the wardrobe."

"June?" Ana asked.

"June is my cat," Laura said with a smile. "I call her my fashionista cat because I found her in the garment district last winter. She was just a kitten."

"Like in a box or something to be adopted?" Ana asked.

"No, not even a box. She was feral and jumped into a pile of fabric swatches to hide when she saw me, but I scooped her up and brought her home."

"Why did you name her June?" Ana asked.

"It's a bit of a story. Do you mind if I finish pinning these trouser hems?"

"I think we're on your schedule," Ana replied with a smile.

"Well, as I said, she was feral. She'd never been around people and was very wild and frightened. When I got her home, she ran and hid from me under a pile of fabric in a corner of my studio. For the longest time, she would only come out when I wasn't around. I could tell she was exploring because her food and water would disappear. And, thankfully, she used the litter box. When she finally showed herself, it was the month of June, so that's what I named her."

"It's a pretty name," Ana said. What made her decide to be friendly?"

"I discovered that she loved soft fabrics, especially velvet. When I wasn't around, she would find scraps of velvet and drag them to her corner. So, I made her a super soft velvet bed and kept it near me. She couldn't resist lying in it, and it was too big for her to take to her corner. She had to come closer and closer to me, and when she finally jumped into her bed, I knew I had won her trust. Since then, we're never apart."

"That's a cute story. I don't think Madison likes cats much. Whenever she tries to be friendly, she gets smacked."

"We'll be sure to keep them apart," Laura said. She hung up the trousers and pointed to an ottoman. "Come sit up here, Madison. I'll be right back." Madison hopped up, sat, and waited expectantly.

"This is exciting, Madison," Ana said, hugging her. "You're getting a special costume to wear onstage."

Laura returned with a small box that was marked "Olivia."

"I made this hair clip just for you, Madison." She pulled out a shimmery purple butterfly with delicate beaded black trim.

"Wow, fancy!" Ana said.

Laura gently held Madison's head in her hands and turned it this way and that. She located a small tuft of fur in front of her left ear and clipped the butterfly on it. "Perfect!"

"Oh, it *is* perfect!" Ana agreed and reached for a hand mirror. "Can I borrow this?" She held the mirror up for Madison to look at herself. Madison had difficulty focusing but was finally able to see her reflection.

It's *beautiful*, she said to herself. I love butterflies.

"Do you think she can see herself?" Laura asked.

"I don't know," Ana replied, "but I can't wait until Garnett sees it." She turned to Madison and added, "I don't know how much your sister will care about your butterfly. She's more about treats."

Madison looked down. She knew *exactly* how much her sister would care.

"I'll be at the theater and elsewhere handling wardrobe," Laura said, "but so you and Garnett know, Madison is to wear this hair clip whenever she is on stage or at a theater event—and, of course, for today's publicity photos. It's Olivia's iconic butterfly."

"I promise she'll wear it whenever she is supposed to," Ana said.

"When you're done with the shoot today," Laura said, "please return the hair clip to me. I'll keep it in perfect condition and make sure Madison has it whenever she is appearing as Olivia. I made a backup, but hopefully, it won't be needed."

"Madison will be very careful with it," Ana said. "Won't you, girl?" Madison looked up at her with a little grin.

"One last thing," Laura said, grabbing her camera, "I need to get some reference photos of her in costume." She unclipped Madison's leash and hung it around her neck with the measuring tape. "Look this way, Madison."

As if she had been directed, Madison tilted her head slightly to the right to show off her butterfly and looked at the camera with irresistibly sweet eyes.

"Oh my. You're a natural star, Madison," Laura said. "I can see why they cast you."

After a few photos, she re-clipped Madison's leash and handed it to Ana. "Okay, that's it. If you don't mind waiting in the hall, I'm sure Claire will come get you soon."

Ana and Madison found Garnett and Carnegie sitting together in the hallway. Carnegie's fluffy behind and rear legs were on the bench with her front feet on the floor—the technique she used when not allowed to sit on the furniture. Keeping two-on-the-floor made it technically permissible.

She got up and approached her sister. "What's that on your head?"

"It's my butterfly hair clip costume," Madison said proudly.

Carnegie pawed the air. "It makes me want to swat it."

"Don't!" Madison said. "I think it's *beautiful.* Besides, I have to wear it for these pictures and whenever I play Olivia. It's iconic."

"What does that mean?" Carnegie asked.

"I don't know, but it sounds important. Did they give you anything to wear onstage?"

"Oh, yeah. They took me to a totally different wardrobe room—just for me—and gave me a special costume."

"What is it?" Madison asked.

"It's an ant clip. Can't you see it?" Carnegie said, pointing to her head. "I'm pretty sure it's iconic."

Madison stood on her tiptoes, straining to look closely at her sister's head.

"Get real, Maddie. Of course, they didn't give me anything to wear. That would be gilding a lily."

"Like Lily at the theater?"

"No, like putting gold on a flower."

"That doesn't make sense."

"Exactly," Carnegie said haughtily. She lifted her nose in the air, spun around, and backed into her two-on-the-floor seating.

CHAPTER FOURTEEN

Sidelined

Claire arrived and escorted the four down a short hall to the photography studio. Carnegie was overly excited and pulling on her leash. Garnett had to stop, take her aside, and calm her down. Claire, Ana, and Madison patiently waited, and they all entered the studio's double doors together.

"Stay here, please," Claire said. "I'll ask Julie where she wants you."

The photography studio was massive. In contrast to the white lobby, it was entirely matte black with high-tech black lighting fixtures. An enormous, exquisitely painted backdrop, supported by tall metal stands, was spread across one wall and extended seamlessly onto the floor. An elegant chaise lounge—a small version of the one used in the theater—was positioned in the center of the backdrop. Massive softbox lights and reflective umbrellas were positioned to create shadowless, even lighting.

Madison noticed that the crew was wearing blue shoe cover booties when they walked on the backdrop. She turned to Carnegie and quietly asked, "Is this when we wear our Pucchi booties?"

Carnegie did not respond. Madison asked again, and still, there was no response. She looked at her sister and found her frozen, eyes wide-open, staring at the bootied crew.

Madison nudged her. "Carnegie..."

Nothing. She nudged her again.

"Carnegie?"

"What?" she finally responded.

"Are you okay? It looked like you were asleep with your eyes open."

"Of course, I'm okay. I was just practicing standing still and not blinking. I don't want to take a blurry picture with my eyes closed."

Madison looked at her sister in disbelief. "Uh-huh."

Claire returned with their directions. "Julie says she wants to get the cast positioned for their photo, and then she will bring Madison and Carnegie in." She gestured towards a seating area off to the side. "You can sit over there and watch. The cast is on the way, and the lighting is mostly set, so it won't be long."

"Here they come," Madison whispered to Carnegie as the ten principal cast members filed in. The cast smiled and waved at them, and Madison enthusiastically wagged her long tail.

"So annoying," Carnegie replied, looking away.

Julie asked Gabriella to sit on the chaise and Vincente, her love interest, to kneel next to the chaise to her right. She arranged the other cast members by height and directed them to stand in a row behind Gabriella.

After some light readings, Julie asked for Madison and Carnegie to join the cast.

A bootied photo assistant came over and greeted them with a smile. "I'll take their leashes if that's okay."

"Sure," Garnett and Ana replied in unison as they both surrendered the sister's leashes.

Carnegie looked down at the assistant's booties and stalled. Madison nudged her and whispered, "I'm pretty sure nobody in the cast is wearing booties."

With that, Carnegie jerked her leash from the assistant's hand and made a beeline for Gabriella's chaise. She skidded to a stop, spun around—twice for dramatic effect—raised her fluffy tail, and planted her rear end in her two-on-the-floor seating style next to Gabriella.

Startled, Gabriella gasped, then laughed and hugged her.

Julie approached and took her leash. "Not here, Carnegie. That's where Madison sits." She moved her over to the right side of Vincente. "You sit over here."

Of course, the *star* sits in the center, Carnegie said to herself resentfully. I'm so far off to the side, I might as well be sitting outside in the limo.

Nevertheless, Carnegie sat like she had learned to do onstage. Julie petted her head. "Good girl." Then, noticing her leash, she said, "We don't want this in our photo, do we? How about if we make a trade?" She unclipped her leash and handed Carnegie a dog treat.

Decent trade, Carnegie thought, momentarily appeased.

When Madison arrived with the assistant, Julie unclipped her leash and directed her to lie on the chaise to Gabriella's left. Madison stepped up and naturally draped herself elegantly with her feathers and tail flowing over the seat cushion.

Staring intently into the monitor, Julie asked Tina, her photo stylist, "Can you move her tail a little towards the end of the chaise?"

Madison watched as Tina picked up her tail and carefully moved it one inch over.

"Too far," Julie said.

Tina moved Madison's tail back about one-half inch.

Julie reached her arm out from behind the monitor and gestured to her left. "A touch more…"

Tina moved Madison's tail one-quarter inch more, which placed it very nearly in its original position.

"Perfect!" Julie said.

"And, Jimmy, brush her tail where it overhangs the chaise."

Garnett quickly grabbed a brush and stood, ready to jump in for Jimmy—but he complied and gently smoothed Madison's tail feathers to perfection.

Carnegie rolled her eyes. Now, Madison's *tail* is getting more attention than I am.

"One final light reading," Julie said.

POP! The studio lights flashed, illuminating the softboxes and silver umbrellas like a lightning strike. Julie checked her light meter.

"We're good to go. Everyone in character, please. Madison, Carnegie…look over here!" Julie said, smiling and holding up her hand just above the camera lens.

For whatever reasons—Carnegie looking for another treat and Madison just because she was asked—both looked in the right direction at the right moment. With a precisely synchronized lighting *POP!*, camera *CLICK!*...and a lot of luck, it was a miraculously perfect shot.

"Everyone hold, please," Julie said as she studied the photo in the monitor. She zoomed in closely and looked at each cast member. "Can you believe this, Tina? It's good of everyone."

Tina looked over her shoulder at the monitor and examined every detail. "You're right. It's flawless," she agreed.

It can't be, Carnegie said to herself. I forgot to smile. What does it matter anyway, sitting all the way over here?

Julie took several more photographs to have some variety, but none quite captured the perfection of the first one.

"Okay, that should do it," Julie said, handing her camera to a nearby assistant. "Gabriella and Madison, please report to Makeup for your close-ups. Carnegie, stay here for lighting, and everyone else, you're done for the day. Well done, thank you."

"What now?" Ana asked Garnett.

"I'll bring Madison back to Nora, and you can stay here while they shoot Carnegie. She's going to stand in for Madison."

"So, Carnegie is just taking pretend pictures?"

"Kind of," Garnett replied.

"I suppose a pretend assistant should be able to handle pretend pictures," Ana said.

"Nothing pretend about you, Anastasia. You're doing a pro job.

I'll see you back here when Madison is done with her makeup."

"Okay," Ana said with newly found confidence.

After Garnett and Madison left, Ana settled into the sofa and grabbed a magazine off the side table. She was thumbing through when she noticed Claire standing over her. Startled, she jumped up and tossed it aside.

"Anastasia, do you mind giving us a hand with Carnegie? Some of our crew's on break."

"Sure!" Ana said. "Over there? Where Julie's taking the photos?"

"Yes, please."

She jogged over and stopped short of the backdrop on the floor. "Should I take my shoes off, Ms. Chase—I mean, Julie?"

"If you don't mind—or we can get you a pair of booties," Julie replied.

"My socks are clean," Ana said, tossing aside her shoes.

Good choice, not wearing those horrid booties, Carnegie commented to herself. She was still seated in her off-to-the-side photo position and waiting patiently to be called for her standing star role.

"Let's get Carnegie center frame where Madison will be," Julie said.

About time, Carnegie thought. Without prompting, she casually walked over and stood in front of the camera.

"*Hmm.* She's good at taking directions," Julie said, amazed.

"Yeah, sometimes," Ana said, also amazed.

"She's standing rather close to the lens," Julie said, then looked at the monitor and started laughing. "Oh my goodness…the size of her nose from this angle! I have to get a picture of this. It's priceless."

Exactly, Carnegie said to herself. My long nose is one of my most priceless Borzoi trademarks. It's probably iconic.

"Sorry for the diversion," Julie said, composing herself. "It's just that your Carnegie is so adorable, Anastasia."

That's what Claire said, too. Carnegie thought. It's unanimous. *I'm adorable.*

CHAPTER FIFTEEN

Gilding a Lily

Up here, Madison," Nora said, patting the black leather seat. Madison easily jumped up and sat on the styling chair in front of the makeup station with its brightly-lit mirror.

Nora closely inspected her face and turned to Garnett. "She's got natural black eyeliner around those gorgeous amber eyes. And a perfect beauty mark on her muzzle. I don't see how I can improve on much. Maybe just a little touch-up…"

Nora put on her leopard-frame glasses, leaned in closely, and with a Q-tip, removed a tiny fleck from the inner corner of Madison's left eye. With Nora so close, Madison could see she still had a light dusting of the white paw powder that Carnegie sneezed onto her face and glasses. I can't wait to tell Carnegie she's still a *Snow Leopardo*, she thought. She'll like that.

"Let me see your paws, Madison," Nora said.

Remembering Carnegie's resistance, she looked to Garnett.

"Go ahead, girl. Shake," Garnett said, and Madison extended her right paw to Nora.

"Look at these long nails. I didn't notice them earlier," Nora said.

"And this is after trimming and filing," Garnett said. "Borzoi are runners, and they dig in for traction. Madison's nails are delicate for a Borzoi. Carnegie's are more like bear claws."

"They're also different colors," Nora said. "Some are clear, and some are black."

"Yes, that's not unusual," Garnett replied.

"I think this is one area we can improve on for the photos. Has she ever had her nails painted?" Nora asked.

"When Ana was younger, she painted their nails pink for a party she was having. I'm sure Madison won't mind…as long as the polish is non-toxic. She might nibble on her right paw."

"Yeah, I remember that from the clown makeup," Nora said, trying not to recall Carnegie's *Sneeze of the Century*. "Oh, don't worry. Do you know how many models bite their nails? There'd be more dead models laying around than clowns," Nora said with her snorty laugh.

Garnett smiled uneasily, finding it disconcerting that Nora measured her products' toxicity by dead clients.

"I'll do an ivory base coat first so they all match," Nora said. "Then, I think an iridescent pearl finish coat will be lovely." She held up the bottle of pearl polish for Garnett to see.

"Lovely like you, Madison," Garnett said, petting her.

"Oh, and there's her back paws, too," Nora said, trying to part her feathers to see them. "I don't think I can paint her rear nails while she's sitting. There's too much fur in the way."

"How about if we have her lie down?" Garnett suggested. "I can move her to the grooming table."

"That should work. I'll bring another light so I can see better."

Madison relocated to the grooming table and reclined with her legs sticking out for Nora to polish her nails. It felt relaxing to be lying there, and Madison closed her eyes. She was reminded of earlier times in their old house in the country. Ana had declared Thursday as "Spa Day" for her and Carnegie. Every Thursday afternoon, Ana would spread big white terry towels on her bedroom floor for them to lie on. Each took turns having Ana trim and file their nails (their *least* favorite part), being brushed (which was pleasant unless there were mats to be combed out), followed by getting a dog massage (their *most* favorite part). Madison recalled the one and only time Ana substituted sparkling mineral water for tap water in their bowls.

What was supposed to enhance their spa experience turned into a disastrous nose-tickling, snorting and sneezing session. "Yeah, maybe not sparkling next time," Ana had said, when she wiped up the mineral water that their sneezing sprayed all around her bedroom.

I miss those days when Ana was home all the time, Madison reminisced, then thought about how Carnegie would say she was getting melancholy. And where is Carnegie now? Madison wondered. Is she still in the studio being the standing star? Did they paint her nails too? I wonder if they're pearl like mine…

Her pondering was interrupted by Garnett lightly shaking her shoulder. "Your nails are done, Madison. We'll do a final brushing, and then we need to wait for Nora at the makeup station for a last look to make sure you're perfect."

Madison obediently stood to have her fur brushed and her feathers combed through, then jumped off the grooming table and followed Garnett back to the styling chair. She hopped up like before, but this time, instead of just a passing glance, her reflection in the makeup mirror caught her attention.

Madison was used to being admired as beautiful. Her dog show fame was based on her being beautiful—the *most* beautiful—and it brought years of countless compliments, awards, television appearances, and cover photos. But she never gave her beauty a thought. After all, she came from a long line of beautiful Borzoi…generations, in fact. And her mom was beautiful. Her sister was beautiful—maybe not in all the spectacular ways she thought—but beautiful. Being beautiful, for Madison, was ordinary. But now, something was different, and for the first time, she saw herself as others saw her…far from ordinary…*EXTRA*ordinary.

She tilted her head to admire how her butterfly hair clip shimmered in the lights and raised a paw to see her iridescent pearl nails sparkle.

Is this gilding a lily like Carnegie said? Madison asked herself. If it is, I don't care, I think I look pretty.

But more than her dazzling physical appearance, there was now an aura around her…an intangible yet undeniable magical glow. Madison was a *STAR.*

CHAPTER SIXTEEN

Royal Crown Collar

"Carnegie, sit!" Ana said for the third time. Exasperated and embarrassed, she tried pushing on her rear end, but Carnegie remained standing statue-solid.

"I'm sorry, Julie, I don't know what's gotten into her. She usually loves to sit on furniture."

"It's okay, we'll figure this out," Julie said. "How about if you sit on the chaise where Gabriella will be? Maybe she'll want to sit next to you."

Ana seated herself and tried to get Carnegie to sit by her, but she remained unmovable.

What is wrong with everyone? Carnegie thought. I'm the standing star. I'm *supposed* to be standing.

"I don't think we can get a good light reading if she isn't in the same position as Madison will be. Maybe her standing-in wasn't the best idea," Julie said.

"I know she can do it. Give me a sec. I'll be right back," Ana said, dashing off to the seating area. She returned with a T-R-E-A-T that Garnett had packed in her show tote.

Ana held up the irresistible star-shaped cookie from the posh dog bakery, and before she could say "sit," Carnegie's furry rear end was firmly planted on the chaise lounge. Munching on the cookie, the *standing* star was now a *sitting* star.

I suppose a star must have range, Carnegie said to herself.

"Perfect," Julie said. "Ana, why don't you sit on the chaise again?

You can stand in for Gabriella and keep Carnegie next to you."

Ana happily sat on the chaise and put her arm around Carnegie.

Carnegie regarded Ana with skepticism. Well, she can *try*, she said to herself. This standing-sitting star stuff takes twice the talent.

"Anastasia, can you take your arm off Carnegie's shoulder?" Julie asked. "It's in the frame."

"Oh my gosh! Sorry!"

"No problem. Who doesn't want to hug Carnegie?" Julie said with a smile.

She's coming in for a hug, Carnegie thought as Julie approached with a light meter. Time to turn on my star power.

"*Aaagh!*" Julie cried, quickly pulling back her hand.

"What's wrong?!" Ana asked, looking to see what Carnegie was doing.

"She's snarling!"

My winningest smile is *snarling?* Carnegie thought, insulted.

"No, no," Ana said, "She's actually smiling...you know, like a person."

"Are you sure? She looks vicious," Julie said, backing up.

"She can't help the fangs. That's just how her teeth are. Look," Ana said, sticking her hand in Carnegie's mouth. "Harmless."

Carnegie narrowed her eyes at Ana. If you're going to stick your hand in my mouth, it better have a cookie attached to it.

"Well, alright," Julie said hesitantly. "But can we have her *not* smile? Her big white teeth will throw off my light reading...unless Madison smiles, too...but I don't think the publicist—or anyone, to be honest—will like this look."

"She sort of smiles on her own, but I can try to make her stop." Ana gently wrapped her hand around Carnegie's muzzle and said, "No smiling."

That won't be hard, Carnegie said to herself. What actor could possibly emote under these working conditions?

When Ana removed her hand, Carnegie's mouth remained shut but with her lips tightly pinched together. The standing-sitting star was now a standing-sitting-scowling star.

Julie squinted at Carnegie. "That's not the best look either...but it'll do for lighting. These are just test photos. We won't be using them."

Of course not, Carnegie said to herself.

After several light readings, test shots, moving lights around, and more test shots, Julie handed off her camera to an assistant.

"Thank you, Ana, we've got everything we need. And thank you, too," she said, approaching Carnegie. "Can I give you a hug?"

Carnegie turned her body away.

"She's probably tired," Ana said.

"I bet not too tired for this," Julie said, taking a dog treat out of her pocket.

Are you kidding? I'm *exhausted.* But a star must make sacrifices for their fans, she said to herself, eagerly snatching the treat.

"Oh, good. I still have my fingers. Thank you, Carnegie," Julie said, smiling, and wiping her hand on her slacks. "Gabriella and Madison will be here soon. You're both welcome to stay and watch."

"Yes, please," Ana replied. "Come on, Carnegie, let's go sit."

Within a few minutes, Gabriella, Madison, and Garnett arrived in the photo studio. Carnegie got up from her seat, expecting Madison to come over, but instead, Garnett handed her leash to Gabriella, and the two of them went over to Julie. Carnegie resumed her seat but didn't miss how Madison was trotting along so cheerfully next to her co-star.

"How did it go?" Garnett asked Ana as she joined her on the sofa.

"It was so much fun. I stood in for Gabriella on the chaise lounge with Carnegie."

"Did Carnegie cooperate?" Garnett asked.

"Yeah, except we had a smiling situation..."

"What do you mean?"

"Well, Julie thought she was snarling, but she was just trying to smile like a person. Although it was bigger than usual and pretty scary. I got her to stop, then she did a weird thing with her lips."

Weird lips?...says the girl who painted hers on this morning, Carnegie thought. She proudly licked her long, thin black lips. Who doesn't love dog lips? Especially mine?

"Well, we can sit back and relax now," Garnett said. "The rest is up to Madison. She looks perfect with Gabriella, doesn't she?"

"Oh, she really does!" Ana replied.

Carnegie looked too—and what she saw surprised her. Yes, it was her sister...but there was something different. Her butterfly hair clip shimmered in the studio lights—and even her nails sparkled. But there was more than that. Madison was beyond happy; she was glowing. She was posing for the camera—so naturally—with those irresistibly sweet eyes. Even her goofy little grin looked endearing. Gabriella was petting, hugging, and praising her. Julie and Tina were complimenting her. Everyone in the entire crew was enchanted by her charm. For the first time, Carnegie truly saw Madison separate from herself—being admired—on her own.

Was it like this at all those dog shows, too? Has Madison always been revered like this, and I just never saw it? Carnegie wondered.

With all the accolades and awards Madison won at dog shows, her sister came home humble and simply happy to see *her.* Madison never even glanced at the display cases filled with her spectacular Best in Show trophies and magnificent multi-color ribbons.

And Carnegie thought Madison didn't care about the fancy collars sent to her by fans from around the world. When Madison was out of sight, Carnegie would longingly stare at the lineup of exquisite collars displayed on glass shelves in their bedroom. Her eyes always lit up at one in particular. It was a wide, black velvet collar set with breathtaking jewels in the shape of a royal crown. She heard it was gifted by a prince, and something about it called to her. It must be what her mom told her and Madison when they were puppies.

Carnegie closed her eyes and tried to remember. Mom said something about our Borzoi ancestors being royal and us having the same noble blood and some boring *blah, blah, blah* history stuff that I really didn't listen to. But then she said the Borzoi live in a real fancy royal palace…or is it a castle?…or a palastle? Yeah, that's right. They live in a real fancy royal palastle with person servants waiting on them paw and paw. They're the most prized and famous-est dogs in the entire world.

So, when Carnegie couldn't go to Madison's dog shows, she imagined she was in her royal palastle instead of being stuck at home. She perfected the technique of discreetly taking the royal crown collar off the shelf and flipping it to land on her head. Looking in Ana's vanity mirror, she pictured herself wearing the sparkly jeweled crown, sitting on a red velvet pillow on an ornate gold throne. How grand she was. How famous. Much more famous than her champion show dog sister. The famous-est. Before everyone returned from Madison's dog show, she would carefully return the crown collar to its place on the shelf.

Carnegie was sure Madison only liked the collars Ana gave them for their first birthday. It's because she wants to look like me, Carnegie told herself. Our birthday collars are *exactly* the same, except Madison's is purple and mine is red, and hers has a heart charm, and mine has a crown charm. But other than that, they're *exactly* the same…like Maddie and me—except one of us (me) is more *adorable.*

At home, everyone loved Carnegie and Madison equally. Carnegie could even be snooty and choose not to sleep on Ana's bed, and Ana would invite her back every night. Everyone loved her no matter what she did and how she acted.

But they were *not* home now. Carnegie averted her eyes from the scene painfully playing out before her in the photo studio.

They all love Madison, and they don't love me.

CHAPTER SEVENTEEN

Balloons

The Thanksgiving holiday was approaching, and the cast was given a several-day break while the stage sets were being constructed. Thanksgiving Eve found Carnegie tossing and turning in her bed, thinking about the Macy's Thanksgiving Day parade they were going to be in to promote the "Hearts Over Broadway" show. In the morning, she and Madison would be marching under parade balloons—big ones, *very* big ones—of their characters' likenesses.

Carnegie's mind was racing, pondering the possibilities. I wonder if my balloon will be cute. I hope they make my nose long enough. Some of the balloon characters look like blobby marshmallows. I don't want mine to make me look fat.

She got up and went over to Ana's full-length mirror. Imagining she was a balloon, Carnegie tried to look at herself from the side. But the mirror was tall and narrow, so she could only see sections of herself at a time.

She looked over at Madison sleeping soundly next to Ana, who was home for Thanksgiving. She tiptoed over to her sister's side of the bed and whispered, "Madison. Madison. Maddie. Maddie. Maddie. Hey, Madison. Maddie. Maddie..."

No response.

Continuing to call her sister's name, Carnegie tried pushing Madison's eyelids open with her paw.

Nothing.

She put her paws on Madison's shoulder and rolled her back and forth.

Still nothing.

Who sleeps this soundly? Carnegie asked herself. She pushed and pulled, back and forth, gaining more and more momentum until, suddenly, Madison rolled off the bed and landed with a dull thump on the carpet.

Oops, Carnegie said to herself, suppressing a laugh.

"*Wuhhaat?*" Madison moaned more than spoke.

"Maddie, are you awake?"

"I am *now*. What am I doing on the floor?"

"I don't know. Since you're awake, maybe it's a good time for us to go to the park."

"Now? In the middle of the night? Whatever for?"

"We can practice walking like we'll be doing in the parade."

"With Ana? She's sleeping."

"No, just us. I know how to work the elevator."

"*Really?*" Madison asked. "When did you learn to do that?"

"Oh, when everyone was busy...maybe sleeping. Do you want to hear how I do it? It's very impressive."

Madison yawned. "Maybe another time."

"I push the button with my nose."

"Uh-huh."

"It's just the right height."

"Your nose or the button?"

"Both," Carnegie said. "That's the secret magic of it. Now, we can go to the park anytime we want."

"But what about dognappers?"

"Sleeping dogs?" Carnegie asked.

"No, dognappers are like kidnappers, only they steal valuable dogs. Haven't you heard the persons talking about them?"

"I don't know. Maybe. I haven't been paying attention."

"I heard Henry say he's being extra cautious when he takes us on walks because of the dognappers," Madison said.

"What do they do with the dogs?" Carnegie asked.

"Sometimes they hold them for ransom. They charge a lot of money for their persons to get them back."

"How much do you think they'd get for us? I think they'd get a *LOT* for me."

"That's not the point, Carnegie. The dognappers aren't nice."

"Well, if we see any, we'll just run away. No dognappers can run as fast as we can."

"I guess not. But why do we need to practice walking? You just walk like normal," Madison said.

Oh, right, Carnegie thought to herself. *Normal*—just like her telling me to walk "normal" in Pucchi booties—only tied to a gigantic helium-filled balloon on a nationally televised show with millions of persons watching. What could possibly go wrong?

"We have to be in Hair and Makeup really early in the morning, Carnegie. That's not long from now. I don't want to have bags under my eyes."

"That's what fur is for. It's nature's concealer."

"*Pleeease*, go back to sleep, Carnegie."

"Will you sleep in your own bed by mine instead of with Ana?"

Madison sighed. "If I sleep there, will you stop talking?"

"Of course. I don't want furry eye bags."

Madison and Carnegie went to their respective beds, circled around three times in unison, and dropped into the soft cushions.

"Maddie, one last thing..." Carnegie loudly whispered.

"*One* thing, and then we're going to sleep," Madison impatiently replied.

"Absolutely. I heard them say we'll be wearing harnesses that are tied to our parade balloons. Have you wondered what would happen if they let go of the ropes tomorrow and we floated up and up and up with our balloons into outer space? I was th—" Carnegie interrupted herself with a deep yawn and closed her eyes. "Oh my. I guess I *am* tired after all. Goodnight, Maddie."

Madison did not respond. She was wide awake, staring at the ceiling, imagining herself tied to a balloon, drifting endlessly into the dark abyss with the earth below, a tiny blue and white ball getting smaller and smaller…

CHAPTER EIGHTEEN

The Parade

The Macy's Thanksgiving Day Parade
Downtown Manhattan, New York

Media personalities, Bob Benner and Gail Langdon, were stationed at their freezing outdoor anchor desk, bundled up against the November cold and wind. As the TV channel hosts, they were announcing and describing the parade participants for the national television audience watching from home. There were massive marching bands, hundreds of clowns and performers, elaborate floats, and more. But the most exciting of all had to be the world-famous giant character balloons. Bob pointed to two just coming into view.

"Well, here they come, Gail! The balloons that everyone has been waiting for! It's Madison! Broadway's newest canine star who plays Olivia in the upcoming 'Hearts Over Broadway' musical…and her sister, Carnegie!"

"From what I hear, Bob, these sisters will be *stealing hearts* when this sensational show opens next month. I can't wait!"

"Me neither!" Bob agreed. "I think we all remember when Madison won 'Best in Show' at Madison Square Garden. What an amazing victory that was for our New York native! And then that big win catapulted Madison onto the Broadway stage to capture such a coveted lead role. And Carnegie, well, she plays her sister."

"These pedigree pooches aren't just impressive *on* stage, Bob. They're descendants of brave and regal wolfhounds. They're Borzoi royalty, in fact."

"Whoa! Do I curtsy when I meet them?"

"No, don't be silly, Bob," Gail said, laughing. "Men just bow."

"Good one, Gail! You know, I'm told that these are two of the biggest balloons to ever grace this hallowed holiday processional!"

"That's right! Each one of those elegant snouts looks as long as a subway car. And the real-life versions of Madison and Carnegie are walking the parade route today...*in person!*"

Bob looked at Gail and then directly into the camera. "I have a question that our viewers at home may be wondering, too. Do you call it in *'person'* if they're *dogs*?"

"Ha! You got me there, Bob. Whatever you call it, Madison and Carnegie are bravely helping those balloon handlers keep their likenesses on the ground in these icy-cold, high winds. Oh my goodness! Look how poor Carnegie is shivering! She's really feeling these record-low temps."

"Yes, Gail. It must be hard to walk in your sister's shadow...quite literally today! Madison's balloon is blocking all of her sun—and it's freezing in the shade. Someone bring that girl a faux fur muffler and some shearling dog booties, STAT!"

Suddenly, a downdraft of wind shear sent Carnegie's balloon straight down onto the handlers, temporarily making them, as well as the real Carnegie, disappear under a massive squashing of polyurethane fabric. Her balloon head abruptly over-inflated, causing an ear to shoot up two stories and one of her eyes to pop out in a disturbing fashion.

"Looks like Carnegie is getting an awfully big head with all this attention!" Bob commented with an uncomfortable laugh.

Under Carnegie's balloon, in her fear and confusion, the real Carnegie bit a hole in the very tip of the long, inflated nose. The balloon quickly lost air from the nose back at an alarming rate, creating a sickening moaning sound and appearing frighteningly distorted.

Bob and Gail were stunned speechless. Finally, he said, "Well, I think I speak for everyone when I say Carnegie has seen better days..."

Humiliated, Carnegie crawled out from under her deflated balloon just in time to watch her likeness be trampled beneath the feet of a high school marching band, coming up from behind.

In extreme contrast to Carnegie's earth-bound indignity, a massive updraft caused Madison's balloon to break free of the real Madison's harness and begin a graceful ascension into the skies above New York City.

Gail grabbed Bob's arm and pointed into the sky. "Did a wolf-shaped cloud just fly by?...because there goes Madison!"

After a short drift, Madison's balloon's ropes gently snagged and anchored it on the spire of the Chrysler Building, where it floated above the city as a glorious promotion for the opening of their "Hearts Over Broadway" musical.

CHAPTER NINETEEN

The Heart

When they returned from their Thanksgiving break, the starring cast members were provided with chauffeured car service to and from the theater for the remaining rehearsals and through the run of the show...which everyone hoped would be a *very* long time.

Garnett picked up Madison and Carnegie at five o'clock and they were waiting in their penthouse's building lobby when a black Cadillac Escalade ESV pulled up.

"Oh, I think that's our ride, girls," Garnett said as Oscar, their building doorman, held open the front doors for them.

Carnegie and Madison recognized the type of vehicle. The Braxtons owned a shorter pearl-white Escalade when they lived in the country. Puppy Carnegie had seen it as her royal carriage. Thinking of it still made her heart skip a beat. But that was a different time and, again, literally another story.

A starkly-uniformed, imposingly-large chauffeur, dressed head-to-toe in dark navy blue, approached them. He removed his patent leather-brimmed cap from his shiny bald head, tucked it under his arm, and briskly bowed.

"Good morning, Madam. I am Klaus, your theater chauffeur."

"Nice to meet you, Klaus. I'm Garnett, and this is Madison and Carnegie." She started to lead them towards the rear of the vehicle. "Can you open the hatch door for them, please?"

"Excuse me, Madam," Klaus said. "They enter here." He opened the side passenger door and gestured inside.

Garnett was stunned to see how the Escalade's stretch interior had been customized to maximize the space, with two sets of ivory leather seats facing each other and a large, carpeted area in between. The seat nearest the door was folded up to make it easy for the Borzoi girls to get in. Once they and Garnett entered, Klaus folded down the seat, briskly bowed again, and closed the door.

Carnegie immediately settled in, sitting in her two-on-the-floor style, and Madison curled up on the seat next to her. Garnett sat in the opposite seat, facing forward. She ran her hand over the gleaming wood trim as she admired the luxurious interior, which had climate controls on every seat, a full entertainment system, and a huge glass sunroof that showed off Manhattan's skyscrapers.

"How do you like this, girls?" she asked, then smiled at their indifference. It takes more than a luxurious ride to impress these two, Garnett thought...although Carnegie might sell her soul for the right cookie.

Before long, the theater district came into view, and they were surrounded by massive Broadway show advertisements, all competing for attention.

"We're here!" Garnett excitedly said as they pulled up to their theater. Looking out the windows and skylight, they were awestruck by the "HEARTS OVER BROADWAY" gigantic show signage and the enormous theater marquee that stood out against the early evening sky. But only one name in lights grabbed them—"STARRING MADISON as Olivia!"

"Look, Madison! Your name in lights!" Garnett cried.

Madison's heart beat faster, but she had to still her excitement. Her heart was back in their bedroom the morning before their roles were cast. Carnegie was waving her paw across an invisible theater marquee in the sky. *"Think about it, Maddie! My name in lights: STARRING CARNEGIE as Olivia!"*

Madison snuck a look at her sister, expecting to be met with a glare and snide remark, but Carnegie was looking down, silent.

Klaus appeared at the passenger door. "We're here, Madam. I've been instructed to have you enter through the lobby today rather than the backstage door."

"Thank you, Klaus. Just let me grab their leashes," Garnett replied. "Girls, let's go."

Madison hopped down off her seat, but Carnegie remained seated.

"Carnegie, come on!" Garnett prompted with a tug on her leash. Carnegie was not listening. She was thinking—thinking about her *perfect* plan, thinking about letters, huge letters in lights on the theater marquee: M-A-D-I-S-O-N C-A-R-N-E-G-I-E. Some of the letters were even the same. It will be an easy swap-out. Satisfied with her calculations, Carnegie exited the Escalade, and they all walked under the marquee with its bright ceiling of lights to the theater entrance. The polished brass doors were flanked with more show posters in illuminated cases. They recognized Julie Chase's photography on the posters from their photo session, but the main poster was a surprise. It featured an irresistibly sweet portrait of Madison in a large red heart over the show title.

"Oh my goodness!" Garnett gasped at the sudden realization. "Madison is featured as the *heart* in '*Hearts* Over Broadway'!"

Carnegie suddenly stopped short and stared at Madison's heart portrait. This is a little problematic, she thought. We look pretty much the same…if they just add a beauty mark to my muzzle. That's what black makeup pencils are for. The Snow Leopardo can do that. I'm sure Madison's butterfly costume will fit my head. Yes, this could work…

"Carnegie, come," Garnett said with a little tug on her leash. "What has gotten into you? You're going to make us late."

On entering the extravagant lobby, they were greeted by Eddie, a young, enthusiastic theater volunteer.

"Good evening, Ms. Dixon and Carnegie," he said. "And good evening, Miss Madison!" He tilted his head, grinned, and made a heart gesture with his hands. "Let me get these doors for you."

Walking through the audience's main entrance doors, it was stunning to see the theater's enormous interior in its full glory. The grand chandelier, a masterpiece of crystal and light, cast a golden glow that highlighted the theater's intricate gilded ornamentation and plush red velvet seats.

During rehearsals, Garnett had been sitting in the audience but mostly in the dark. It suddenly struck her how big this production was, how important, and how very fortunate they were to be a part of it.

As she, Madison, and Carnegie walked down the center aisle, they were surprised that the bare stage they'd been rehearsing on had been completely transformed. As if by magic, it had become a dramatically lit, glamorous Art Deco-style bedroom with high, mirrored walls and miles of artfully-draped, shimmery white satin fabric.

Gabriella's plain bed that was used for rehearsals, was now elegant and glamorous. A tall, stately headboard was tufted in the same silky white satin with crystal buttons that glimmered like diamonds.

The worn wood slat stage floor was covered with a high-gloss, slick black surface.

A sleek light fixture with long, lush fringes of sparkling crystal prisms hung center stage from the invisible ceiling.

Getting closer to the stage, they noticed that the orchestra pit was now completely filled with chairs and music stands holding sheets of music.

Randy was already in the theater with Precious and Glory. The break had not improved their attitude as they greeted Carnegie and Madison with barely suppressed snarls.

Carnegie cringed and whispered to her sister, "Have you ever heard the expression, 'Absence makes the heart grow fonder?'"

"I think so," Madison whispered back.

"Apparently, it doesn't apply to understudies," Carnegie said.

"Uh-uh," Madison replied with a wince.

Ruby greeted them from the lip of the stage.

"Welcome back, everyone!" she said, clasping her hands and smiling. "Madison and Carnegie…Congratulations on the Macy's Thanksgiving Day Parade! I watched you on TV. The whole nation tuned in—over thirty million viewers!"

"Yeah, that was quite a dramatic performance Carnegie's balloon put on," Randy said with a sarcastic smile.

"Well…every year, there seems to be a little mishap with one of the balloons," Ruby said, smiling sympathetically at Carnegie.

"*Little* mishap? The press is calling Carnegie the Hindenburg Hound," Randy said with a mean-spirited laugh.

"Anyhow…" Ruby said, raising her eyebrows and trying to ignore Randy's snide remark, "Madison's balloon looks fantastic floating above the Chrysler Building! Our marketing department couldn't believe the lucky break to have all that free publicity. Opening night is already sold out, so thank you, Madison!" Ruby said, applauding her.

Garnett joined in the applause, and Madison slowly wagged her tail and looked down. She didn't want to see the expressions on Precious' and Glory's faces…or even her sister's.

"Today, we start dress rehearsals, which will be so much fun!" Ruby said, clasping her hands.

"She keeps promising fun," Carnegie whispered to Madison. "I don't know about you, but I'm still waiting for it to kick in."

Madison lowered her eyes. "I think it's been pretty fun."

"Except the Glory-trying-to-eat-us part," Carnegie replied.

Madison snuck a look at Glory, who was hunched over with her perpetual sneer and the growl that was too low for Ruby to hear but clearly loud enough for the intended "growlees."

"Yeah, she's not fun, but I *really* love singing show tunes and dancing with Gabriella," Madison said with a little grin.

"And I *really* love being a piece of furniture," Carnegie said with an out-loud sarcastic scoff that got a questioning look from Ruby, who paused a moment, then continued.

"In addition to this beautiful stage set you see here, there are other scenes that have moving set pieces that your dogs will have to become accustomed to.

"We have our full backstage crew from now through the run of the show. Nora will be doing your dogs' makeup, if needed. Garnett, I think you met her at the photo shoot."

"Yes. She did a wonderful job on Madison."

Madison looked at Carnegie to see if she had a bad reaction to Nora, but she seemed pleased.

Ha! The Snow Leopardo, Carnegie said to herself. Just as I planned.

"And for your dogs' hair…or fur," Ruby continued with a smile, "we have the award-winning stylist, Mia."

Garnett breathed a sigh of relief that it was not Jimmy. "Can we give her some grooming directions that are specific to the Borzoi breed standard?"

"Of course. She's also a professional dog show groomer, but I'm sure she'll be open to suggestions," Ruby replied.

"Laura, who was at the photo shoot, is our theater's wardrobe supervisor in charge of all the cast costumes. She's setting up our wardrobe room backstage and will keep Madison's butterfly there.

"Amelia and Lily will still be helping out, but since they also go to school, we may have other volunteers pitch in with their duties.

"We've just had a small band for rehearsals, but now we have our full orchestra—around 30 musicians—playing in the orchestra pit.

"Garnett and Randy, you'll notice the stage floor is super shiny. It's also super slippery. Both Nora and Mia have paw wax to apply to the dogs' pads that will prevent them from sliding. Brad and I will be directing their entrances, but should the occasion arise, please do not, I repeat, do *not* let them on the stage without it. We don't want any accidents. And, if you apply the paw wax yourselves, make sure it's rubbed into their pads, so it doesn't leave a messy residue on this beautiful stage flooring.

"We don't want the dogs leaving the theater for potty breaks so there is now a fenced-in artificial grass area they can use backstage. Running around on the grass can remove their paw wax, so walking only. Amelia or Lily can take them on potty breaks if you want.

"Our stage manager, Brad, and I will be on headsets and in constant communications. We'll be dressed in show black—which means black head-to-toe—so the audience won't see us in the wings. The dogs need to get used to me being less visible, so you can say goodbye to my red hair. I'll be wearing a black cap during dress rehearsals and performances.

"And starting today, Carnegie will move into Madison's dressing room. It'll be a lot more efficient for Mia, Nora, and Laura to have them in the same place."

Even better, thought Carnegie. I'll already be in the star's dressing room.

"Princess and Glory will remain in their same dressing room. We've installed dog gates in both rooms so the doors can be kept open if needed. You're Borzoi owners, so I don't have to tell you to make sure the gates are kept latched.

"You have some time this morning to resettle in your dressing rooms before we start rehearsing. Any questions?"

"I've got one," Randy said, raising his hand and wiggling his fingers. "Or maybe two questions because it's about Precious *and* Glory…and about three things. Is that six questions?"

"What's your question or questions?" Ruby asked.

"Do Precious and Glory get the same hair, makeup, and wardrobe as Madison and Carnegie?" Randy finally asked.

"We'd like both of your dogs to check in with Nora and Mia so they know how to style them, should they have to step in. Only Precious will need to meet with Laura in Wardrobe."

"For a wardrobe fitting?" Randy asked with a mocking laugh. "For that bug Olivia wears on her head?"

Madison lowered her eyes at Randy's belittling comment, and Carnegie glared at him in defense of her sister's beloved butterfly.

Ruby stared at Randy with impatience, then composed herself and replied, "Madison's butterfly hair clip will probably fit, but just to be sure…"

Carnegie thought she heard Glory whisper to Precious: "Oh, it will fit all right. I can see it on your head right now."

CHAPTER TWENTY

Fashionista Cat Attack

Backstage, in their newly shared dressing room, Carnegie leaped onto the long, luxurious sofa. "Dibs!"

Madison walked over to her sister who was lying on her back, fully stretched out, taking up the entire length.

"I called 'dibs.'"

"I heard you. You can have the sofa," Madison said. "I like my pillow bed on the floor. I just have a question."

"If it's about the goose-down cushions on this sofa, I'm not allergic to feathers, but thank you for asking," Carnegie replied.

"Actually, I was wondering what a dress rehearsal is."

Carnegie sighed in exaggerated disbelief. "You don't know?"

"That's why I asked."

"Everybody knows what it is."

"I don't. Tell me," Madison said.

"Well, if you need me to dogsplain it..."

"I do."

"Obviously, Maddie, it's when the…dresses...rehearse," Carnegie hesitantly said.

"But we don't have dresses," Madison replied with concern.

"We rehearse like regular."

"My butterfly can rehearse," Madison said sweetly.

"Uh-huh," Carnegie absently replied, her mind on a sudden realization. When she appears as Olivia on opening night, she will need her own butterfly hair clip costume. Carnegie abruptly rolled over and stared into Madison's eyes, nose-to-nose.

"What happens if your butterfly gets messed up?"

"You mean when it rehearses?" Madison asked.

"Oh, anytime. Is there like another one somewhere?"

"Laura said she keeps a backup with all the wardrobe...but *nothing* is going to happen to my butterfly, Carnegie," Madison said with a warning look.

"No, of course not. I was just curious."

Curious about how I'm going to break into the wardrobe room to get that butterfly, Carnegie said to herself. I need to formulate another *perfect* plan.

"Excuse me," Carnegie said stepping off the sofa and brushing past her sister. "I'm going to take a tour of my new dressing room." She casually walked around, not looking but consumed by scheming—although she did stop to snag a gourmet treat. She smiled with self-satisfaction as her butterfly heist plan emerged.

She ended her dressing room tour by sitting at their doorway gate. Within minutes, Laura rushed by with costumes draped over her arm. Carnegie's eyes followed her as she disappeared into a room on the other side of the hall. When the door closed, the sign on it read "WARDROBE." Yes!

She narrowed her eyes and calculated. I'll have to time it when Laura is not in the wardrobe room. Let's see...I'm free during my mid-morning and afternoon breaks. Madison likes to take naps on breaks, and the staff usually leaves us alone. And there's lunchtime—but I can't miss that. Tomorrow morning when Laura is still fussing with all the persons' costumes will be perfect. I'll have to figure out how to slip away, but that shouldn't be a problem. Everyone only cares where Madison is. They won't notice I'm gone.

The next day, like clockwork, Carnegie's plan fell into place. When she and Madison were released for their morning break, they were left alone in their dressing room. And, as expected, Madison settled in for a nap.

Carnegie went to the doorway gate and could see the wardrobe room door was closed. Suddenly, the door flew open, and Laura appeared with a portable steamer and gown on a hanger. This is almost too good to be true, Carnegie thought, as Laura rushed by.

She nibbled on the gate latch to see if it would move, but it held firm. She tried pushing it up with her nose, then grabbing it with her teeth and twisting it. Then variations and combinations of nibbling, nose pushing, and twisting. Carnegie tried pawing the latch with her right paw, then her left paw, and then both paws. Nothing worked.

This horrid latch thinks it's smarter than me. We'll see about that.

She backed up two steps, took a leap and easily sailed over the dog gate, surprising herself.

Hmm? So…Borzoi can jump high, too? I only thought we can run fast. Good to know.

Carnegie looked up and down the hall and no one was there. She tiptoed to the door marked "Wardrobe." Like their penthouse doors, it had a lever doorknob conveniently positioned at her mouth height. She easily turned the knob and quietly pushed the door open. She entered slowly, being careful to not let the door slam behind her. It was dark inside, but she could make out racks of costumes like she had briefly seen at the photo shoot. Carnegie's eyes adjusted to the darkness as she scanned the room. Varieties of hats hung above the tightly-packed costume racks and bins, filled with shoes, were stacked on the floor. Beyond the hats, racks, and bins, her sharp sighthound eyes made out a wall of shelves, and on one near the top…there it was!…A small box labeled "Olivia's backup."

Easy peasy, she thought. I'll just grab my butterfly box and be on my merry way. She made her way to the shelves, stood on her hind legs and reached for it with her mouth.

Watching from a higher shelf, Laura's fashionista cat, June, had a very different plan to protect *her* wardrobe.

"MerrROOOWWW!!!" June yowled as she leaned out and swiped her sharp claws across Carnegie's forehead.

"Help, help!!!" Carnegie yelled, falling backwards into a bin of shoes. She frantically scrambled out of the wardrobe area and lunged at the doorknob. She ripped open the door, sped down the hall, leapt over their dressing room dog gate and onto her sofa. Panting heavily, she curled up in a frightened ball.

Awakened by the commotion, Madison looked up from her floor pillow. "Are you okay?"

"Wh-aat *huff-huff* do-oo you *huff-huff* me-ean?" Carnegie stammered through her panting.

Madison looked at her sister with concern. "You're all out of breath."

Carnegie tried get her panting under control. "How *huff* could I be? I've *huff* been sleeping."

"And you don't look good."

"I had a nightmare."

"Your forehead is bleeding!" Madison said with alarm.

"It was a vivid nightmare."

Madison looked at her questioningly.

"I must have scratched myself," Carnegie casually replied. "Does it look bad?"

"It can probably be covered up with some white clown makeup."

Just perfect, Carnegie sarcastically said to herself. I don't have a butterfly to play Olivia, but I can appear onstage as a clown.

CHAPTER TWENTY-ONE

Fur Bags

Dress rehearsals were over and the evening before opening night arrived. Unable to sleep, Madison tiptoed over to her sister who was lying upside down in bed with her legs straight up in the air.

"*Pssst!* Are you awake?" Madison whispered.

"No, I'm sleeping," Carnegie replied.

"*Pssst!*" Madison tried again.

"I said, 'I'm sleeping.'"

"Wake up, please. I'm scared."

Carnegie turned right side up and sighed. "Of what?"

"Of tomorrow. Of opening night."

"You said you love singing show tunes and dancing."

"I do. But I can't remember any of my lines."

"You just have to howl."

"Yeah, but I can't remember any of my dance steps either."

"You've been doing them at all the rehearsals."

"I know, but now it's all a blank," Madison said. "Can you help me?"

"It will come back to you when the music starts. Don't worry."

"I *am* worried. What if I freeze on stage, like you did in Pucchi booties? That would be devastating."

Not a good sales pitch for getting help, Carnegie said to herself. "We better get some sleep, or we'll have fur bags under our eyes."

"*Pleeease*, Carnegie, you're such a good dancer."

"Well, that's true…but I haven't been paying much attention. I guess I can see if I remember a few moves," Carnegie replied, stepping out of her bed.

In truth, Carnegie had been closely watching and memorizing *all* of Madison's performance in preparation for her planned takeover. She knew the dances by heart.

Illuminated only by the moonlight streaming in their bedroom window, Carnegie patiently went through all the dance steps side-by-side with her sister. She told herself that the practice would be useful for when she secured the lead…but when Madison kissed her on the cheek and whispered, "Thank you, Carnegie. I feel happy about playing Olivia now," she felt an unfamiliar pang of guilt.

The next morning found Carnegie standing on Ana's vanity stool, intently looking down into a hand mirror that was lying on the vanity table. She frowned, then picked up the mirror by its handle, carried it over to Madison's bed, and dropped it on her sleeping sister's head.

"Oww!" Madison cried.

"I've got them," Carnegie said.

"Got what?"

"Fur bags. Not just under my eyes…they're all over my face! That's what I get for staying up all night dancing, showing you your steps. I look like one of those droopy hounds."

"Bloodhounds? I heard their extra skin helps them smell and track things," Madison said.

"Who cares? It looks droopy. I don't want to look like that."

"You *don't.*"

"I *do!*" Carnegie climbed into Madison's bed and stood over her. "Hold up the mirror so we can both see me."

"How can I do that?" Madison asked.

"Grab the handle with your mouth and hold the mirror so I can see myself, and then you look at me at the same time."

Madison gently picked up the handle in her mouth and tried to aim the mirror towards Carnegie's face. "Like this?"

"No, I can't see myself. I just see the ceiling."

"How about this?" Madison asked, trying to rotate the mirror handle with her tongue.

"You're pointing it at the window," Carnegie said.

"How about now?" Madison asked, twisting the handle with her teeth.

"No, that's worse. Forget the mirror. It's too complicated. Just you look at me and tell me what you see."

Madison set down the mirror and looked straight up at her sister.

"You look like you usually do, but maybe a little jowly."

"Jowly?!"

"That's only because you're leaning over me. And you just drooled on me."

"I can't help it. I'm a droopy, jowly, drooly Bloodhound now. And on opening night!"

"You're *not*. Go look at yourself straight-on in a regular mirror."

Carnegie deftly climbed out of Madison's bed without stepping on her. Unfortunately, the same couldn't be said of Ana's hand mirror that cracked under the weight of her rear foot.

Oops, Carnegie said to herself. That's not going to be very good luck for Ana. She looked to see if Madison had heard the *CRACK!*, but she had already turned over and closed her eyes. Carnegie carefully picked up the mirror and placed it broken side down on the vanity table. Looking in Ana's large vanity mirror, she turned her head in all directions, admiring herself.

"You're right, Maddie. I'm still adorable. It must have been that unlucky mirror." She walked back to her bed, circled around three times, and dropped into her pillow. "I don't know why we're awake so early. Our call time isn't until five tonight. I'm going back to sleep."

CHAPTER TWENTY-TWO

Secret Magic

At 4:30 p.m., Ana was dressed and nearly ready to leave for the theater when Catherine entered her bedroom. "You look lovely, Anastasia."

"Thanks, Mom. Do you think it's okay if I wear sneakers and bring my dressy shoes for later?"

"Oh, yeah. That's a good idea. Are you sure you want to get to the theater so early?"

"Yes! I'm going to help Garnett get Madison and Carnegie settled in their dressing room," Ana said, stuffing her heels into her backpack. "Besides, I get to ride in their chauffeured car."

"Alright then. We'll meet you at the theater at seven when the doors open. You know where our seats are?"

"Yup. Garnett has my ticket."

"Better take this in case it's chilly backstage," Catherine said, handing her daughter a sweater. "And you'll need help getting the girls to the lobby."

"I can do it,"

"Not both of them. Dad will help you."

Spencer appeared in Ana's bedroom doorway. "Did I hear something about Dad?"

"Yeah, you're going to help me take Carnegie and Madison down."

"...*Please?"* Spencer added.

"Sorry. I mean, will you, please, Dad?"

"Yes, when you ask so nicely. You don't want to come with your mom and me? It's a big family event."

"No, thanks. Besides, half of our family is leaving now. Can you grab Madison's leash? I'll take Carnegie. Hey, where *is* Carnegie? She was here a minute ago."

"Maybe she's at the living room windows," Spencer suggested.

"Yeah, she's probably guarding her cookies from those dogs who walk in 'her' park," Ana said.

"I don't know how she can even see them from so high up," Spencer said. "And when's the last time a Golden Retriever scaled our apartment building to steal dog cookies?"

"Proof positive we're keeping them away," Carnegie had told Madison when she asked the same question.

"I'll go get her," Ana said. "Be right back."

But Ana did not come "right back" with Carnegie. She did not return at all.

"Carnegie! Carnegie!! Carnegie!!!" Ana's voice increased in volume and anxiety as she went from room to room to room. Finally, she breathlessly reappeared in the doorway. "She's not anywhere!"

Her parents joined the search, opening closet doors, looking under beds, behind sofas and chairs. Still, no Carnegie.

"Carnegie, here's a treat!" Ana called out, which usually elicited an immediate response. She opened and closed the refrigerator door and jiggled the dog cookie jar lid. Nothing. "Oh my goodness! She's *really* gone!"

"Don't panic, Princess," Spencer said, trying to hide his own concern. "She didn't just disappear…unless…"

Suddenly stunned into silence, no one dared say the unspeakable: *Carnegie had been dognapped!*

A text notification broke their terrible trance. "Wait! A message from Garnett," Ana said. "Carnegie is in the lobby, and she doesn't have a leash. Garnett's wondering where *we* are."

"What?!" Catherine and Spencer exclaimed in unison.

"Carnegie's down there alone?" Catherine asked.

"I know!" Ana said, "That's insane! I'll text Garnett we're coming right down."

Ana quickly leashed-up Madison and grabbed her backpack and Carnegie's leash while Spencer called for the elevator. In the ride down, the Braxtons looked at each other in disbelief. How on earth did Carnegie end up in the lobby? Madison tried to look equally perplexed.

The elevator doors opened to find a confused Garnett holding a self-satisfied Carnegie by the collar. While the Braxtons and Garnett discussed her mysterious lobby appearance, Carnegie proudly whispered to her sister, "See, what did I tell you? Secret magic."

"You had everyone worried, Carnegie," Madison whispered back, annoyed.

"I knew where I was and isn't that the most important thing?"

"Next time you're going to take the elevator on your own, tell me."

"Oh, so you can be the big hero who finds me?"

"No! They even thought you might have been dognapped."

"*Really?* Like for a big ransom? How much?"

Exasperated, Madison turned away.

"Well, thank goodness, she's here safe and sound," Garnett concluded, clipping on Carnegie's leash. "We better get going, or we'll be late. See y'all at the theater!"

Klaus, who was waiting at the curb, came around their car, briskly bowed, and opened the passenger door. Carnegie instantly broke away from Garnett, jumped into the car, spun three times, and backed into her two-on-the-floor seating.

"Oh dear. It's going to be one of those nights," Garnett said, rubbing her leash-burned hand.

It was 4:55 p.m. when Klaus pulled up to the stage door entrance. Carnegie darted to the passenger door and started in with her impatient brat barking. “HERF! HERF! HERF!”

“Carnegie, *shh,”* Ana said. “Madison is being good, and she’s the star.”

For *now,* Carnegie said to herself. She looked over her shoulder at her sister, who was still curled up on the seat. Madison looked back with apologetic eyes.

“We’ve arrived, ladies,” Klaus announced over the car intercom. Garnett took Carnegie’s leash, wrapped it around her wrist twice, and picked up her dog show tote with the other. “Ana, you take Madison. Carnegie is out of her mind tonight.”

Klaus opened the Escalade passenger door with a bow and said, “Break a leg tonight.”

“More like break a paw,” Ana replied with a laugh.

“Let’s get them inside before we break *a-ny-t-h-i-n-g.*” Garnett’s voice trailed off as Carnegie leaped from the car, dragging her by the wrist and sending her dog show tote flying. With the precision of a matador, Klaus jumped out of Carnegie’s way and then—with the grace of a male ballet dancer—caught Garnett before she landed on the ground. He carefully set her upright, retrieved her tote, and then stared at Carnegie in a manner that instantly calmed her into an obedient sit-stay. With a crisp heel click, he presented her leash to Garnett.

“Your dog, Madam,” he said. “And your bag.”

Regaining her composure, Garnett smoothed out her evening dress, took her tote and Carnegie’s leash. “Thank you, Klaus. Opening night is a little too exciting for some of us. Sorry.”

Klaus bowed briskly in response. “No problem, Madam. I’ll meet you back here after the performance.”

CHAPTER TWENTY-THREE

Good Bad Luck

"Wow! What's all this?" Ana asked as they approached Madison's and Carnegie's dressing room—or what they could see of it. Huge, spectacular flower arrangements nearly blocked the entrance. Some were on tall stands and pedestals, some in crystal vases, and others in white wicker baskets with large round handles. Shipping boxes and beautifully wrapped gift boxes were stacked on a wheeled cart. Lily and Amelia darted in and out of the doorway, grabbing items and bringing them inside.

"Hi, Ms. Dixon," Lily said when she reappeared in the doorway. She held up a cut crystal vase with long-stem white roses and a wide white satin ribbon embellished with "MADISON" in gold letters

"Look, how pretty! We're getting things organized for you," Lily said, disappearing inside with the roses.

"Is there room in there for us?" Garnett asked Amelia, who had replaced Lily at the doorway.

"I hope so. Come on in…watch your step."

Madison with Ana and Carnegie with Garnett entered the dressing room in a state of awe. The beauty and fragrance of all the floral arrangements was overwhelming. Madison, who especially loved flowers, was in sniffing heaven. She was immediately attracted to a standing arrangement in the shape of her iconic butterfly. It was artfully composed of tightly packed roses dyed the perfect color purple. Madison raised her nose to inhale its sweet scent.

I love it, she said to herself with a little grin.

Next to the butterfly was a standing arrangement of white carnations shaped like a gigantic horseshoe.

"Did we win the Kentucky Derby?" Carnegie whispered to Madison sarcastically.

"I think horseshoes are for good luck," Madison whispered back.

"Isn't it *bad* luck in the theater to wish someone *good* luck?"

"I hope not," Madison said. "It would be horrible for us to have bad luck tonight."

Suddenly, Carnegie remembered the hand mirror that broke that morning. *Ana's* mirror. The bad luck falls on the mirror owner, not the mirror breaker. That's the rule, she assured herself.

Garnett went around the room, reading gift cards on the arrangements. "Are all of these for Madison?"

"There's one for Carnegie," Lily replied, pointing across the room.

Carnegie looked over enthusiastically only to find a bouquet made of flower-shaped fruit.

"It's an edible fruit arrangement," Amelia said.

Carnegie rolled her eyes. Edible fruit? Isn't that a contradiction?

"Do you mind if we have a couple of strawberries?" Lily asked. "We haven't had dinner yet."

"Please, help yourselves," Garnett replied. "I'm sure Carnegie won't mind."

"Yeah," Ana said. "Fruit isn't her thing. She's more of a meat and cookie girl."

"Oh, I'm sorry," Garnett said. "I forgot you haven't been introduced. Amelia and Lily, this is Anastasia Braxton. Madison and Carnegie are *her* dogs."

Lily and Amelia looked at Ana with wide-eyed admiration. "You're their owner? Seriously?" Lily asked.

"Uh-huh, but I don't think they like to think of themselves as being owned—especially Carnegie."

"You're *soooo* lucky, Anastasia!" Amelia said.

Is she? Carnegie wondered, thinking about her broken mirror.

"She's also my assistant when we take them on photo shoots," Garnett said with a discreet wink at Ana.

The young girls gawked at Ana with "you're-what-I-want-to-be-when-I-grow-up" looks.

"Yeah, sometimes," Ana said humbly. "I heard you guys wrangle the dogs during the show. That must be fun...and kind of stressful."

"Totally," Lily said. "One time, at their audition, Glory—"

"That's Carnegie's understudy," Amelia added.

"Right. Glory stepped on Carnegie's tail so she couldn't go onstage," Lily continued. "We tried to move her foot, but it was like lifting the wheel of a car. And when we finally got Glory to move, she had some of Carnegie's long white tail fur stuck under her foot."

"Ouch! That had to hurt having her tail feathers pulled out," Ana said. She looked sympathetically at Carnegie, who responded with dramatically pained eyes.

"I know!" Amelia said. "Sometimes, I almost think Glory has it in for Carnegie."

Sometimes? Almost? Carnegie commented to herself. My, isn't she the intuitive one?

"Anyway," Lily said, "Glory and Precious—"

"Precious is Madison's understudy," Amelia added.

"Uh-huh," Lily said. "Precious and Glory are supposed to stay out of the way. They're only needed if something drastic happens. You know, like if Madison or Carnegie trips onstage and breaks a leg."

"Or if they pass out during a performance," Amelia added in a way that sounded unintentionally cheerful.

Feeling the uncomfortable silence in the room that their disaster statements produced, the girls backtracked. "Uh…um," Lily stammered, "but that's not going to happen."

"No, no, not at all. Zero chance," Amelia said, grabbing Lily's arm. "We better get the rest of the stuff out of the hallway." The girls quickly made their exit.

A cracked mirror, good-bad-luck horseshoe, broken legs, passing out. Is there a black cat that can walk across my path before I go on-stage? Carnegie thought. She turned to Madison and quietly asked, "Maddie, what color is that June cat in Wardrobe?"

"I barely saw her, but I think she's kind of gray, why?"

"No reason."

Ana picked up a stack of telegrams from the dressing table. "Lots of people sent well wishes and congrats, Garnett."

"Nice. Who are they from?"

"Let's see..." Ana said, thumbing through. "Some friends and family, Madison and Carnegie's talent agent, the Borzoi Club of America, *Hound Beautiful* magazine, and M-House Editrice. Wow! They're in Milan, Italy."

"They are," Garnett replied. "They publish lovely books and the *Beauty & Performance Review* that's devoted to sighthounds."

"I can't read Italian, but I've seen the English version," Ana said. "It's really cool. I wonder if they know the Pucchi people who sent all the cute dog booties. They're in Milan, too."

"Did someone say, 'Pucchi?'" asked Lily cheerfully, carrying an international shipping box.

"Yeah, it's from the House of Pucchi," said Amelia, closely following Lily. "Oh no!" she cried with sudden realization. "We probably missed Luca!"

"Who's Luca?" Ana asked.

Amelia and Lily looked at each other with dreamy eyes.

"Just some guy who delivered Madison's Pucchi booties," Lily said casually. "He was kind of crushing on us, but he's too old."

"Way too old," Amelia added.

"Can we open the box, Ms. Dixon?" Lily asked.

"Sure," Garnett replied.

"It's got tons of tape on it," Amelia said. "See if you can find those scissors, Lily."

"Silver scissors with gold handles and a pink jewel on the hinge?" Garnett asked.

"Exactly. Have you seen them?" Amelia asked.

"Not recently," Garnett replied with a long sigh. Not since I threw them away after they were destroyed probably opening a similar box, she added to herself.

"Look in my dog show tote, Amelia. There's a box cutter."

Carnegie kept her distance when Amelia and Lily opened the shipping box and tore into the designer tissue paper.

I hope it's not more of those Pucchi booties, Carnegie said to herself. What if we're supposed to wear them tonight?! she thought in a panic. Carnegie suddenly saw herself onstage in those dreadful booties. She is frozen—and it's devastating—just like Madison said. The entire audience is focused on her, watching…wondering…then snickering and laughing, louder and louder. Her dream of stardom is dashed! Over! Forever! All because of those dreadful dog shoes. She started to pant heavily and sway back and forth, lightheaded.

"Carnegie, are you okay?" Ana cried, just as she passed out and hit the floor with a dull thump. "Help! Garnett, help!"

Garnett rushed to the now limp Carnegie. "Oh dear! What's wrong, girl?" she said, petting her side. She looked at Carnegie's gums, and they were a healthy pink. "I just can't imagine…"

"It's like she fainted," Ana said. "She did that when she was a puppy, and we revived her with a cookie. I have some in my backpack."

"Let's try it."

Ana quickly returned with a star-shaped cookie and waved it under Carnegie's nose. No response. She and Garnett exchanged desperate, worried looks. Madison came over and sniffed her sister's face, then settled into a sphinx position next to her.

Across the room, Amelia whispered to Lily. "When I said one of them might pass out, I didn't think it would really happen."

"Is Glory going to take her place?" Lily whispered back.

GLORY?! Take MY place?! The hateful prospect cut through Carnegie's semi-consciousness. She bolted upright with dazed eyes. While everyone watched breathlessly, she looked around, oriented herself, and snatched the cookie out of Ana's hand.

"YAY!" Ana cried, hugging her tightly. Madison licked her sister's face, then circled joyfully while everyone applauded wildly.

What's the big deal? Carnegie thought, licking the crumbs off her lips. I eat cookies every day. At least they finally gave a star cookie to the real star. I'll applaud *that*.

With Carnegie recovered, Ana brought the House of Pucchi gift box over to her. "Let's see what gorgeous gift they sent. I'm sure it will perk you up."

Carnegie's eyes crossed as Ana removed the box lid.

"Oh, look! Pretty Pucchi cashmere sweaters for you and Madison, embroidered with your initials.

Carnegie breathed a sigh of relief. *Cashmere.* I can work with that.

After they were settled in, Garnett said to Ana, "You know, we're in good shape here. Our stylists have a 6 o'clock call, about twenty minutes from now. If you want to take a look around the theater, it's a good time."

"Really? Okay!" Ana replied, slinging her backpack over one shoulder. "I'm going to take a quick look at the lobby. Text me if you need anything." She threw a kiss to Carnegie and Madison. "Be good girls!"

Glad she was wearing her sneakers, Ana jogged down the corridor that led from backstage to the lobby. She was expecting a lot of show-themed merchandise but what she saw, stopped her in her tracks. Madison as Olivia was everywhere! Madison plushie dogs of all sizes from tiny to life-size dominated the lobby display. Her heart image was on posters, tote bags, hats, socks, t-shirts, hoodies, PJs, mugs, key chains, pins—practically any merchandise imaginable had Madison featured on it. New York's iconic "I ♥ NY" slogan had been replaced by "I ♥ Madison."

A tall, slender man wearing a Madison heart pin on his suit jacket lapel approached Ana.

"Hello, Miss. I'm Ethan, the director of merchandise sales. We're actually not open for another hour."

"That's okay," Ana replied. "I'm here with Madison and Carnegie, and I just wanted to see what you're selling."

"Oh, you know Madison?"

"Uh-huh. I'm Anastasia. She's my dog."

"She's *your* dog? Come with me!" He led Ana to the main display and called out to his sales team.

"Hey, everyone. This is Madison's owner!"

They all looked up, smiled, and made a heart with their hands. Ana wasn't sure what to do, so she made a heart back.

Ethan handed her a Madison plushie. "You've got to have one of these," he said.

"Oh, I love it…but I didn't bring my wallet," Ana said, slightly embarrassed.

"It's on the house."

"Really? That's so sweet. Thank you! We'll keep it in her dressing room. Is there a plushie of Carnegie?"

"No, but she's in cast photos that are on lots of things," Ethan said. He handed Ana a rolled-up poster. "Would you like this? Carnegie's in the photo."

"Sure, if you can spare one. Do you mind if I take a look around?" Ana asked.

"Feel free," Ethan replied.

Ana browsed around and then checked in with Ethan.

"There's so much cute stuff. Maybe I can come back at intermission." Ana carefully put the Madison plushie and poster in her backpack and checked her phone for the time. "I better get backstage. Bye, everyone. Thanks again!"

Back in the dressing room, Ana held up her backpack. "I went to the lobby. You should see all the merch! They gave me some awesome stuff!" She produced the rolled-up poster. "Maybe we can hang it up here? And…look!" She pulled out the Madison plushie.

Carnegie's head jerked up. It's a known fact that all stuffed animals belong to her. She stepped forward and snatched it out of Ana's hands.

"No!" Ana said, taking the Madison plushie out of Carnegie's mouth. She wiped off the dog drool and set it on the dressing room table. "This is Madison's Olivia…but you know what, Carnegie? It looks a lot like your stuffed puppy, Ike. I don't think I unpacked him when we moved. There's a box in my closet with some dog stuff. I'll try to remember to check it."

Didn't unpack my puppy?! Carnegie said to herself. She's going to *try to remember* to check if my puppy is lying in a cold, dark box with some random dog stuff? Some mother Ana would be. I've been grieving all this time because I thought we left Ike behind.

Madison looked at Carnegie sympathetically and wondered if her Little Puppy bean bag toy—her dear L.P.—was in that same box.

CHAPTER TWENTY-FOUR

Opening Night

Outside, as the twilight sky dramatically transformed from tangerine to indigo, the dazzling "Hearts Over Broadway" marquee stood out as if no other show in the theater district existed.

Elegantly dressed patrons lined up at the entrance, their attire ranging from classic black tie to flamboyant. It was an eclectic gathering of celebrities and New York society's "Who's Who," as well as those who scrimped and saved to splurge on the most anticipated show of the season. Besides the usual enthusiastic theatergoers, dog lovers from all over couldn't wait to see Madison, and matinees for kids were sold out months in advance.

Photographers jostled for position, their cameras capturing the glamour and excitement of opening night. Journalists and podcasters whispered into microphones, sharing the evening's unfolding magic with an eager audience watching on television and online.

When the theater's street doors opened, the crowd jammed the lobby to buy glossy souvenir show programs and Madison's heart merchandise. Inside the house, white-gloved ushers in vintage-inspired red and black uniforms with rows of gold buttons and gold braid trim, handed out Playbill programs. With flashlights at the ready, they guided the audience to their seats in the orchestra, mezzanine, and balcony sections. Some fortunate patrons enjoyed rather regal seating in elevated box seating along the theater walls. Among those patrons were Garnett, Spencer, Catherine, and Anastasia who were dressed in their best—almost.

"Oh my gosh!" Ana suddenly exclaimed. "I forgot to change my shoes!" She reached into her backpack, pulled out her heels, and discreetly swapped them for her sneakers.

"I hope no one noticed."

"Probably not with us being up here," her mom said with a smile.

"Yeah, these are awesome seats, Dad," Ana said, leaning over the box railing to view the stage below.

"Thanks, but the credit goes to Garnett."

"Don't thank me," Garnett said. "These seats were in Madison's and Carnegie's contracts."

"We'll give them 'thank you' cookies when we get home," Ana said.

"That's going to take a lot of cookies to cover the ticket price of these seats," Spencer said.

"Have you seen the price of their favorite posh dog bakery cookies?" Catherine asked with a laugh.

"They're worth it," Ana said. "At least Carnegie thinks so."

Backstage, it was an adrenaline rush of final touches. The dog gate had been removed and their dressing room door closed to avoid any distractions. Nora was powdering Madison's foot and buffing her nails while Laura was making sure her butterfly hair clip was secure. Mia was re-combing Carnegie's long feathers that she managed to get tangled after being brushed minutes before. Both Nora and Mia had anxiously checked and double-checked their paws to make sure they had the perfect amount of paw wax applied to their pads. Two stylists, two dogs, four paws each, times two checks equaled thirty-two paw checks.

"They're going to wear our paws out before we take a step onstage," Carnegie whispered to Madison.

"I know. I thought *I* was nervous," Madison quietly replied.

"They're a wreck," Carnegie said. "So unprofessional."

Three knocks and everyone jumped when their dressing room door flew open. An assistant stage manager dressed in show black and wearing a headset loudly announced, "Thirty minutes to curtain!"

Even though they were expecting the next announcement, everyone jumped again when he returned to announce, "Fifteen minutes!"

Fifteen minutes felt like fifteen seconds when the assistant stage manager returned, this time to announce, "Five minutes to places!"

And then, finally, he returned with Ruby and announced, "Places!"

"Okay, girls, it's time," Ruby said, clipping on their leashes.

Madison's and Carnegie's hearts suddenly beat so fast, it was hard to breathe. It wasn't like being out of breath after a full-out run. That was *thrilling*. This was entirely something else. Madison looked down at her right front paw, longing to lick it.

"Don't even think about it!" Nora said.

"Oh, they're just a little nervous," Ruby said. "That's normal on opening night. Let's get you onstage, and all your jitters will go away."

Jitters? Carnegie thought, trying to still her shaking rear leg. More like exhilaration. Tonight, I become a star!

As soon as they arrived in the stage right wing, they could hear and feel the audience impatiently waiting in the theater behind the closed curtains. The air was electric with excitement.

"This isn't making me feel less jittery," Madison whispered to Carnegie.

"That's funny," Carnegie replied. "I'm cool as a cucumber."

Madison regarded the "shaking cucumber" for a moment and then kissed her on the cheek. "Good luck, sister."

"You mean good-bad-horseshoe-break-a-paw-luck."

"Uh-huh," Madison replied, her eyes wide with a mix of elation and fear.

Ruby first took Madison to sit in her place next to Gabriella, who was already seated on the chaise, center stage.

"Watch for my directions. I'll be right over there, okay?" Ruby said, unclipping her leash and pointing to the stage right wing. She offered Madison a treat, but she turned her head away.

Ruby then took Carnegie upstage to sit in her background spot next to Gabriella's bed. She unclipped her leash, gave her a treat and said, "Remember to watch for me," again pointing to the stage right wing.

Ha! YOU watch ME! Carnegie said to herself, munching her turkey jerky.

As the orchestra struck up the overture, Gabriella hugged Madison and reassuringly whispered to her.

No hug for me? Carnegie resentfully thought.

When the massive red velvet theater drapes slowly parted, Madison and Carnegie got their first-ever view of a fully packed house, the audience with their eyes glued on the stage, holding their collective breath in anticipation.

"Oh, Olivia, what am I to do?" Gabriella's emotionally delivered opening line to Madison kicked off the eagerly anticipated "Hearts Over Broadway" musical.

When Madison sympathetically put her paws on Gabriella's lap, the audience's wild applause swept over the stage like a windstorm of love. Sitting in the background, it hit Carnegie like a gust of disgust. It was leftover love—not the genuine love reserved for the stars.

While Gabriella and Olivia's heartfelt scene was playing out, Carnegie was getting increasingly bored sitting in the background, feeling like a piece of furniture.

This dull scene needs some punching up, Carnegie thought. She jumped up on Gabriella's bed, circled three times, and sprawled out dramatically. The audience started to titter as they noticed her and elbowed their neighbors.

In a panic, Ruby tried to catch Carnegie's attention. *Off! Off!* she silently signaled, frantically waving her hands to the left for her to get off the bed and back to her spot.

Intentionally misinterpreting Ruby's signals, Carnegie snidely snickered to herself. *Oh, she wants me to rollover. I can do that.* She turned onto her back with her fluffy rear end and tail pointed towards the audience and extended her long legs straight up. Now, the audience was in full laughter, confusing Gabriella and Madison, who had no idea that there was an upside down dog "table" on the bed behind them.

Looking at the monitor, Brad, the stage manager, pointed at the screen in alarm and disbelief. "Ruby, is that Carnegie's legs sticking up?" he urgently asked over the headsets.

"I'm afraid so."

"Get her back in place, please!"

"I'm trying. She's ignoring me!"

By now, Carnegie had added a swishy wag of her long plume tail that had the audience doubling over in laughter.

"I don't care what you have to do," Brad said, trying to keep his voice down. "She's destroying this scene!"

"Hold on. I have an idea."

Ruby dashed behind the backstage curtain and calculated where the bed was. She reached her hand under the curtain and tossed some turkey jerky on the floor next to the bed. Instantly sensing a treat, Carnegie rolled off the bed and snatched it.

I wasn't expecting a treat so soon! Carnegie happily said to herself. I figured intermission, at best...but they just couldn't wait to reward my talent. Well done, ME! I think I'll just sit here until my next big part. Carrying this production is exhausting.

With Carnegie back in place, Ruby resumed her spot in the wing. Everyone breathed a sigh of relief and the play progressed as intended... that is, until near the end of Act I, when the lights dimmed, and the spotlight focused on Gabriella and Madison for their emotional scene.

The time has come to claim *my* spotlight! Carnegie said to herself. Under the cover of darkness, she crouched low and launched her tried-and-true combination of sliding her front paws and scooting her rear end to silently move around the stage but *wait! NO!* Her paws did not slide! She was stuck…fixed…riveted…glued four-on-the-floor. She could move her paws up and down like a marionette, but her stealth sliding was finished.

This is horrible! she inwardly screamed. Even more devastating than Pucchi booties…well, maybe. Why didn't I test this hideous paw wax during the dress rehearsals?

As Carnegie's mind raced, searching for what to do, Madison began singing with Gabriella. "*AAAWWOOOooo…*"

And then it struck her. She lifted her head high into the air and loudly howled, *"OOOoooWaaAAwwOOoooow!"* in a hair-raising attempt to harmonize with Madison.

Brad immediately called over the headsets to Samantha, the audio director. "What is that horrific sound I'm hearing when Madison is singing?!"

"I hear it too! I've been trying to locate the source," Samantha replied, baffled. "It's not feedback or an echo…"

"OOOoooWaaAAwwOOoooow!"

"There it is again, Sam!" Brad exclaimed.

"I know! I know!" Samantha turned up her monitor volume, pressed her headphones tightly against her ears, and listened closely. "It's coming from upstage. I think it's…it's Carnegie."

"Is she hurt? She sounds like she's in pain."

"No, I think she's singing along—or trying to."

"Ruby!" Brad called into the headsets. "Make her stop!"

Ruby frantically launched into her "no bark" signals which Carnegie not only ignored, she turned her body away so they had no eye contact.

"I'm so sorry! We're not in communication anymore," Ruby said in exasperation. "Madison's song is almost over. Hopefully, Carnegie will stop singing when she does."

And with a final ear-piercing, *"OOOoooWaaAAwwOOoooooow!"* Act I was over. It was time for intermission.

Instead of exiting stage right with Madison and Gabriella, Carnegie rushed to front center stage and took her best Gracie-taught bow. While the audience laughed and applauded, she remained in her downward-dog bow and added a wide tail wag.

"Close the curtains! Close the curtains!" Brad ordered.

The heavy theater curtains swept in from the sides, leaving Carnegie's head sticking out where they met in the center. Encouraged by the reaction to her protruding long nose dog face, she added her biggest winningest smile, confusing the audience who couldn't decide if they should continue laughing or run in terror.

"What *is* she doing?!" Brad asked.

"I can't see from back here," Ruby said. "I'll grab her."

Carnegie's smiling face abruptly disappeared from the audience's view when Ruby pulled her back inside the curtains.

Brad called to her on the headsets. "Ruby, after you drop off the dogs in their dressing room, we need to talk."

"Let me guess," Ruby replied. "Carnegie?"

"I'm afraid so. We can hope she went off-course because of opening night nerves but if the second half is anything like the first..."

"Her understudy needs to step in?"

"Exactly. Glory will be a major change for the audience, but we can't let the show go totally off the rails."

"If it's any consolation, the audience thought Carnegie was *very* funny."

"In all the wrong places," Brad added.

"True," Ruby replied with a sigh. "I'll let Nora and Mia know and make sure Glory is set and waiting in the wings. What about Precious?"

"Madison couldn't be more perfect, but it wouldn't hurt. And let

Laura know Precious needs a butterfly hair clip."

"On it."

Ruby leashed up Madison, who was sitting offstage, and took her and Carnegie to their dressing room where Lily and Amelia were waiting.

"It's intermission break," Ruby announced.

"Yeah, we've been watching on the monitor," Lily said, laughing.

"OMG! Can you believe what Carnegie did?" Amelia added with a too-loud giggle.

"Never mind that now," Ruby said. "We've got bigger fish to fry."

Is fish on the catering menu today? Carnegie wondered. I prefer salmon, FYI.

Ruby clapped her hands and snapped Lily and Amelia to attention mid-giggling.

"Please! I need your full attention. We've got to get Precious and Glory ready quickly, so you need to watch Madison and Carnegie until Nora and Mia can get here. I see their water bowls are full, but they may need a potty break. I'll be back before intermission ends."

She unclipped their leashes, and Madison ran to her pillow bed, circled three times, dropped, and closed her eyes. Carnegie leaped on her sofa and stretched out with her back to everyone. While Lily and Amelia went back to discussing her outrageous stage antics and whether or not she was going be replaced by Glory, Carnegie covertly examined her paw pads.

This paw wax is ruining my act, she thought. *It's got to go!* Very quietly, she started licking her paws. The wax wasn't coming off her feet, but it *was* making her tongue and lips terribly sticky. This won't work, she said to herself. I need another way to get it off.

She hopped off the sofa and casually walked to her water dish. After making sure no one was watching, she dipped her right paw and swished it around. To her dismay, the water had no effect on the wax. *It's waterproof. Now what?* I'm going to have to scrape it off...

but how to do that with those silly girls here?

Suddenly, it hit her. The sure-fire potty demand. She went to the dressing room door, pawed it, whined, and looked over at Amelia and Lily expectantly.

"Oh, look!" Amelia said. "Carnegie has to pee. I'll take her."

"What about Madison?" Lily asked.

"Nah, let's not wake her up," Amelia said. "Be right back." Amelia clipped on Carnegie's leash, led her to the backstage potty area, opened the gate, and released her inside.

Now that she was on the artificial turf, Carnegie pretended to be sniffing and looking for the perfect place to pee. She walked in circles over and over, shuffling her feet, using the friction from the turf to remove her paw wax.

"You can't find the right spot?" Amelia asked with a laugh. "So picky!"

Carnegie looked up at Amelia in disgust, then put her head down and continued to shuffle in circles all around the enclosure.

"Hurry up! We need to get back."

That should do it, Carnegie thought. She faked a squat at the distant end of the enclosure and then loped back to the gate.

When they arrived back in the dressing room, they found Mia and Nora in a panic. Getting Precious and Glory ready had taken longer than expected, and intermission was nearly over.

"There you are!" Mia cried, rushing to Carnegie with a brush in her hand. "And all tangled again. You're due back onstage any second."

Right then, the assistant stage manager knocked on their door, opened it, and announced, "Places!"

Ruby instantly appeared and, ignoring Mia's frantic brushing of Carnegie's feathers, clipped on both dogs' leashes. "Sorry, gotta go."

Mia brushed Carnegie's exiting tail as Ruby led them to the stage right wing to make their entrance with Gabriella. Suddenly, she gasped and turned to Nora. "Did you check to see if they needed more paw wax?"

Nora stared back wide-eyed through her leopard-frame glasses. "I barely got Madison's makeup retouched…but I'm sure they're still okay," and then added, "I hope."

CHAPTER TWENTY-FIVE

I Meant to Do That

Standing in the wing, Madison whispered to Carnegie, "Where were you? I was worried."

Carnegie tried to answer, but her lips were stuck together from licking the paw wax.

"What's going on with your lips?" Madison asked.

Carnegie forced her lips apart, and they made a little popping sound. "Nuthwing."

"And why are you talking like that?"

"Nwwwhat dnoew yneuw meann?"

Ruby interrupted their exchange when she unclipped their leashes and whispered, "Madison, get ready to heel. Madison, go!"

"It's so lovely this time of year, Olivia…" Gabriella theatrically delivered her line as she gracefully stepped onstage with Madison closely walking by her side.

Ruby pointed to upstage. "Carnegie, go!"

Whoa! Carnegie silently cried when she stepped on the shiny stage floor and felt her feet slip…and then, *YAY! My paw wax removal plan worked!* Placing her feet carefully, she slowly walked upstage and sat on her "X" mark with regained confidence. She was just one irresistible performance from her name in lights on Broadway, shining bright for all the world to see. One charming performance away from Madison only playing her sister, onstage and off. One delightful performance away from being a *STAR!*

She looked to the stage right wing to see if Ruby was giving her a "thumbs up" for properly sitting in place. But what she saw was not just Ruby. It was Ruby *and* Glory *and* Precious. Glory's and Precious' big white snarling teeth stood out like grinning Cheshire Cats in the dark wing.

And, as if it couldn't be worse, Precious was wearing Olivia's backup butterfly hair clip costume…the very one that would be hers if it hadn't been for that vicious June cat in the wardrobe room.

With a musical flourish, the stage lights dimmed, and the spotlight focused on Gabriella and Madison at center stage for their most moving scene.

Now's the time! she said to herself. She crouched close to the floor, slid her front paws forward and scooted her rear end to move into the spotlight…but she underestimated how slippery the stage was and began to accelerate. After a few increasingly speedy slide-scoot combinations, her long legs suddenly splayed in four different directions like an uncoordinated spider on ice skates as she slid and spun out of control.

The audience gasped as Carnegie appeared as a blur of fur sliding in and out of the spotlight, dangerously careening toward the edge of the stage. Gabriella screamed, and Madison howled, *"No, Carnegie, NOOOO!"*

Time slowed as Carnegie made a desperate scrambling attempt to save herself by frantically pawing the slick stage. The theater was shocked into silence with only the strangely magnified sound of Carnegie's toenails scraping the stage floor before she sailed over the edge, still pawing the air…and disappeared into the orchestra pit.

BOOOOM! The silence was broken by her landing on a big timpani drum. She bounced off onto a drum set, smashed her rear foot through the snare drum and dragged it with her as she slammed into the cymbals with a *CRASSSSH..SSssSH!* With her head ringing, Carnegie "cycloned" through the string and brass sections, terrifying the musicians and knocking over music stands. Dizzy and blinded by flyaway sheet music, she collided with the horn section and staggered off with her front leg through a bent trombone slide.

The conductor, in disbelief and horror, stood frozen with his baton mid-air as the startled musicians screeched and honked out a bedlam of discordant notes, trying to dodge the one-dog destruction band. Carnegie finally came to an abrupt stop when she tripped over a toppled chair, and her head lodged in the bell of a tuba.

The conductor, recovering from his state of shock and hoping to salvage what was left of the orchestra, dropped his baton and descended on Carnegie. He hastily stripped off her instrument wreckage and dislodged her head from the tuba with a *THRUMP* sound.

Dazed but undaunted, Carnegie had only one ambition—to get back onstage—*her* stage—and claim her dream of stardom. She jumped on the piano and slid down the keyboard in a glissando of notes, then leaped from the keyboard to the stage.

Back onstage, she proudly bowed to the stunned audience and proclaimed to herself, *"I meant to do that."*

CHAPTER TWENTY-SIX

Top Billing

Ana breathlessly burst into the Braxton's kitchen with a stack of newspapers. "The reviews are in!"

"Let your mother and me get a cup of coffee, please. It was a late night," Spencer said.

"I don't know why you need coffee to read or listen to reviews, but okay. I'll go get Madison and Carnegie."

Ana returned with the sleepy and unenthusiastic Borzoi sisters. Madison curled up to go back to sleep. Carnegie sniffed the kitchen counter in hopes of finding bacon, then sat on a dining room chair in her two-on-the-floor style.

"Here, take these," Ana said, handing her parents different newspapers. "I've got the *Times*. That's the important one." She anxiously thumbed through until she found the entertainment section. "Here it is. Wow! 'Hearts Over Broadway' is a Critic's Pick!" As Ana read the review aloud, her smile changed to a frown.

> *The opening night of the 'Hearts Over Broadway' musical made rare theatrical history when newcomer canine actor, Carnegie, who plays canine Olivia's sister, gave a disastrous and unintentionally sidesplittingly hilarious performance the likes of which has never been seen—or should ever be seen again—on the Broadway stage. Carnegie, who you may recall was dubbed the Hindenburg Hound after her Macy's Thanksgiving Day Parade balloon deflated in a horrific and humiliating manner, fared no*

better in her acting debut. While the audience chuckled at her silly background antics, covered their ears for her disharmonious 'singing,' and didn't know how to react to her terrifying smiling face stuck in the curtains, they found themselves aghast when her quest for the spotlight landed her in the orchestra pit and created musical mayhem that literally and figuratively stopped the show. Short of the stage bursting into flames and screams of 'Oh, the humanity!' Carnegie's performance could not have been more catastrophic.

"That doesn't sound...good," Ana said, with a questioning look at Carnegie. She was beaming with wide-eyed pride that her name was mentioned before Madison's.

I think that's what you call "top billing," Carnegie smugly thought. *Goodbye* to starring "Madison as Olivia" *and* a big *HELLO* to starring "Carnegie as Olivia."

Whether or not she could have understood the review, Carnegie didn't bother to listen to anything but her name. She closed her eyes and reveled in how marvelous it felt to be the lead.

"Go on, Ana. It probably gets better," Spencer said.

"I hope so." She read on:

Mandi Marin, as the charmingly emotional Gabriella, was simply superb, as expected. But to everyone's delight, Olivia, played by new canine sensation Madison, captured hearts, not just 'Over Broadway' but this reviewer believes, will capture hearts the world over. The silky-furred superstar gave a Pony Award-worthy performance on her debut night!

"That's a glowing review...for Madison," Catherine said. "A little mixed when it comes to Carnegie."

"Mixed?!" Spencer asked, looking at his wife in disbelief. "It's

highly descriptive...I'll give it that. Let's look at these other papers."

And the other papers' reviews were, unfortunately for Carnegie, no better—and unanimous in their sky-high praise of Madison. As the Braxtons sat in silence, absorbing their dogs' drastically different reviews, the phone rang. It was Garnett.

Spencer picked up, and Ana and Catherine leaned in, listening intently to his side of the conversation.

"Yes, we just read some reviews. We're proud, too. Uh-huh… Uh-huh. Oh, I know. Well, those reviews were rather harsh, don't you think?…I guess that's true. Oh, no, really? Starting with tonight? So soon? Yes, I understand it's an insurance issue. No, please, it's not your fault. I'm sure you did everything you could. I'll tell them. It'll be okay. So, you'll pick her up here in our apartment at 5:30 for a 6 o'clock call? We bought tickets for tonight, but we're not leaving that early. No, she'll be fine alone. We can have Oscar, you know, our doorman, look in on her. Yes, we're sorry too. Thank you, Garnett."

Spencer slowly hung up the phone.

"What, Dad?" Ana asked anxiously.

Spencer responded to his daughter with a sad, silent nod toward Carnegie. Ana ran to Carnegie and hugged her. "Oh, no!"

Oh, no, *what?* Carnegie asked herself sarcastically. *Oh no, Madison is getting replaced?* That *is* sad. I'm sure Garnett did her best. Madison had a good run. Very short but good.

Half-awake, Madison sensed her sister's happiness but also the concern in the room. Something didn't feel right. Was that the mixed review? She slowly got up and quietly slunk back to her bed.

"Who wants some breakfast?" Ana asked Carnegie, hugging her again and trying to be cheerful. "Should we call your sister back?"

Carnegie stood and wagged her tail. "So brave," Catherine said with a sympathetic smile.

Brave to want breakfast? Carnegie asked herself. What's wrong with everyone?

After Carnegie consumed her breakfast and Madison picked at hers, they retired to their bedroom. Madison went straight to her bed and, after her compulsory circling, settled in. She tried to ignore her sister pacing back and forth...and back and forth...and back and forth. Finally, Carnegie stopped in front of Madison's bed and thoughtfully addressed her.

"You know, Maddie, it's really better."

"What's better?"

"Not having to go to that theater every day."

"What do you mean?"

"It's better to relax at home. I'll represent for *both* of us."

"Represent what?"

"Being a star."

"I think you've always been a star, Carnegie," Madison said.

"Oh, I know. But not so much on Broadway like now."

"I guess not."

Carnegie went to their bedroom window and tried to see the theater, but a mile of buildings was in the way.

Right now, is a person up on a ladder on the theater marquee changing "Starring Madison as Olivia" to "Starring CARNEGIE as Olivia?" she wondered. Oh, and the posters and programs. They must be scrambling to redesign and print those. There's already pictures of me from the photo shoot—not with my winningest smile—but still adorable. But it's probably going to take a while to make a plushie of me. I hope they don't over stuff me like that horrible parade balloon. The way they kept blowing it up, bigger and bigger, anyone could see it was bound to pop...

As Carnegie continued with her musings, Madison tried to not think about the gloom in the room after Garnett called. She wasn't sure why, but it made her want to lick her paw.

Later that day, Ana appeared in their bedroom doorway with Henry. "Look who's here!"

"Your favorite dog walker," he added in a sing-songy voice. "Ana and I are going to take you to the park."

The word "park" was good for an enthusiastic ears-up/jump-up on Carnegie's part and a slow rise on Madison's.

"Come on, lazy girl," Ana coaxed. "You can move faster than that. You're a Borzoi. That means *swift* in Russian, remember? I'll take you. Henry will take Carnegie."

It was a sunny, crystal-clear winter day in Central Park. Along their path, graceful trees held out their lacey, bare branches in anticipation of the first snowfall. It was the kind of day when your breath makes little puffs, and you're happy to be bundled up against the frost.

Borzoi, who are native to snowy winters, are invigorated by the cold. Breathing the brisk air, Madison felt revived by her natural Borzoi instincts and relieved of the pressure of stardom.

Quite the opposite, Carnegie, was exhilarated, believing in her newfound stardom. She proudly trotted along with her chest puffed out and her head held high—until…

"WOOF! WOOF!" she barked and plunged into the bushes.

"Carnegie!" Henry exclaimed as she jerked him off his feet and ripped the leash from his hand. "What are you doing?!"

She emerged from the bushes with a tiny mouse. She had it by the tip of its tail, dangling from her mouth like a pull toy.

"Eek!" Henry screamed.

"Seriously, Henry?" Ana said. "Eek, a mouse? Do people really say that?"

"I don't like rats," he said, getting back on his feet and brushing off his pant knees.

"It's just a tiny little mouse."

"For now. Give it a while, and it'll be a big sewer rat."

"Mice don't grow into rats, Henry. Anyway, it's cute…but we can't take it home. Carnegie, drop it."

Carnegie considered Ana's order for a moment, then dropped the mouse, and it skittered back into the bushes. Before Henry could grab her leash, Carnegie dug in her feet and took off. Within seconds, only her fluffy white tail bobbing up and down could be seen in the distance.

"Where's she going?!" Ana screamed. "She runs so fast. We'll never catch her! Mom and Dad and Garnett are going to kill me!"

"Okay, don't panic," Henry said. "She's probably headed to a picnic area. She likes to look for snacks that people leave behind. I'm sure Madison can find her."

They didn't have to ask. Madison pulled on her leash and dragged Ana, along with Henry, through the park's many meadows. Exhausted, they finally found Carnegie lying on the Great Lawn across from Belvedere Castle. She was surrounded by discarded snack wrappers with her long nose stuck in a Pringles can. Henry quickly grabbed her leash, and Ana pulled the can off her nose. Madison licked her salty snoot, then gave her a sniff inspection to learn her route through the park.

With Carnegie under control, Ana looked at the impressive medieval stone building with its high grand tower sitting atop a tall, massive outcropping of rock.

"Wow, a castle in the middle of Central Park. It even has a lake in front—kind of like a big moat."

"That's Turtle Pond. Yeah, Belvedere Castle is a famous tourist attraction," Henry said.

"I can see why. It's so regal. I'd like to get a closer look, but it's getting late. We better get back," Ana said.

"Let me pick up after Carnegie's snack fest," Henry said. He stuffed the wrappers in the Pringles can and tossed it in a nearby trash can. "Okay, let's go, girls."

As they headed home, Madison whispered to Carnegie. "What was that about?"

"You mean my mouse pounce or my dramatic exit?"

"Both," Madison replied.

"How can you help *not* catching a mouse? They're just asking for it. And it reminded me that I should hunt for woofs."

"You mean wolves?" Madison asked.

"That's what I said...*woofs*," Carnegie replied, annoyed. "We *are* woof hunters, are we not?"

"I don't think there's any woofs—I mean *wolves*—in the park, Madison said.

"I must have scared them off. At least, I didn't find any."

"It looked like you found some potato chips."

"Just one at the bottom of the can. But you know what, Maddie? I found that royal palastle."

"Palastle?"

"You know...on the other side of that pond with turtles...what Ana and Henry were just talking about."

Madison, who had not been paying attention to their conversation, stared back at her sister blankly.

"...the fancy palastle place our famous royal ancestors live. Remember? Mom told us about them," Carnegie prompted.

"I guess," Madison replied.

"They're the famous-est dogs in the entire world. More famous than show dogs or Broadway star dogs."

"I think that was a long time ago," Madison said.

"I'm pretty sure I could live there with them now," Carnegie confidently replied, looking back over her shoulder at Belvedere Castle.

"*You?* Live in that palastle?" Madison asked.

"If I wanted to."

Madison looked at her sister with hurt eyes. "Without me?"

"Oh, no, never," Carnegie promised.

That afternoon was eerily quiet in the Braxton's household. When Ana announced dinner, Carnegie high-pranced into the kitchen and dove into her dish. Madison walked in slowly, sniffed hers, and took little nibbles.

Noticing how daintily her sister was eating, Carnegie ceased her gulping. I don't want to look plump, she thought. I've heard the spotlight adds ten pounds.

"Aren't you feeling well, Carnegie?" Ana asked, then whispered to her mom. "She never just picks at her food like that."

"Do you think she *knows?*" her mom asked.

Knows that I have to watch my figure now that I'm a star? Carnegie answered to herself.

"I thought she'd enjoy the special steak bits we added to her dinner. Y'know, because…" Ana said.

"Yes, me, too," Catherine agreed.

Steak bits? Carnegie snapped to attention and examined her dish. I missed those with all this precious nibbling. Careful to avoid the broth-soaked kibble, she picked out a piece of steak—YUM!—and went back to gulping her food. So much healthier! Who wants to be supermodel scrawny like Madison? I embrace my extra cuddly body image! My fans will, too.

When it was time for Madison to leave for the theater, you could hear a pin drop in the household. Ana cautiously stuck her head in their bedroom doorway and quietly said, "Madison, time to go."

Carnegie instantly hopped out of bed, beat Madison to Ana, and stood at attention. Ana knelt and gently petted her.

"No, Carnegie. You stay. Mom, Dad, and I are going to the theater later, too…but Oscar will come by to check on you."

Who? When? What?! That's not right! Maddie is the one *staying*. I'm *going*. I'm the STAR!

She whipped around and glared at her sister. Madison withered in Carnegie's anger, and tears welled up in her eyes.

"I'm sorry," she whispered. "I wish it was you."

"Don't waste your wishes. I'm glad it's not me," Carnegie replied. She snootily raised her nose and tail high in the air and whispered to Madison, "I've got bigger fish to fry."

Madison was wondering *what fish?* and *when did Carnegie start cooking?* when Ana clipped on her leash.

"Time to meet Garnett. She's picking you up here," Ana said. "We'll see your sister when we get home after the show."

Madison watched Carnegie's fluffy rear end walking away, sighed with resignation, and slowly followed Ana to the foyer.

CHAPTER TWENTY-SEVEN

All Alone

Ding! At 5:30 p.m., the Braxton's penthouse elevator arrived with Garnett to take Madison to the theater.

Ding! At 7:00 p.m., the elevator returned to take the rest of Carnegie's family away. The doors closed on smiles, waves, and thrown kisses. And abruptly, Carnegie was alone.

She sat statue-still, staring at the elevator doors, stunned by disbelief and emptiness. She waited…and waited…forever in dog-time, but no *dings* brought Madison back with apologies that they made a mistake—and she was the real star.

Well, this is boring, she thought. Carnegie got up and stretched, then decided to walk around the apartment. With no one there, she was free to do absolutely anything she wanted. Anything at all.

Consulting her mental list of all the "no's," "don't touch that's," and "off's," she went room by room, lying on off-limits furniture, licking forbidden objects, and jumping up on prohibited surfaces.

Tiring of that, Carnegie decided it was the perfect time to snoop around. She looked on the coffee table to see if there was anything in the candy dish. Just a wrapper Ana probably left. It smelled like chocolate—which was never, ever allowed—so she tried eating it. It didn't taste nearly as good as it smelled, so she munched on it for a while and spit it out. With a wet, gooey *SPLAT*, it landed on a *Hound Beautiful* magazine—and not just any issue—her family's prized edition with Madison featured on the cover. She snickered at her sister's glossy, glamorous close-up that now featured a drooly, chewed-up wrapper covering one of her "irresistibly sweet" eyes. How embarrassing. Glad *I* wasn't available for *that* photo shoot, she said to herself.

Moving on…what was in all those dressers and behind closet doors? She struggled pulling open the drawers with her teeth. Some of the knobs were just impossible, and the contents were not worth the trouble. The closets, however, were more promising—especially Ana's—which was always kept closed. Carnegie turned the knob with her mouth and pulled open the door. She was surprised that the interior lit up as if to welcome her.

"Oh, hello," she said as she walked inside. There were the usual dull racks and racks of clothing. How horrible to have to wear all these things and different ones depending on the weather. I'm so glad I have built-in year-round beautiful fur, she said to herself. And there were shoes—lots of shoes. She recognized a few pairs that bore her puppy teeth marks. It was not a happy day when Ana discovered her chewing on her new designer boots. Carnegie remembered Ana, red with anger, saying, "You're lucky that you're cute," whatever that meant. She wondered why shoes were so irresistible when she was a puppy, almost as good as Ana's socks she found in her dirty laundry basket.

"AAAAGH!" Suddenly, her blood ran cold—the dreaded Pucchi booties! She roughly dug through the stacked boxes until she found the Leopardo booties that were the source of so much humiliation. She ripped off the box lid and latched onto one bootie by its elegantly shaped toe and violently shook it back and forth.

"GRRRR! Rrrruff!" Shake! Shake! Shake! *"GRRRR! Rrrruff!"*

Dropping the bootie on the floor, she held it down with her front paws and, with great effort, ripped off the precious Leopardo fabric in one piece—*R-I-I-I-I-P!*—and flung it aside, where it landed like a game hunter's miniature leopard trophy rug. She took the other bootie to Ana's bathroom and dangled it with delight over the toilet bowl.

"*Arrivederci!* Isn't that how you say 'bye-bye' in Pucchi words?" She dropped the bootie in with a *SPLOOSH*—and with a *SWOOSH* flushed the toilet with her paw. Leaning over the bowl and grinning with self-satisfaction, she watched the swirling water swallow up the shoe. That is, until the water began to rise…and rise…quickly filling the bowl to the brim, running under the seat, and forming a waterfall that spilled onto the white marble floor.

"*Oops,*" she said, backing away from the river that was flowing towards Ana's bedroom carpet. "That Pucchi bootie is going to be in a lot of trouble." She ran back to Ana's closet and kicked the bootie boxes to the side. "Bad booties! Now, where was I?"

Her eyes scanned the shelves and she spotted a box with a sticker of a cartoon dog. The box was labeled "Carnegie & Madison." And it struck her. Was that the box Ana talked about at the theater? The one she never bothered to open after we moved? Standing on her hind legs, she nosed under the overhanging box and eased it off the shelf until it landed at her feet. The lid easily lifted off to reveal its treasures. There were photos of her and Madison with Ana at their old house, a little ball, a tiny plastic bag with some puppy teeth, a short, thin, chewed-up leash, and large white envelopes with their American Kennel Club pedigree papers. She removed the envelopes with her teeth, and underneath…

"My puppy!" Carnegie cried. She carefully lifted the soft, stuffed dog out of the box. He had a long nose, was white with black markings, and looked remarkably like her. The pale blue heart-shaped felt tag on his collar read, "Ike." She licked her plushie puppy affectionately like her mom had licked her when she was little. Ike was a prize from her sister's first major puppy show win, and Madison brought him home to her. It wasn't that Carnegie didn't want to compete in that prestigious show (oh, she did!) or wasn't beautiful enough (she was!) but show attendance was by invitation only—and based on her previous dog show antics, she was excluded. Nevertheless, Carnegie considered herself deserving of winning first place.

And there in the box was Madison's tiny, black and white spotted beanie-bag dog. It was a pathetic, saggy little thing, as if it didn't get its full share of beans. But Madison loved it. Garnett named it Little Puppy or L.P. for short. Carnegie took it out of the box and put it on Ana's bed, where Madison had been sleeping. She returned to get Ike and balanced him on their bedroom windowsill.

"See out there?" she asked her stuffed puppy, pressing her nose against the chilly window and fogging it with her breath.

"That's where *I* should be. In *my* theater with *my* name in lights. Starring in *my* Broadway show. *ME*, not Madison. I should report the theater management to the Animal Humane Society for cruelty to *me*. So, I had a tiny little mishap? Is it my fault the stage floor was more slippery than a black-ice rink? I blame that cracked mirror and those bad luck horseshoe flowers in the dressing room."

If nothing else, Ike was a good "listener," but he wasn't making Carnegie feel any better. In fact, looking out into the darkness, the theater seemed a million miles away—and her dream to be a Broadway star hopeless.

She carried Ike to her bed and circled three times before lying down and setting him next to her.

"Who cares about being a Broadway star, anyway?" Carnegie asked Ike. "These days, they make Broadway shows about absolutely anything. It's ridiculous. Like *What I Ate For Breakfast This Morning: The Musical.* And the shows close every day. And then what? You're just a washed-up has-been, and if you're lucky, you get to be a pathetic contestant on a *Dancing With The Dogs* TV show. At best, you win a Mirror Bone trophy. It's sad, really…although I *am* a spectacular dancer. *I* want to be truly famous, the famous-est!"

Ding! Carnegie jumped up. "Never mind. They're back! I'm going to be a Broadway star, after all. See you later, Ike."

She speed-pranced to the elevator and beat the doors opening.

Sitting proudly, she told herself to be humble. Madison must be very disappointed.

The doors parted, and Oscar stepped into the penthouse foyer. "Hello, doggie."

The doorman? *Not Madison?* It was a stab to Carnegie's heart.

"How're you doin'?" He reached down to pet her, but Carnegie pulled away.

"No smiles tonight?" Just as well, he thought. Those big teeth are scary.

"I guess you're pretty upset. I didn't see your show, but the whole town's talking about it." He shook his head sympathetically. "Too bad. Not everyone is meant for the stage."

Carnegie resentfully followed Oscar as he briefly looked around the apartment, ending his inspection in the kitchen. "I see your water bowl is full. Well, it looks like you're okay. G'night, doggie."

After Oscar left, Carnegie slowly walked back to her bedroom and collapsed into bed. She thought about her telling Madison she had bigger fish to fry. What was she thinking? She didn't even have a tiny goldfish. And the harsh reality was that no one was coming back until *after* the show. *After* her understudy, Glory, had taken over her role of playing Olivia's sister, and *after* Madison, once again, triumphed as the star. They wouldn't be home for hours. Hours and hours of Madison being the toast of the town.

"We might as well go to sleep," she told Ike. She was positioning him to be a head pillow when Madison's collar display caught her eye. There, on its glass shelf, sparkling enticingly, was the crown collar—the *royal* one.

She stared at it—at first blankly—and then with a growing realization. She got up and carefully took the crown collar off its shelf and brought it to her bed. She propped up Ike next to the collar and looked into his little black button eyes.

"Don't you see, Ike? It's no wonder I didn't become a silly show dog. No wonder I'm not some dumb dog actor on a stage. Those were not my destiny. Not with *my* noble blood. My destiny is *ROYALTY!* And when I'm royalty living in my big palastle, I'll be *way* more famous than my champion-show-dog-Broadway-star sister. I'll be the famous-est dog in the entire world. I just have to…go…live there…"

There, not *here*. With a surprising sense of sadness, she thought about leaving her luxurious home—the cushy furniture and pillows, the kitchen with its bottomless cookie jar, the big windows where she and Madison watched for enemy Golden Retrievers far below in Central Park, their bedroom with its comfortable familiarity. Her eyes landed on her sister's empty bed, and she felt a sudden pang of loss. And didn't she tell Madison that she would never go live in the palastle without her?

Well, that was before I knew I was kicked off the show, she said to herself. All bets are off now. Besides, Maddie can come live in my palastle after her Broadway show closes. We can share a bedroom and run up and down the tower stairs. That will be fun.

But, first, she had to get to her palastle, and her inner dog clock told her that she had to leave before her family returned.

She got up and gently placed Ike in the center of her bed's pillow.

"I'm sorry I can't take you," she told him. "I need you to pretend you're me. After I'm settled in my palastle, I'll send one of my servants for you. I promise." She licked her stuffed puppy on the cheek and headed for the foyer.

Carnegie stood in front of the elevator call button, suddenly frozen by a mix of anticipation and fear.

It's just my usual secret magic elevator trick, she tried to reassure herself. Push the button with my nose, and away I go. *Easy peasy.*

She'd done it before, just yesterday, in fact, on their opening night. And everyone was so amazed when she magically appeared in the lobby. So, why are her paws sweaty now? Why is her heart racing? Finally, summoning all her courage, she closed her eyes, flattened her ears, and resolutely pushed her large black nose squarely on the button. The distant swoosh grew louder as the elevator traveled to her floor. She jumped inside and located the "L" for Lobby among the wall of buttons. It was one of the two buttons she saw the persons push. "L" and "P" for Penthouse. *Hmm*, that's the nickname for Madison's Little Puppy, she said to herself. Funny that I never noticed before. I should tell Maddie, she thought out of habit. And then she stopped herself. Maybe not.

Carnegie sat bolt upright in the elevator car, swaying slightly as it dropped from the top floor all the way to the lobby, where it landed with a *ding!* After a short pause, the doors parted, and she craned her head around the open doors to peer into the dimly lit lobby.

Oh no! A security guard! And worse! That annoying Oscar was helping some residents carry packages toward the elevator.

"Hold the door, please!" he called out.

She pulled her head out of sight and pressed her back against the elevator wall while the doors closed—snail slow—as she frantically punched the "P" button with her paws. Eyes big as saucers and holding her breath, she rode her way back up and leaped out into their penthouse foyer in a panic.

That…*huff-huff*…was...*huff*...close. *Huff-huff*…I…*huff*…need… *huff-huff*…an escape plan, she thought, panting. My perfect-est… *huff*…plan ever.

She mentally listed and checked off some of her favorite personal attributes: Smart √, Sneaky √, Adorable √ (not relevant in this case but nonetheless important). What should smart-sneaky-adorable me do?

She closed her eyes and pictured a 3-D tour of the lobby. Let's see…the walls are a lovely white like me, so I won't stand out. That's good. There's some columns and tall plants and furniture I can hide behind. Excellent. And the lobby floor matches this foyer floor—slick like at the theater. She remembered her stealth slide-scooting around the stage. As long as she stayed out of the spotlight no one had noticed her, and they all had their eyes pinned on the actors' every move. The security guard won't be looking for her. Even better.

Carnegie did a practice run silently slide-scooting around in circles in the foyer. Thank goodness for my thespian skills, she thought. One last thing…

She ran back to the royal collar on her bed pillow and told Ike, "I probably should take this. I may need a stand-in crown while mine is being fitted. Don't worry, Madison won't notice it's gone…but just to be sure no one does…" She went to the display shelf, stood on her hind legs, and nudged the collars to fill in the gap the royal crown collar left, then stood back and admired her cleverness.

She lifted the crown collar with her teeth, flipped it on her head, and checked herself in Ana's vanity mirror. It was sitting loosely, so she pushed her crowned head against the vanity to make it fit snugger.

"Ouch!" she yelped when the crown slid down and pinched her ears. Too tight. Well, at least it won't fall off.

She gave Ike a farewell kiss and said, "Stay and be a good boy, okay?"

She dashed back to the foyer and without hesitation this time, pushed the elevator button with her nose. She paced impatiently for the familiar *ding!* When the doors parted, she dove in, hit the "L" button, and rode down to the lobby again.

CHAPTER TWENTY-EIGHT

Glory-ous

Madison arrived at the theater *without* Carnegie but *with* an empty and guilty heart. Lily and Amelia greeted her at the dressing room door, took her leash from Garnett and unclipped it.

"Hi, superstar!" they cried in unison.

Head down, Madison made a beeline for her bed. Without her compulsory circling, she dropped directly onto the pillow with her back to everyone.

"*Aww,* I bet she's missing her sister," Amelia said. "We miss Carnegie, too."

Soon after, Randy appeared with Glory, who as Carnegie's replacement, would now share Madison's dressing room. He dramatically handed her leash to Amelia.

"Here's our new super co-star!" he gloated, "She's all ready for her *glori*ous debut!"

Amelia nodded. "Uh-huh."

"Get it? Glory-ous?" Randy asked.

"Yeah, we got it," Lily said, exchanging a "look" with Amelia.

"I've got to take Precious to her understudy dressing room…for now, that is," Randy said with a snide snicker. "Something tells me she'll be moving into this dressing room, too…"

"Gosh, I don't know about that, Mr. McCormick," Lily said. "Everyone loves Madison."

When Amelia unclipped Glory's leash, she possessively strutted around the dressing room, smelling Madison's flowers, and gobbling up the gourmet dog treats that were set out. She jumped up on Carnegie's sofa, walked up and down the full length, snootily sniffing it all over. She finally settled down and planted herself on the center cushion. She narrowed her eyes and growled in Madison's direction, "*Mine!*"

Madison pretended to be asleep and resisted responding. How can they treat Carnegie like this? Is it *my* fault? she asked herself, feeling overwhelmed with guilt and sadness.

When Nora and Mia arrived in the dressing room, Glory got off the sofa and sauntered over to the makeup table. Ignoring her, Nora called, "Madison, it's time to get ready."

Madison tightly closed her eyes and tried to be invisible.

"Madison! Now, please. Come!"

She reluctantly rose and limped over to Nora.

"Gracious! What's wrong?!"

Madison sat and raised her right paw.

"Your paw! It's all wet! Have you been licking it all this time? It's so red, honey. I don't know if I can even cover it up."

"Worse than that," Mia said. "Can she even walk without limping? How on earth will she dance? We better call Brad!"

Brad rushed in the dressing room with Dr. Jamie Ina, the on-site veterinarian and Ms. Jenko, the representative from the Animal Humane Society.

"Tell me! What's wrong with Madison?!" Brad asked anxiously.

"It's her paw," Nora replied. "You know the one she sometimes licks. She really went to town on it. I'm *so* sorry. None of us saw her doing anything."

Dr. Ina knelt next to Madison and gently took her paw in her hands. After examining it closely, she said, "Well, it's definitely red and irritated, but it's nothing serious."

"Can she perform tonight?" Brad asked.

"I believe so," Dr. Ina said. "I'll clean it and add a soothing ointment. Her paw will feel better if she leaves it alone. I'm going to have to bandage it to make sure she does."

Brad, Nora, and Mia all gasped simultaneously.

"I'll use a white wrap, so it won't be obvious. But, please, watch her like a hawk so she doesn't try to pull off the bandage."

"What about her slipping on the stage?" Brad asked.

"Right. We can't have that," Dr. Ina said, looking in her medical kit. "I've got some non-slip tape, so she'll have traction."

Madison patiently watched as a non-slip sole was added to her bandage.

"What a good girl," Ms. Jenko said, petting her. "So, you are *sure* she is fine to perform, Jamie?"

"Let's see you walk, Madison," Dr. Ina said, leading her by the collar. She took one hesitant step, then sat and held up her right paw.

"*Hmm.* I can't tell if it's her paw or the bandage that's bothering her. Or if she's just anxious about something, which is why she licks her paw in the first place."

"I have an idea," Brad said. "Let's get Gabriella in here."

When Gabriella appeared at the door, Madison grinned and instantly ran over to her, wagging her long tail. Completely forgetting about her bandaged paw, she followed Gabriella around the dressing room, joyfully trotting and even added some of their dance steps.

"I'll sign her medical release," Dr. Ina said with a smile.

"Thank goodness," Brad said. "Alright, everyone. Back to your places, please."

CHAPTER TWENTY-NINE

Rat Suit

When the elevator car landed in the lobby, Carnegie flinched at the *ding* it made.

"Shhhh!" she shushed and then peeked around its parting doors. This time, she only saw the security guard. He was facing away from her with his head down.

Maybe he's sleeping? Carnegie hoped. She silently scooted out of the elevator, hugging the lobby walls as the elevator doors closed behind her. No turning back now. Her sharp sighthound eyes darted around the dim lobby as she plotted her way out:

Slide-scoot to behind the tall potted plant ⇢ to behind the big marble column on the left ⇢ to behind the big marble column on the right ⇢ *Hold.* Sneak a peek at the security guard to make sure he doesn't see me ⇢ *Slide-scoot* to behind the fancy sofa near the front door that I'm not supposed to sit on ⇢ to that roll-ey thing with the suitcases and hide behind the tallest ones ⇢ *Hold.* Make sure that annoying Oscar is not around, and then ⇢ *RUN!!!* as fast as I can to the revolving door, jump up on my hind legs, and with a standing-paws-push ⇢ *SPIN* to the outside.

Okay, I've got this, she reassured herself. *Ready, set, go!*

The security guard never raised his head as Carnegie silently slid by with the covertness of a ninja. Gaining confidence, she also gained speed as she entered the revolving door enclosure. Spinning too fast, she missed her first two attempts to exit the building. On her third time around, she was ejected onto the sidewalk and landed in a heap.

Dizzy and disoriented, Carnegie stumbled to her feet and scurried to a dark doorway of the building next door.

"Huff-huff-puff-huff-huff-puff-huff-huff" she gasped, trying to catch her breath. She cautiously looked around, then grinned and congratulated herself. "I *huff* made it!"

She could see Central Park, across Fifth Avenue—four lanes away. The evening traffic was light, but she had never crossed the street on her own.

This can't be too hard, she thought. Henry does it every day and he's not that bright. I just have to walk between those white lines. She crouched down and slithered out of the darkness onto the sidewalk. She crept alongside the cars parked at the curb until she found the open area with the pedestrian crossing. She waited for the cars to pass in both directions, then blasted off at her top Borzoi-blur speed, not stopping until she entered the park.

The park was icy cold and eerily dark. Rather than offering a sense of safety, the illumination cast by the lamp posts added a frightening misty glow. Carnegie had never been at Central Park alone at night. She had never been *anywhere* alone at night—a fact that she instantly realized when she heard rustling in the nearby bushes and felt the fur raise on her back.

Could that be a woof?! she anxiously wondered, wishing she had her woof hunter sister by her side. She braced herself and tried to look fierce. But instead of a wolf, a gang of tough hoodlums emerged from the bushes.

Oh, thank goodness…my fans! Carnegie said to herself.

"Hey! Check out the furry Greyhound with that bling on her head!" Rosa, their female leader, called out. "She must be worth some big bucks. Grab her, Vinnie!"

Yes, thank you. I *am* valuable, Carnegie commented to herself and smiled at the hoodlums.

"Yikes!" Vinnie cried, jumping back from her large white teeth.

"*You* grab her."

Please, please…don't be shy, Carnegie tried to say, approaching the gang with her winningest smile, flashing her huge fangs.

Recoiling in terror, Rosa cried, "Not me! I'm outta here!" She took off with the entire gang screaming and following her.

Being famous can be so intimidating to the general public, Carnegie said to herself, yawning. Oh, my. It's getting late. I better get to my new home.

She set out at a trot, but in the darkness, the park looked different—with endless paths and grounds—all diminishing into blackness. She stopped and tried to recall the route she took the day before that led to her finding the palastle.

Maybe I can find where the mouse was and start from there, she thought. She sniffed the air and followed a faint rodent scent until it increasingly got stronger and stronger and led her to…*what?* A discarded pizza box!

Even better, she thought. I missed my bedtime snack (which was actually a nutritional supplement pill disguised in a cheese ball). Still, it counted.

She nosed open the pizza box lid, and what met her was not just a slice of pizza. It looked like that same little mouse was nibbling on the crust.

"RUFF!" she barked and lunged at it.

"Squeak squeak squeak!!!" it squealed in its tiny voice and backed into the corner of the pizza box, shivering in terror.

A rodent in your food…that's disgusting! I'm not crazy about the crust anyway, she said to herself, taking a bite out of the cheese end. Not New York's finest slice, but not bad in a pinch, she thought.

While Carnegie was absorbed munching away, she didn't notice that an enormous rat—the baby rat's mother—was now boldly sitting up behind it. The rat bared her long yellow teeth and squealed at her.

I thought Ana said mice didn't grow into rats, Carnegie commented to herself. Well, what's a big old rat to a brave royal woof hunter, anyway?

"Go away, pesky rodent," Carnegie growled. "You're disturbing my evening snack."

The rat pointed at the pizza slice and squeaked a warning. "Give it up, fur ball, or you'll get it!"

"I already got it," Carnegie smugly replied, taking an extra-large bite. "For your future reference, I prefer pepperoni with thin crust."

The mother rat twirled her pink paws in the air and squealed in a pitch so loud and shrill, it made Carnegie's ears ring. A massive wave of gray swarmed in from every angle and ran up Carnegie's legs and tail. Within moments, she was wearing a full, plump bodysuit made entirely of swarming rats.

"EEEEW!!!" Carnegie shivered at the creepiness. She flung the pizza slice and sprung to her hind legs. With a full moon as her spotlight, she gyrated around like a deranged disco dancer. The rats, unfazed by her frantic shuffling, spinning, and twirling, hung on as if directed by a 1970's dance choreographer.

I can't go to my palastle looking like this, Carnegie thought. A royal ermine fur-trimmed robe is one thing…but rats? Not a good look.

Finally, dropping to all fours, she performed "The Mother of All Wet Dog Shakes," sending rats flying off in all directions. As quickly as the rats appeared, they disappeared.

"Vanquished!" Carnegie proudly proclaimed, shaking her fur back into un-rat-infested form.

"Not exactly!" the baby rat squealed in its tiny voice, clinging to the discarded pizza crust with its little pink paws.

"You again?!" Carnegie asked in disgust.

"Yes, me! What are you going to do about it, fur ball?" it asked with a smug look. The baby rat looked over its shoulder, but the big mother rat was not there—a fact that Carnegie did not miss either.

"Oops!" it squeaked.

"Oops, indeed," Carnegie replied. "How about if the 'fur ball' does *this* again?" With her mouth, she picked up the baby rat by its tail and dangled it, pizza crust and all. "Remember yesterday?" she managed to say with a little rat tail between her front teeth.

"No. I've never seen you before."

"I dramatically lunged into the bushes, caught you by your tail like now, dangled you around pathetically, and when I let go, you skittered off into the bushes?"

"That wasn't me."

"Seriously? I was here with my sister. She looks like me but less adorable."

"Uh-uh."

"Maybe this crown is throwing you off? I wasn't wearing it yesterday."

"Nope. Not ringing a bell."

"Hmm." Carnegie spit the baby rat/pizza crust combo into the bushes. That's odd, she thought. I suppose there is more than one little rodent in the park. But where *am* I then? Looking around at the heavily wooded surroundings, she realized she had never been in this area before. Her erroneous rodent tracking had taken her in the opposite direction from Belvedere Castle—to Central Park's dark North Woods.

I can hardly see my paw in front of my face. I'll have to smell my way to the palastle, she thought. Not ideal for a sighthound, but surely, my noble blood will guide me. Two hours of walking later, neither her nose nor noble blood had guided her to the palastle door. Exhausted and shivering in the icy darkness, Carnegie stopped in front of a tall pine tree. Didn't I see this tree before? she wondered. Didn't I see *all* these trees before? Maybe I should take a little rest and think about it. Carnegie crawled under the tree's branches and curled up against the trunk, hidden by the low boughs.

It reminded her of when she convinced Madison to run away from their old house to find a different royal palace. She trembled at the memory of that cold and scary night when they hid from terrifying coyotes under a similar tree. Then, at least, she had her sister by her side. Should she have brought Ike along for company? No, he has a job to do, she decided.

Lying alone in the dark, on the hard, frigid ground amongst the prickly, dry pine needles, she pictured her warm, cozy bedroom with her soft cushion bed.

BRRR, it's freezing, she said to herself with chattering teeth. I should have worn my Pucchi cashmere sweater—then remembered she'd need Ana or someone to put it on her. *So* inconvenient.

It must be late, she thought. Is Maddie home yet? Will anyone miss me? Does it even matter now? Carnegie curled up tighter against the harshness of the elements and her emotions, sighed deeply, and closed her eyes.

CHAPTER THIRTY

Disappearance

Carnegie! Carnegie!" Anastasia called out the second she stepped into their penthouse foyer. "We're home!" Ana was answered by silence. The kind of silence that is quieter than silence. The silence of emptiness.

Madison nearly knocked Ana over making a dash for their bedroom, then stopped short, stunned into stillness in the doorway. Her quick sighthound eyes scanned the room, and she spotted Ike on her sister's abandoned bed pillow. Carnegie must have found him in that box Ana talked about, she thought.

Ana rushed to the doorway behind Madison and was joined by her parents.

"Is that Ike in her bed? Ana asked incredulously. "How did he get there? But where's Carnegie?"

"Maybe she's asleep on one of our beds," Spencer suggested. "Call her again."

"Wait! Why is my carpet wet?" Ana asked. She followed the saturated pathway to her bathroom, where water was puddled up on the marble floor and dripping from the toilet bowl rim.

"Mom, Dad, I think something bad happened while we were gone."

"Oh my goodness!" Catherine cried. "Quick! Find Carnegie!"

The Braxtons took off on a panic-search around their apartment for Carnegie, but Madison stayed put. She already knew they wouldn't find her. Before Ike got stashed away in that box, Carnegie always carried her stuffed puppy everywhere. If her sister was here, Ike would be with her, not laying on her pillow. Did Carnegie think they would mistake Ike for her? Was that to buy her time to get away?

Madison's eyes went to her collar display shelf. She stood on her hind legs to look closely—and as she suspected—her crown collar was missing. She never let on, but she knew Carnegie admired it and tried it on when she thought she was alone. It was Madison's favorite, too, but she pretended to ignore all her fancy collars and awards to not make her sister jealous.

From standing height, Madison spotted Little Puppy on Ana's bed. In one sweeping move, she leaped across the room and onto the bed, picked up L.P. in her mouth, settled into a sphinx position, and gently placed him between her front legs.

"Carnegie found you?" she softly asked her little beanie bag dog. "When it was time to leave our old house, I looked and looked, but I couldn't find you. I didn't want to leave you behind...honest."

As abruptly as they left, the Braxtons reappeared in Ana's bedroom.

"We never checked my closet," Ana said, approaching the open door. "Wouldn't it be crazy if she was in there sleeping while we were searching all over the rest of the apartment?"

"Crazy-good," Catherine said.

"Wow!" Ana exclaimed.

"Is she there?!" both her parents cried in unison.

"No, but I think she's been here. There's an open box on the floor and Pucchi booties thrown all over the place."

Ana came out of the closet holding up the Leopardo bootie "skin."

"She ripped up this one," Ana said, tossing the torn fabric in her waste basket. "You know, we haven't looked *under* my bed. She's gotten stuck under there before, although it seems like we would hear her..."

As Ana approached the bed, Madison quickly tucked L.P. under her feathered chest.

"What have you got there? What are you hiding?" Ana asked accusingly.

Madison leaned her chest forward to completely cover her Little Puppy, narrowed her eyes, and snarled. Ana and her parents gasped. No one—absolutely no one—had ever seen Madison snarl. Seeing her huge wolf hunting fangs shocked them into the sudden realization that their dogs are docile by choice.

"Back off, Anastasia," Spencer said urgently. "She's protecting something."

When Ana moved away, Madison relaxed and gently pulled L.P. from under her chest feathers. She placed him between her front legs again and began licking him.

"It's Little Puppy!" Ana said. "Carnegie must have found him with Ike. They were probably in that box on my closet floor."

"*Ohh*, it's Madison's *baby*," Catherine said in her "mom voice." "She's afraid you're going to take him away."

"Well, she shouldn't snarl under any circumstances," Spencer said with a frown.

"She's not being mean, Dad. Look…"

Ana slowly re-approached Madison and cheerfully said, "That's so good you found your Little Puppy! Can I see him, sweetie?"

Madison thought about it for a moment, then nosed L.P. toward Ana. Under Madison's watchful eye, Ana gently took Little Puppy, gave him a kiss on his damp fabric, and then returned him. Madison apologetically licked Ana's hand and wagged her tail.

"Well, that's good at least," Spencer said, "but it doesn't help with Carnegie. I'm going to call Oscar. Maybe he knows something."

"He would have called or texted us if she was missing when he came to check," Catherine said.

"*If* he came to check," Ana said.

"Oscar is very reliable. I'm sure he did," Spencer said, dialing the front desk. Setting down his phone after a concerning discussion, he turned to Catherine and Ana, who were waiting breathlessly.

Catherine asked the question she and her daughter feared: "Is it possible someone took Carnegie?"

"No one is talking dognapping right now," Spencer said. "Oscar confirmed that Carnegie was here at eight o'clock, and the security guard said no strangers came in or out of the building all evening. By the looks of the place, I'd say Carnegie was here for quite a while. Long enough to lie on all the furniture and snoop around."

"Yeah, I don't think anyone else tore up Pucchi booties," Ana said.

"Or left their lick marks on all my good crystal," Catherine added. "But who cares about that now?"

"No one *ever* cares about your crystal, Mom."

"That's uncalled for, Anastasia," Spencer said.

"Sorry."

"We've got to support each other and put our energy toward finding Carnegie."

"Yeah," Ana agreed. "We all have to stick together, right, girl?"

She sat on the bed and hugged Madison, who had started whimpering, wishing she could tell them about Carnegie's secret magic elevator trick. Madison suddenly pawed Ana, jumped off the bed, and ran to the elevator foyer, where she whined and paced in circles. Ana followed Madison and then called out to her parents.

"Come here! I think she's trying to tell us something."

They joined her in the foyer to watch Madison's frantic behavior.

"Seems so," Spencer agreed. "She can certainly help us look for Carnegie, which is the best thing we can do…and as quickly as we can!"

They leashed up Madison, threw on coats, grabbed flashlights, and searched the streets around their building and what they could of Central Park, which wasn't much in the dark.

"This is hopeless, Dad," Ana said, shivering. "Henry told me the park is over eight hundred acres. There's all kinds of meadows and wooded areas. She could be anywhere."

"Or not even in the park," Catherine added.

Spencer and Ana stared at her in horror. "Oh, please don't say that, dear. Not right now, anyway," he said.

"We'll never find her. She's gone forever," Ana said tearfully.

Catherine pulled a tissue from her jacket pocket and wiped her daughter's icy cheeks. "No, she's not. It's just too dark to find her now."

"Madison can track Carnegie better in the daylight," her dad added.

"Right," Ana agreed, petting Madison's head. "She found her yesterday."

"What?!" her mom exclaimed. "Carnegie ran away *yesterday?* And you didn't tell us?"

"Uhh…" Ana stammered. "I guess I forgot to mention it. When we were in the park with Henry. But we found her almost right away."

Both of her parents looked at her, annoyed,

"It wasn't like tonight. There was this mouse and…"

"We'll talk about this later, Anastasia," her dad interrupted. "I think we better call off our search until morning."

Back in their apartment, Catherine called Garnett, who was equally distraught after hearing the news and offered to come right over.

"No, thank you, Garnett," she said. "There's not much we can do in the middle of the night. We'll call you in the morning."

"Did Garnett have any suggestions?" Ana asked her mom after she hung up.

"She's going to notify the Borzoi Rescue Network and all of her contacts. You know, she reminded me about Carnegie appearing in the lobby by herself on opening night."

"Yes," Spencer said. "That one remains a mystery, but maybe it eliminates her being dognapped. I hope so, anyway. I'll give the police a call and make a report."

His call to the New York Police Department was of limited help. The police don't investigate missing dogs but said they would alert patrol cars to keep an eye out for her.

Next, Catherine called Animal Control and the local animal shelter. Both were closed for the night, so she left messages.

"I still have the 'Missing Dogs' flyer artwork files on my laptop," Ana said. "Remember?...from when they both ran away from our old house?"

"Who could ever forget that?" Catherine said with a sigh.

"I can change the info and photo to just Carnegie missing and post it on social media and our neighborhood app. I'll print a bunch of flyers, too. We can put some up and hand them out in the park."

"That'll be good, Princess," Spencer said, putting his arm around her. "Oh, sorry. I forgot I'm not supposed to call you that anymore."

"No, it's okay, Dad. Really."

Staring out the penthouse's large windows into the blackness, they all desperately tried to picture Carnegie somewhere safe and warm—not frightened, alone, and in the freezing cold.

CHAPTER THIRTY-ONE

The North Woods

Lying on the icy ground and covered with a layer of frost and fallen pine needles, Carnegie shivered herself awake at first daybreak.

Well, this isn't particularly comfy, she said to herself. I must have fallen asleep while I was thinking.

She stood and shook, but the dry pine needles stuck in her chest, legs, and tail feathers, dangling as an unsightly fringe. She tried to pull them out with her teeth only to find them stubbornly woven into her fur.

I can't show up at the palastle wearing tree debris, she thought, although it's an improvement over wearing rats. I'll have to freshen up before I get there.

Crawling out from under the tree limbs, Carnegie was greeted by the serenity of the early morning sun filtering through the frosty foliage and birds chirping in the distance. She arched her back and stretched like a cat, then dropped into a downward dog bow and then back up. Morning yoga done!

Her feet crunched on the frosty forested floor as she trotted off with renewed purpose and vigor. Within a short while, she found a rock-bordered footpath and followed it.

Maybe this way? she wondered. I hope there's some picnic areas. I could really use a breakfast snack. When her stomach growled, she upped her craving to a breakfast burrito.

The path meandered through the woods to a rustic wood bridge with a waterfall and stream below. The sound of running water reminded Carnegie of something. *Oh right,* the dreadful Pucchi shoe that clogged the toilet. She pictured everyone coming home and discovering the watery mess. I hope they don't blame Ike, she thought.

She carefully made her way down the rock bank to a still part of the stream. She lapped up some water then leaned out and gazed at her fluid reflection. Her crown collar was still perched on her head but with pine needles sticking out that coordinated with the pine needle fringe on her body.

I'm not loving this matchy-matchy tree debris look, she said to herself. Will these things wash off?

She dipped her right front leg and swished it around to wash off the pine needles, but when she lifted her dripping leg out of the water, they still clung to her feathers.

Maybe I can blow them off? She climbed up the bank and looked for an area where she could run all out. When the trees and heavy foliage thinned out into an open grass meadow, she took off running. The cool air rushing through her long fur felt thrilling. This would be even more fun if Maddie was running by my side, she thought, then put that out of her mind.

Sensing a picnic area, she skidded to a stop, digging divots in the grass and muddying her rear feet.

A granola bar! She pounced on the wrapper and stuck her long nose inside. *Pathetic,* she said to herself, licking the few crumbs stuck at the bottom of the wrapper. What did my royal woof hunter ancestors eat for breakfast before the persons built them a palastle? She closed her eyes and tried to conjure up her natural food-gathering instincts, but all that she could envision was scrambled eggs with a side of bacon.

EWW! I'm drooling like one of those droopy Bloodhounds. *So* unattractive. I can't go to the palastle covered with sticky-outy tree debris *and* slobber, she thought, shaking the saliva off her long lips. I think now's the perfect time to try intermittent fasting. When I get to the palastle, I can un-fast and fill up on any food my royal-self desires. Mom said surf and turf is good…*mmm*…filet mignon and lobster, Carnegie thought dreamily. *EWW!* I'm drooling again!

Shaking off her second slobber incident too violently, Carnegie's feet flew out from under her—and with a sickening SMACK!—she landed headfirst on a rock.

CHAPTER THIRTY-TWO

Grand Theft

With the first light—after a sleepless night—the Braxtons resumed their search for Carnegie. They posted missing dog flyers around their neighborhood and then headed across the street to Central Park. Madison pulled on her leash and urgently led them to where Carnegie had found the mouse.

"This is where we were yesterday," Ana told her parents. "Before… you know…"

"Before Carnegie ran away and you forgot to tell us?" her dad reminded her.

"Yeah, sorry…but Madison knows where Carnegie went next. She tracked her and led Henry and me there. It was by some castle."

"Belvedere Castle?" Catherine asked.

"That sounds right. Maybe she went there again."

With hope in their hearts, they let Madison lead the way. Even though it had been over a day since she tracked Carnegie, her sister's scent still clung to the pathways, grass, and foliage she had brushed past. In fact, it still faintly lingered in the air. Madison followed Carnegie's route to the picnic area, where they found her with the Pringles can.

"Good girl!" Ana said. "This is the place." She pointed across Turtle Pond. "See, there's the castle."

The picnic area was there, the pond was there, the castle was there—everything was there but Carnegie.

Discouraged, they nevertheless searched for several more hours.

At around nine a.m., the Braxtons decided to return home, have some breakfast, and regroup. On their way out of the park, they left some small stacks of missing dog flyers on park benches.

In their apartment lobby, Spencer picked up the morning *Times* newspaper. "I doubt there's any missing dog news, but it doesn't hurt to check," he said.

As soon as the elevator arrived on their floor, Madison headed to her bed and, despite Ana's pleading, would not come to the kitchen to eat her breakfast. Nor would Madison eat it when presented at her bedside.

"What can I do? She won't eat anything," Ana asked her parents.

"She's upset. I don't have much of an appetite either," her dad said as he thumbed through the newspaper. When he turned to the entertainment section, a headline caught his eye.

"Well, look at this," he said as Ana and Catherine read over his shoulder:

'Hearts Over Broadway' Cast Update:
UNLIKEABLE and LACKLUSTER

Thank goodness for vegan materials because this reviewer has to eat his hat. The much-maligned canine actor, Carnegie, AKA the Hindenburg Hound, proved that one doesn't need to be perfect to be adorable and adored. Abruptly cast out after her rather unorthodox (to be generous) performance on opening night, Carnegie's understudy, Glory, replaced her in the role of Olivia's sister. Somehow managing to be simultaneously haughty and robotic, Glory delivered both an annoying and boring performance that left us all desperately yearning for Carnegie's endearing and uniquely entertaining antics. I enthusiastically join the theater going public with my demand for Carnegie's reinstatement and immediate return to the 'Hearts Over Broadway' stage!

"This review would have made Carnegie happy," Ana said.

"Let's not talk about her in past tense," Spencer said, setting the paper down.

When Catherine's phone rang, everyone jumped.

"Hello?" Catherine anxiously answered.

"Hi. It's Garnett. Any sign of Carnegie?"

"We wish. We searched for her this morning and we're going to go back out and search some more."

"Well, unfortunately, I have some news to add to our troubles. I just got an urgent email from the theater, and they want Carnegie back…tonight."

"Mom! Mom!" Ana cried, tapping on her shoulder.

"Just a minute. I'm talking to Garnett."

"I think she'll want to know about this," Ana said, holding up her phone. "*Carnegie Missing* is trending all over the internet. They must have seen our postings—but they're saying she was dognapped. Some people think Randy did it to keep Glory onstage."

"Randy? That's ridiculous," Catherine replied. "Did you hear what Ana said, Garnett?

"I did."

"Do you think the theater knows?"

"Hold on, Catherine. My phone's blowing up. I'm getting texts and emails from the theater and Carnegie's agency…and, oh my goodness, the news media wants interviews. Yes, they know. Everyone knows!"

Shortly after Catherine and Garnett finished talking, the front desk called. Officers from the NYPD were in the lobby and wanted to come up and talk to the Braxtons.

As they anxiously lined up in their elevator foyer to greet the police, Ana asked, "Was Carnegie dognapped, Dad? Is my bedroom going to be a crime scene, like with yellow tape across the door?"

"I don't know any more than you, Ana," he replied. "Let's not overreact and be grateful if they can help."

The Braxtons greeted Detective Lee and Officer Miller and invited them to sit in their living room. The detective explained that the reports of Carnegie being captured had escalated her from being a missing dog to a case of suspected dognapping, which is a crime of theft.

"You mean like stealing property?" Spencer asked.

"That's right," the detective responded. "The punishment for stealing a dog is like for stealing a laptop."

"But they're family!" Catherine objected.

"I understand how you feel, ma'am, but that's the law. In the case of Carnegie being a valuable purebred dog with celebrity status, it would be grand theft."

Ana brought her phone over to the detective. "Is this what people are reporting?" she asked with tears in her eyes. She quickly scrolled through disturbing photos of Carnegie cruelly chained up, guarded by an evil Glory and Randy. There was even one of Carnegie locked up in a terrifying prison. "I think these are AI images, but still…"

"I suggest you all stay offline for now. Our department monitors postings and investigates any that seem legit," Detective Lee said.

"Have you gotten any real leads?" Spencer asked.

"Not yet. We hope you can provide some information. What do you know about this Randy person?"

"Not too much," Catherine said. "His last name is McCormick. He's got the two Borzoi, Precious and Glory, who are understudies for Madison and Carnegie. He's maybe jealous, but he doesn't strike me as a dognapper."

The detective jotted down the information about Randy and then asked, "So, where was Carnegie when you saw her last?"

"She was in her bed. I can show you," Catherine replied, getting up and leading everyone to Ana's bedroom. She pointed to Carnegie's bed with Ike still laying on her pillow. "When we left for the theater, she was right there."

The detective knelt at Carnegie's bed. He put on gloves and picked up Ike. "What's this? Her toy or something?"

"Yeah," Ana said. "That's Ike. Carnegie likes to carry him around. He wasn't there when we left for the theater, though."

Across the room, Madison was lying in her own bed facing the wall. She didn't acknowledge their presence even when Officer Miller noticed her and excitedly cried, "Whoa! That's famous Madison. My kids won't believe I saw her in person."

Detective Lee gave him a "look."

"Sorry, sir," he replied, standing at attention.

The detective noticed the stream of wet carpet and followed it to the puddled-up bathroom. "What happened here?"

"No idea. We found it like this when we got home from the theater," Spencer replied. "The closet is messed up, too. We assume Carnegie did that though."

"Yeah? How so?" the detective asked.

"She wasn't a fan of wearing dog shoes, and they're thrown all over," Ana said.

The detective used a pencil to pick up the torn-up Leopardo fabric from the wastebasket. "Is this from one of the shoes?"

"Uh-huh," Ana said. "She hated those the most."

"My Rottweiler wouldn't be caught dead—," the officer started to say.

The detective interrupted him. "Bag this, Miller. Bag the stuffed dog, too. We'll check for DNA."

"Can you please return Ike when you're done?" Ana asked.

Spencer put his arm around his daughter's shoulders. "Carnegie will want him when she comes home," he added compassionately.

"I'll make sure of it, Miss," Officer Miller said with a smile.

The detective handed out his card and asked the Braxtons to call if they think of anything. He promised the department would notify them of any breakthroughs in Carnegie's case.

When the police were leaving, Ana handed Officer Miller a show poster with Madison's paw print. "Your kids might like this," she said. "Madison personally signed it."

With the police gone, Catherine gathered up their coats. "It's good the NYPD's looking for her, but we should go out ourselves and search some more."

Before they could call Madison, she was standing in the foyer, ready to be leashed up.

When they arrived in the lobby, Oscar rushed up to stop them. "I don't think you should leave right now. There's a crush of press and paparazzi outside."

Loud and repeated shouts of "There's Madison!" and flashing cameras confirmed Oscar's warning and forced the Braxtons back up to their penthouse.

Looking out the window at the large crowd below, Ana asked, "How are we going to go out and look for Carnegie now? And how is Garnett going to take Madison to the theater?"

"*Is* she taking her?" Spencer asked.

"Oh, yes," Catherine said. "She texted me. Madison is still under contract to perform."

Whoever coined the phrase, "The show must go on," couldn't have been more accurate for "Hearts Over Broadway." After confirming that Carnegie was officially missing, the theater management held an emergency meeting to strategize. Carnegie was not just an unfortunate missing dog. She was the beloved canine star that the public was now clamoring to have back onstage...the same beloved star the theater management fired the night before she disappeared. The publicity implications were horrific. And the potential financial loss was devastating. Already, demonstrators had gathered in front of the theater with signs to boycott the show that proclaimed, "*HEARTLESS* Over Broadway Fired Carnegie!" and "No Carnegie, No Audience!"

Whether it was to save the "beloved canine star" or the show's future, the theater management immediately set up a non-profit organization to help find Carnegie and made that evening's performance a benefit.

Word spread quickly, with pet-friendly companies jumping on to add their support. Within hours, the organization's mission expanded to rescuing all missing dogs—especially in light of the recent dognappings. It was named the *Carnegie Missing Dog Foundation* with her likeness featured on the logo.

The strategy paid off. Tickets for that evening's performance sold out within minutes of the benefit being announced, and the signs boycotting "Hearts Over Broadway" were replaced by theater-friendly signs that featured Carnegie and called for the rescue of all missing dogs.

CHAPTER THIRTY-THREE

Shakespeare Garden

Where am I? Carnegie asked herself when she awoke lying on the ground with her head on a rock pillow. I must have fainted from hunger. *And how long was I here?* The sun was higher in the sky and her internal dog clock told her it was around ten a.m., which is the time she expected to get her mid-morning snack, at least in her *old* life.

From her reclining position, Carnegie noticed a paper that clung to a scraggly branch. She removed it with her mouth and set it on the ground. She smoothed out the damp, wrinkled paper with her paws and stared down at her own image on the Braxton's missing dog flyer.

I'm missing. *Huh.* They noticed. It looks like they cut Madison out of this photo, she commented to herself in disgust. They couldn't find a picture of just *me?*

She wondered what her family was doing to find her besides littering the park. She might have been pleased to know that the police had been in her apartment investigating her mysterious disappearance. But definitely *not* pleased that her beloved puppy, Ike, was no longer waiting on her pillow but was in a sealed plastic bag to be sent to a DNA laboratory.

"Look!" an approaching jogger suddenly yelled to their partner. "Is that the missing dog?!"

Carnegie quickly ducked behind the bushes. She tore at the flyer with her nails but found her photo was still intact. Not sure what to do, she decided to eat it. Swallowing the paper wad, she tried not to make a gagging sound as the joggers passed by.

She'd been on the lesser-traveled paths but now, as she approached the more popular areas of the park, she would have to be careful, especially being publicly known as "missing."

She slyly grinned, remembering how she snuck past the security guard in her apartment lobby. I'll have to engage my thespian ninja skills again, she thought. Using the bushes for cover, she attempted a slide-scoot.

YOW! she yelped when the abrasive rocky dirt path scraped her behind. She couldn't decide if it was a matter for the Actor's Union, the Animal Humane Society, or the Park Department...but someone should answer for the precious fur she was now missing off her fluffy rear end.

Carnegie stuck her head up over the bushes and, with no persons in sight, decided to abandon her more exotic skills and simply travel on four feet. Naturally swift and stealth, she made fast progress—sticking to the shadows and hiding behind large rocks and trees to avoid being spotted by the park visitors. As she neared the reservoir, she stopped dead at a shocking sight.

"RUFF! RUFF!" she barked. Hippopotamuses! Just like the ones on the wildlife TV show Garnett used to play when we were rehearsing. But don't they live far away with lions and giraffes? Did I go past the palastle? she wondered.

As the fur on her back raised, she crouched down and cautiously approached. Out of the corner of her eye, she spotted a child jumping up and down on one of the hippopotamuses, yelling "Hippo! Hippo! Hippo!" and she realized they were sculptures. Oh, of course they're fake hippos, she said to herself. Delusional child. He thinks they're real.

Suddenly the child ran towards her shouting, "Papa! Papa! It's Maddyson!"

Before she could react, the little boy threw his arms around her neck and held on tightly, screaming, "I wuv you! I wuv you! I wuv you! I wuv you! I wuv you!"

Now what? Carnegie thought in a panic. This is wrong on *so* many levels.

Her mind racing, she frantically explored the options:

Option One: Run off and drag this hysterical "boa constrictor" child with me to the palastle.

Two: Stand still and be discovered by "Papa" after which it will be revealed that I am not Madison but, in fact, her adorable sister, Carnegie, who is missing, leading to me being captured, never making it to the palastle and forever giving up the dream of claiming my rightful royal destiny and becoming the famous-est dog ever, or

Three: Do a slight-of-hand—or in this case—slight-of-head trick and slyly slip away…NOW!

Hmm, do I really need to do a comparative analysis?

Selecting Option Three, she thanked her natural Borzoi flexibility for being able to quickly twist away from the child's choke hold. She dashed out of the Safari playground and didn't look back when she heard cries of, "Weawy, Papa. It was Maddyson!"

Carnegie ran the long length of the reservoir, keeping to the bushy areas off the park's paths. Past the reservoir, she came upon the sprawling Great Lawn and, with sudden familiarity, her instincts led her to a picnic area.

"I know where I am!" she proudly proclaimed. Her mind became a swirling montage of smells and memories—walks and runs, Henry and Ana, leftover snacks, and Pringles. And Madison! Carnegie raised her long nose in the air and inhaled deeply. Maddie's been here recently…like *this morning?* And she sensed the Braxtons were with her.

An orange snack bag suddenly distracted her. Are those my favorite cheese puffs? She pounced on the bag, stuck in her nose and rooted around. She didn't find puffs, but she certainly found orange.

Her white snout emerged resembling a giant cheese puff.

A-a-A-CHOOooo! she sneezed an orange cloud. She snickered remembering when she sneezed on Nora and transformed her into a Snow Leopardo. It seemed so long ago when she and Madison were getting styled for their photo shoot, she thought wistfully. Absently, her eyes followed the orange cloud as it drifted away and floated over Turtle Pond and beyond to...*what?!*

Lightheaded by near disbelief, she sat and stared at the vision before her—*her dream come true*—her palastle! There, perched atop the dramatic Vista Rock stood the majestic Belvedere Castle. Suddenly realizing that she should have remembered its location, she smugly said to herself, *It's exactly where I knew it would be.*

Keeping her palastle in sight, she took off running toward it. Frosty stone walkways took her through the serene Shakespeare Garden to the steps that led up to the palastle. Taking them three at a time, she bolted to the entrance terrace—where she skidded to a stop.

Tourists! Uninvited persons standing in line to get into *her* palastle. How dare they? Before she could be spotted, she ran back down the stairs. Breathing heavily, Carnegie backtracked to Shakespeare Garden. The winter foliage was bare, and the rose bushes were covered with thorns, so she hid under a large bench made from rustic tree limbs. Visitors would call the bench romantic, but to Carnegie, it felt like a cage. Scrunched in the darkness, she watched persons' legs pass by and sit on the bench, unaware she was underneath.

*Some*times, the bench sitters read passages from Shakespearean plays out loud to each other. *Some*times they just read silently. *No* times did they drop any snacks on the ground.

Trying to ignore her empty stomach, she listened to the persons recite Shakespearean scenes, playing kings, queens, princes, and princesses. The old Shakespearean language sounded noble to her. This must be how they talk in my palastle, she thought. How smart of me to stop here to learn royal talk.

She grew bored listening to the persons blather on and switched to pondering her soon-to-be royal life. Things like, will I have ruling responsibilities that cut into my essential nap times? Will I be required to wear white gloves and greet commoners? What if my royal chamber carpeting is green? I hate green, except forest green is tolerable… and so on, with every concern avoiding her real fear of missing her pampered life with Madison.

As the shadows grew longer and the evening approached, the park visitors grew fewer and fewer until there were none. Carnegie cautiously crawled out from under the bench and stretched out her long limbs. Looking around at the deserted Shakespeare Garden, she said to herself, *Time to take-eth me ~ to mine own palastle-ee.*

She snickered at her clever, noble rhyme, dismissed all worries about becoming royalty, and happily hightailed it to Belvedere Castle.

CHAPTER THIRTY-FOUR

Broken Heart

"Madison, please get up…please!" Ana pleaded. "Garnett is in the lobby. It's five o'clock. Time to leave for the theater."

No amount of begging or bribing could get Madison to move from her bed, lying facing the wall, and pretending to be asleep.

"What do we do?" Ana asked her parents.

"Text Garnett and ask her to come up. She may have better luck," her dad suggested.

Garnett approached Madison's bed and calmly but firmly said, "Madison, come." She slowly rose and stood to be leashed up.

The Braxtons stared at obedient Madison in amazement. "How did you do that?" Catherine asked. "We've been trying to get her up all day."

"Borzoi and I have an understanding," Garnett said with a wink, *…that I don't put up with their diva attitudes*, she added to herself. Garnett knelt to pet Madison, and she responded with a sad sniff kiss.

"Oh dear," Garnett said. "She's been licking her front paw again. What happened to her bandage?"

"She pulled it off, and it was all dirty from searching for Carnegie, so we threw it away," Spencer said.

"Do you have a white cotton sock you can spare and some tape?"

"Sure. Be right back," Ana said and returned with one of her dad's socks and some white adhesive tape.

"Perfect," Garnett said. She pulled the sock over Madison's right front paw and taped it around her lower leg. "This should work until we get to the theater. But, first, we've got to get her past all the reporters and cameras."

"They're going to scare her," Ana said, petting Madison.

"I know, dear. Oscar said I can sneak her down the freight elevator and out the back door. Klaus is already parked, waiting for us there."

Looking out the SUV's windows as they approached the theater, Garnett gasped when she saw Carnegie's photos on the "missing dog" signs the demonstrators were carrying. She looked down at heartbroken Madison, tightly curled up on the seat next to her with a now-damp white sock on her paw.

"Oh, you licked your sock," she said sympathetically. "I'm so sorry, dear. I know you're hurting. We'll get your sister back…somehow."

The paparazzi had discovered the stage door and were anxiously waiting for the cast's arrival. As Klaus pulled up, they descended on the car with noise and flashing camera lights that felt like terrifying thunder and lightning to Madison. She scrunched down and shivered in fear. Two theater security guards came out to push back the crowd so Klaus could open the rear passenger door. He reached in and handed his overcoat to Garnett.

"Here, Madam. I think Madison will be less frightened if you cover her with this. I can get it back later."

Garnett cloaked Madison in Klaus' dark navy overcoat, leaving just enough uncovered for her to see. Flanked by a security guard on each side, they made a dash for the stage door.

Madison's dressing room was barely visible for all the sympathy flowers waiting to be brought inside. Their beauty and fragrance rivaled the ones sent on opening night, but their messages of support and concern were far from congratulatory and cheerful.

Garnett and Madison were met at the door by Amelia, who was carrying an arrangement of tall gladiolas in a silver vase.

"We're so sorry, Ms. Dixon. We wanted Carnegie back onstage and now she's missing all together."

"We hope it won't be for long," Garnett replied. "Madison is quite upset, so please be patient with her."

Amelia peered around the arrangement. "Where *is* Madison?"

Garnett responded with a questioning look at Amelia, then saw that Madison was now lying at her feet, curled up in a ball and completely covered by dark navy fabric.

"Oh my." Garnett removed Klaus' coat and draped it over her arm. "See what I mean?"

"Poor girl." Amelia knelt and hugged Madison, then unclipped her leash. "Would you be more comfy in your bed?"

"Be careful of the flowers!" Lily called out as Madison got up and threaded her way through the standing arrangements to her bed at the far end of the dressing room.

As Garnett was leaving, Randy approached with Precious and Glory.

"Who died?" he asked with a smirk.

Garnett gasped. "Why on earth would you say such a thing?"

"Oh, gee. I don't know…all the sympathy flowers? But as they say, the show must go on. Right, Glory?" Randy said, unclipping her leash. "Precious will be waiting in her dressing room right next door—all ready to take over for Madison…just FYI."

Garnett left without responding, but Madison could feel her anger all the way from her bed. Glory sauntered into the dressing room and intentionally knocked over the gladiola arrangement, sending the long stems everywhere. While Amelia and Lily scrambled to recover the arrangement, Glory continued her rude tour around the room, ending at Madison's bed.

"Too bad you'll never see your no-talent sister again," she sneered, then flipped her tail in the air and headed to Carnegie's sofa.

From a complete recline, Madison leaped in the air and landed between Glory and the sofa. Standing firm with fierceness in her eyes, Madison loomed much larger than her slender self. With a deep growl, she slowly pulled back her lips in a huge snarl. It wasn't a warning snarl like when she was protecting her Little Puppy. This was a primal snarl that came from the depths of her Borzoi soul. It was a terrifying snarl meant to stop a ferocious wolf.

"DON'T YOU EVER MENTION MY SISTER AGAIN!" Madison growled so viciously that Glory cowered and peed on the floor.

"AND STAY OFF HER SOFA!" she threatened as Glory whimpered and meekly crawled into a corner.

Satisfied that Glory was staying in her subservient spot, Madison returned to her bed. With her eyes closed tight, she pretended to be asleep—actually, beyond asleep—completely unresponsive.

Nora and Mia did what they could with Madison lying dead still on her left side. Dr. Ina changed out her sock for a white bandage. Laura stood by with her hair clip.

"We better get Brad," Mia said. "We can't send a half-made-up, half-brushed dog onstage."

Brad quickly arrived and stood over Madison with concern.

"There's no way I can put her butterfly on," Laura said.

"True," Brad agreed, "but I'm afraid that hardly matters if she won't get up. We can't drag her onstage in her bed. Let's see if Gabriella can work her magic again, or we'll have to go with her understudy. No one wants that, but we better get Precious set to go on, just in case."

Gabriella, half-ready to go onstage, rushed in and knelt at Madison's bed while Mia, Nora, Laura, and Brad anxiously looked on.

"Can I have a moment alone with her, please?" When they stepped aside, Gabriella leaned into Madison's bed, kissed her cheek, and whispered into her soft fur ear.

"I understand this is hard, and you miss your sister. We all do.

You know the people who watch us onstage? They love you, and they love Carnegie. Most of them are coming tonight because they want to help find her. We need to be brave and go on for Carnegie's sake. Can you do that, Madison?"

Whether it was because Madison understood what Gabriella said or it was out of love for her—to everyone's joy and relief, she got out of bed.

Madison obediently took her opening place seated next to Gabriella, leaned against her legs and looked up at her with sad eyes. When the curtains parted, the entire audience jumped to their feet, wildly applauding and yelling, "We love you, Madison!"

The response was so overwhelming that Gabriella had to hold for the cheering to die down before she could deliver her first line.

Quite the opposite, Glory's stage entrance was met with loud boos and taunts of "Get off the stage!" and "We want Carnegie!"

Madison was driven by the love she felt coming from the audience for Carnegie and to everyone's delight, she was perfectly performing her role as Olivia for the first act.

When the lights dramatically focused on center stage, Brad addressed the crew on headsets.

"Okay, we're coming up on Gabriella and Olivia's emotional scene. We don't have to worry about a Carnegie disaster tonight, but let's get to intermission without any mishaps."

Gabriella moved into the light and gracefully sat on the chaise lounge. Madison trotted over and sat at her feet. On cue, she put her paws on Gabriella's lap and looked up at her…but Madison's eyes were soon drawn to the orchestra pit where her sister had crashed in such a disastrous and humiliating way.

Carnegie only wanted to be in the spotlight…to be adored like she deserves, Madison said to herself. But all the focus was on *me. Only me*. And now Carnegie is gone. Maybe forever.

She turned her attention back to Gabriella and looked deep into her eyes—piercing through to her heart—to silently say, *"I'm sorry to let you down."*

And then, with a prolonged, pain-filled yowl, Madison—out of grief and guilt—collapsed onto the stage.

The audience collectively gasped as Gabriella dropped to the floor and cradled Madison's limp body in her arms.

"Close the curtains! Close the curtains!" Brad yelled over the headsets as Precious gleefully ran onstage to claim her role as Olivia.

"Call Dr. Ina and get Precious off the stage. She's practically standing on Madison."

The show was announced "closed until further notice" but much of the audience remained in their seats, stunned by the dramatic scene they had witnessed.

Behind the abruptly shut curtains, Madison was examined, and no physical reason was found to be the cause of her collapse or unresponsiveness. After Dr. Ina decided she would recover better at home, Madison was wrapped in a thermal blanket and carried out of the theater by Security.

In reverse of the earlier evening's theater arrival, the guards forced their way through the crowd of frenzied paparazzi to reach Madison's car. They handed her off to Klaus, who was standing at attention, waiting at the passenger door. He stepped into the car and gently placed Madison in distraught Garnett's arms.

"Here, Madam," he said. "My condolences."

Lifelessly lying across Garnett's lap, the beloved canine star was driven home. Spencer met them at the curb and carried Madison upstairs.

Still in the thermal blanket she had been wrapped in when she was whisked out of the theater, Madison lay motionless in her bed at home. Ana, Catherine, and Spencer stood at her bedside, watching for her to awaken from her earlier collapse onstage.

"Are we sure she's breathing?" Ana asked.

"Oh, I'm sure she is, dear," Catherine replied.

"I think I should check." Ana knelt and gently pulled back the blanket and intently stared at Madison's chest until her silky fur barely rose and fell.

"Oh good, she's breathing…but is she in a coma or something?" Ana asked.

"Dr. Ina said her vitals are okay. It's hard to know what's wrong," Catherine replied.

Suddenly, Ana stood and turned toward her parents with tears streaming down her cheeks. "I *know* what's wrong! Madison has a broken heart. And she won't wake up until we find Carnegie—and that may be never!"

Ana snatched a tissue from the box on her vanity and ran out the door. Her parents exchanged concerned looks and followed her to the living room, where she was standing at the tall windows.

"Look how big this city is!" Ana cried, waving her arms at the endless view. "Carnegie is hardly the size of a dot out there."

"Try not to think of it that way. It looks different when we're on the street," Spencer said.

"Like we can go anywhere with the press all over us. Madison's been home for hours, and they're still out there. It's almost midnight."

"That's temporary, Ana. This will all die down."

"Yeah. When they stop caring what happened to Carnegie and move on to the next story," she replied.

Ana looked at her parents, who were staring at her sadly. "I don't mean to be so negative. I think I'm just tired. I'm going to sleep next to Madison tonight."

Ana grabbed a pillow and a comforter off her bed and settled on the floor next to Madison's bed. Madison was lying in the same position as when they left her—but with one major and perplexing difference. Little Puppy had been moved from Ana's bed to Madison's bed and was tucked up close to her.

CHAPTER THIRTY-FIVE

Royal Palastle

At dusk, Carnegie left Shakespeare Garden behind and raced up the stairs to Belvedere Castle's entrance terrace. This time, no one was there. Sitting in a pool of light under a lamp post, she craned her neck to take in the three-story medieval stone building with its sky-high tower.

Majestic, Carnegie nervously commented to herself, suddenly feeling overwhelmed by the imposing palastle and the choice she was making.

Go Big or Go Home, she decided. I just need to spiff up a bit. She shook herself to fluff-out her fur and imagined her renewed elegant, noble appearance. A reality-mirror check would reflect an alarmingly odd creature with an orange snout, wearing a fancy collar on its head as a ridiculous royal crown. Adding to her strangeness was the pine needles that stuck out and dangled, making Carnegie look like a huge, scary, porcupine.

The front palastle door was closed but not locked, with an ideal Borzoi-nose-height handle. She grabbed it with her mouth, backed up to pull the door open, and entered. It was dark inside, with only moonlight streaming through the tall arched windows. Carnegie stepped forward, raised her long nose in the air, and puffed out her chest.

"Thy royal-eth woofhound, Carnegie, hath arrive-eth!" she barked.

Her pompous proclamation was met by the flapping wings of two startled pigeons. She quickly ducked as they flew past her, circled over her head, and landed on a high ledge. The pair looked down at Carnegie and cooed their annoyance at her presence.

EWW! Filthy flying rats! she said to herself. This palastle needs a deep cleaning. Where are the maidservants?

Carnegie took another step forward and re-announced her presence. "HERF! HERF! HERF!"

Her irritatingly loud signature brat bark was answered by a quieter but still irritating "HERF! HERF! HERF!" bouncing back at her off the hard stone walls.

Who said that? How rude! she thought, hearing her echo. Not very welcoming, she complained to herself

Frowning, she looked around at the stone walls, which were bare except for some signs and framed historical photos.

Well, this isn't very regal, she said to herself.

Her mother, Gracie, had described the glorious palastle having lavish rooms, decorated with glistening gold everywhere. This dull, empty stone room was *not* that. And Gracie told her there'd be royal Borzoi lounging on velvet sofas in front of a massive marble fireplace, *not* ratty pigeons perched overhead amid cobwebs—and worse—bird poop.

Mom wouldn't make up stories about our noble ancestors, she thought with a sinking heart. And then it hit her. *Of course!* This is where they let the commoners visit. The real royal stuff is happening somewhere else.

With renewed hope, Carnegie approached the next room which appeared to be a little shop. The sign read "Gifts."

That's nice, she said to herself. I'm quite fond of gifts. How thoughtful! It was dark inside, but she could make out a display of shiny royal gold crowns.

"Behold!" she happily cried, as she ran over and snatched one off the table.

PHTFFF! She spit the paper crown out in disgust. What *is* this cheap thing? It's like what kids get at a burger joint. Not that I don't like burgers…(Extra meat and cheese, please. Hold the onion, pickles, tomato, lettuce, any kind of sauces, and bun. Maybe I just like meat and cheese?)…Anyway, those burger crowns are pathetic—like this one, she thought, stomping it flat with her paws.

Kicking the souvenir crown aside, she explored the rest of the gift shop. There were books, t-shirts, and souvenirs that persons seem to like. She found it all boring but then she spotted a dark, narrow staircase off to the side. A thick, heavy red velvet rope suspended between two gold metal stands blocked the visitors from entering.

What was I thinking? she gleefully reprimanded herself. The royal Borzoi would not be living on the lowly ground floor where those nosy persons poke around. Obviously, the regal living quarters are on-high.

She ducked under the velvet rope and excitedly scampered up the steep enclosed circular tower stairs, around and around to the second floor. Slightly dizzy, she found herself in a room smaller than the first floor. It opened out to a roofless terrace with two round turret-style balconies. She did a short tour of the terrace and decided it was perfect for dining al fresco. The chilly night air was a little too "fresco" for her comfort, so she went back inside. The second-floor room had stunning views of the park on all sides but nothing else. Literally, it was bare. She strutted around, enjoying the absence of green carpet and admiring the room's "good bones." A perfect blank canvas for *mine own* palastle designer to work their majestic magic, she thought.

She went to one of the large arched windows and looked out. In the distance, her sharp sighthound eyes spotted two annoying dogs being walked at night on the path around the Great Lawn.

Oh, yes, this will be perfect for me, she thought, then wistfully added…Maddie too, after her show closes. We can watch for enemy dogs in all directions, all over my entire kingdom.

Satisfied with her royal chamber, she went to the next staircase and excitedly said to herself, *Onward and upward to meet-eth mine own royal-eth family!*

Her heart swelling with anticipation, she quickly climbed the dark, narrow winding steps higher and higher until she reached the top tower stair. Before entering the third and final floor, Carnegie paused to catch her breath and regain her composure. Feeling sufficiently dignified, she elegantly pranced into the room with her head held high and her tail fluffed into a majestic plume.

"Thy royal-eth woofhound, Carnegie, hath arrive-eth…at last-eth!" she barked…to absolutely…no one.

Carnegie, shocked into stillness, stood staring ahead. Without daring to move, her eyes swept a 180-degree view of the small round bare stone room. Slowly, very slowly, she turned in a circle. It was hardly a room at all—just the entrance to the vacant top floor outdoor terrace. Her palastle was as empty as her dream of being royalty.

No! No! This can't be! Carnegie internally screamed.

In a panic, she blindly ran back down the winding staircase, around and around, not stopping on the second floor, around and around, faster and faster…until she blasted out on the ground floor and smashed into the red velvet rope. Unable to stop, she dragged the rope with its gold stands across the gift shop.

The dog/rope/stands jumble came to an abrupt halt when it crashed into the souvenir crown display with a loud metallic *CLANG!* and sent the paper crowns flying.

After the collision debris settled, Carnegie lay motionless underneath, pinned by the velvet rope that she believed would lead to claiming her royal destiny—to being the famous-est dog in the world—to being more famous than her sister.

Carnegie dragged herself from under the gift shop heap and crawled out of the room. She curled up in a dark corner of the "pigeon room" and, out of exhaustion and despair, fell into a sorrowful sleep.

CHAPTER THIRTY-SIX

Kind of a Hero

Early the next morning, Ana burst into her parents' bedroom holding up her phone, waving it wildly.

"Mom! Dad! Call Animal Control now. The NYPD found the missing dogs. They might have Carnegie!" Ana cried, sitting on her parents' bed.

"Lemme see," Catherine responded sleepily, reaching for her daughter's phone.

It was true. In the middle of the night, the dognapper ring had been arrested. Animal Control rescued the captive dogs and was in the process of identifying them to return to their owners. The Braxtons' optimistic news was interrupted when Spencer's bedside phone lit up with a blocked number.

Spencer anxiously answered. "Yes?"

"Good morning, Mr. Braxton. It's Detective Lee. Sorry if I'm calling too early."

"No, no, it's fine."

Spencer raised his eyebrows and mouthed "it's the detective" to Catherine and Ana.

"You may have heard about the missing dogs being rescued…"

"We just did," Spencer replied hopefully.

"Well, I'm sorry to report Carnegie wasn't with them," Detective Lee continued. "It's mostly pugs and Frenchies. We haven't ID'd them all, but there aren't any fitting her description."

"Yeah, she'd stand out in a crowd of little dogs," Spencer replied.

"It's disappointing, I know...but her missing dog foundation led to the dognappers being caught," Detective Lee said. "And we'll be making another plea to the public that your dog is still missing. There's a press conference at five p.m. this afternoon in front of Carnegie Hall."

"That's appropriate," Spencer said.

"I know. The theater marketing department set it up. The mayor and the Chief of Police will be there, and we expect coverage from the major networks. We'd like to have your family present...and bring Madison if you can. She'll draw a lot of attention."

"We'll try. She's kind of under the weather right now," Spencer replied, realizing what an understatement that was.

He thanked the detective, said goodbye, and stared down at his phone.

"What, Dad?! Did they find Carnegie with a bunch of little dogs?"

"I'm afraid not, Ana. It was *just* little dogs that they found. But her foundation led to them being rescued."

"Well, that's something," Catherine added, trying to sound positive.

"Yeah, Carnegie is kind of a hero. Too bad she couldn't save herself," Ana said sadly. "I'm going to check on Madison."

"Before you go...There's a press conference about the dog rescue at five this afternoon. It's at Carnegie Hall."

*"Aww...*that's so sweet," Ana said.

"The detective asked us to come. And they'd like Madison to be there, too. Let's hope we can rouse her."

"For that and other reasons...like eating," Catherine said.

"How about just being awake?" Ana said. "I'd settle for that."

CHAPTER THIRTY-SEVEN

Magic Mushrooms

After a miserable night spent curled up on the hard stone floor in a corner of the palastle, Carnegie opened her eyes to a pigeon perched on her long nose. It was pecking at one of the crystals on her crown collar. Another pigeon was plucking out pine needles and flying with them up to their ledge.

"Excuse me…?" Carnegie said sarcastically.

"No worries, mate," the pigeon on Carnegie's nose replied. "Popcorn and I can work around ya."

"Who's Popcorn?"

"That's me mate up there on our ledge. And they call me Skittles. Just so you know, this shiny thing seems to be stuck."

"That *shiny thing* is a jewel," Carnegie replied haughtily, "and why are you assaulting my stand-in royal crown?"

"We're building a nest for our babes, mate."

"I'm *not* your mate," Carnegie said, "and my crown is *not* nesting material."

"Looks like it to Popcorn and me," Skittles said.

"Sure does, mate. Definitely nesting material," Popcorn said, flying down and landing on Carnegie's tail. "Ace building material on this end, too, Skittles."

He plucked a pine needle from Carnegie's tail and pulled out a clump of tail feathers with it.

"OWW!" Carnegie hollered. "Leave me alone! Can't you see I'm in mourning?" she added dramatically.

"Oh yah, mate? Who died?" Skittles asked.

"Not *who* but *what*. I'm mourning the loss of my royal destiny. At this very moment, instead of lying in this cold, dingy corner, I should be in a lavish room that's decorated with glistening gold everywhere, lounging on a velvet sofa in front of a massive marble fireplace."

"That's very specific, mate," Popcorn said. "Clear as day ya ain't doin' none of that."

"And we ain't chillin'-out on an ace Aussie beach with some prawns on the barbie, neither," Skittles added. "Roll of the dice, mate."

"At least you have that ledge. I'm homeless. No one cares what happens to me," Carnegie said.

"Ya mean you're feral, mate?" Popcorn asked.

"Probably…maybe…what's feral?"

"A feral dog lives on their own without a lick of human kindness, mate," Skittles said. "The poor doggies barely stay alive by scavenging for scraps of food."

Carnegie recalled being cruelly kicked out of the theater and only finding one potato chip in the Pringles can.

"Yes, that pretty much sums it up," she said.

"Sorry, mate, that's tough. There's a stone arch in the North Woods some homeless animals live under. We could guide ya there."

"No, thank you. I know the way. I used to live in the North Woods," Carnegie replied. Sure, it was for one night, she thought, but that counted. "I guess I'll just ramble around feral-like. Some family might take pity on me and want to adopt me."

"That'd be first-rate, mate. Maybe ya could even live indoors, like in a house," Skittles said.

"Uh-huh," Carnegie said.

"The persons will start showing up in a bit. If ya ain't too afraid, ya otta sit out there at the entrance and try to look adoptable," Popcorn suggested.

"That sounds like a good plan," Carnegie replied, thinking it was her warning to leave the palastle before she got discovered. She got up and tugged at her crown collar with her paws, wriggled her head out, and let it fall to the floor.

"I don't need this fake crown anymore," Carnegie said and disdainfully kicked it into the corner. "Have at it for your nest."

"Good on ya, mate," Popcorn said. "We'll name our first egg after ya. By the way, what's ya name?"

"Just call me the 'not-famous-forgotten-one,'" Carnegie replied on her way out of Belvedere Castle.

With nowhere to go, Carnegie lazily loped around the perimeter of the castle and found herself overlooking Turtle Pond. She'd seen the pond from the lower park level but now, looking down at its harsh rocky bank from the high-up castle, made her dizzy. She backtracked to the entrance terrace and instead of returning to Shakespeare Garden, she took a pathway that led in the opposite direction—to a large, forested area called the Ramble.

That's funny, she thought. I told those flying rats I was going to ramble around. I must have had a premonition. Is this my new, true destiny? Rambling around in the Ramble?

It was a crisp morning, and the sun was shining brightly, making the morning dew sparkle like diamonds. Carnegie breathed in deeply, feeling renewed—reborn—in harmony with nature.

Who wants to live a superficial, pathetically pampered royal existence anyway? Carnegie resentfully thought.

"I'm feral and free! YAY!" she exclaimed. She dug her rear claws into the moist earth and leaped into the air—again and again. After a short time, her elation wore off and she decided to find something to eat.

I just have to tap into my natural instincts, she thought. That shouldn't be too hard here. I don't have to scavenge for junk food. Everything in this forest is so healthy and organic, she said to herself.

Yum! She surveyed her culinary surroundings. Dirt, rocks, moss, leaves, a trail of ants. *Yum?*

A Blue Jay fluttered down and began pecking at the forest floor right in front of her. Carnegie froze. Should I pounce on it? Then what? Eat it raw? I might as well have eaten those flying rats. She silently leaned in to watch the Blue Jay up-close and realized it was devouring the ants…alive.

EWW! This wild kingdom nature stuff is so gross! she thought.

Thoroughly repulsed and with her stomach growling, Carnegie tried to remember the Food TV shows that she and the Braxtons watched. She recalled an episode about truffles—a mushroom-like fungus that's one of the world's most luxurious gourmet treasures. The show host said Italian white ruffles are the rarest and can only be found and dug up by pigs (which Carnegie considered to be bloated and boring) and Italian truffle hunting dogs—yes, dogs!

If I can hunt woofs, hunting truffles will be a cake walk, she thought.

She'd never eaten a truffle but at six thousand dollars a pound like the Food TV host said, they had to be delectable. She plunged her nose into the soft earth and began sniffing all around for the rare fungus.

And then finally—*"Successo!"* she cried, trying to sound Italian. She began digging and digging, deeper and deeper until she was able to grasp the Food TV-show-worthy-prize in her mouth. She gently set it on the ground and wiped away its mud covering to find the most mouthwatering…*rock?*

After sitting and staring at the rock in annoyance, her eyes wandered to a patch of golden cap mushrooms at the base of a tree.

"Oh hello!" she said. My expert truffle hunting skills have kicked in! And how much more convenient to hunt them above ground. I'll never go hungry again!

Had this wolf-turned-truffle hunter known that the "convenient truffles" she found were actually magic mushrooms that cause hallucinations, she may not have leaned over and bit off a mushroom cap—but she did!

It had a slimy texture and crude earthy taste. Out of hunger, she forced herself to swallow it whole.

"I don't care how much this truffle costs," she commented, "it tastes like icky dirt. This forest is only getting a one-star restaurant rating from me."

Wearily, she looked for a place to lie down and think what to do next. She found a thickly leafed area and circled around her usual three times. To her surprise, the circling made a nice nest in the leaves. So that's why Maddie and I do all that circling before we lie down. Who knew? What else have we been doing and don't know why?

As Carnegie contemplated the mystery of instincts, her dog nest leaves slowly came to life. They swirled around to hug and comfort her as her mind floated off in a mushroom-induced psychedelic haze. Becoming one with nature, Carnegie saw and heard everything, everywhere in the forest...magnified and in vivid surreal colors. Neon-pink worms wriggled their way through the glittery purple earth, illuminated lime-green bugs skittered along electric blue branches, a million saffron-yellow insects buzzed in the prismatic air. High above, glowing rainbow trees waved and twisted and then leaned in toward her. Mesmerized, Carnegie stared wide-eyed as the trees spoke in a silent language that she somehow understood.

"I understand the trees because I am a tree," she murmured in a trance. *"Not with horrid pine needles, though...I am a beautiful regular leaf tree...A beautiful regular leaf rainbow tree..."*

And then, the trees weren't trees anymore. They shape-shifted to become Carnegie's Borzoi ancestors. They were calling her to join them as they floated overhead in a kaleidoscopic sky.

Wait! I am still a tree!

Before her distorted mind could panic, rainbow-tree-Carnegie transformed into Borzoi-ancestor-Carnegie, and she lightly floated up to join her phantom ancestors.

"I am one with my ancestors and one with myself. I used to be a tree but now I am myself—although not exactly because I am my own ancestor which is kind of confusing—but no worries because all is oneness and peace and harmony...peace and harmony...peace and..." BLAAH!

In a painful purge, Carnegie was jolted back into reality when she threw up the hallucinogenic mushroom cap she had eaten. Head pounding and panting, she dragged herself onto some soft moss and tried to calm her confused mind and aching stomach.

"Those truffles are seriously overrated," Carnegie said with a loud burp.

CHAPTER THIRTY-EIGHT

At the Same Time

Ana left her parents' room to check on Madison with the faint hope she had woken up. She'd slept on the floor by her all night and Madison had not stirred. Ana stopped in her bedroom doorway and gasped in terror. Madison's bed was empty! With her heart beating out of her chest, Ana's eyes swept the room and stopped at the furry lump lying on her own bed.

"Oh, thank goodness!" she cried. She raced to Madison's bedside and knelt to hug her. "You scared me! I thought someone took you." She noticed that Little Puppy was tucked into Madison's chest. "I see L.P. is with you. That's sweet."

Madison responded by slowly wagging her long tail.

"You're awake!" Ana said with happy tears in her eyes. "You had us all so worried!"

To everyone's relief and joy, Madison came into the kitchen to drink some water and eat a small meal. Instead of returning to bed like the Braxtons expected, Madison went to the tall living room windows and sat looking down at Central Park, like when she and Carnegie watched for enemy dogs. And she stayed there all day until it was time to go to the press conference at Carnegie Hall.

At 4:30 p.m., the same time Madison and the Braxtons were leaving by their apartment building's rear entrance to evade the paparazzi,

Carnegie was leaving the Ramble. Unsure what to do or where to go, she thought she'd to return to the palastle and sort out her options. She cautiously approached and hid behind a bush near the terrace entrance stairs. Some of the tourists were leaving but she could tell some were still there. She decided to hide out at Turtle Pond until the coast was clear. Keeping a low profile, she followed a ridge in the steep rock face that took her to the water's bank where she scrunched down in the tall reeds. The amber sun was setting, and the pond had taken on a glorious coating of gold.

Ahh...such a peaceful place to dream up my next perfect plan. Maybe I should take a nap and do some dream planning, she thought, taking herself literally—and besides, a nap was always a good plan for Carnegie. She rolled on her back so the last of the sun could warm her soft pink belly. She stretched her long front legs over her head and quickly fell asleep with her legs in the air.

"Psst."

"What?" Carnegie abruptly woke up and was shocked to be in darkness. The peaceful golden pond had changed into an unsettling blackness with a swatch of moonlight.

"Psst. Come 'ere," the little voice whispered.

"Who said that?" Carnegie flipped upright and peered through the reeds to see who was talking, but she could only see more reeds.

"I said, 'come 'ere.' I want to show you something."

Curious, Carnegie crawled toward the little voice. "I don't see anything."

"Come closer..."

She took another step. "This is annoying, whoever you are. What do you want to show me?"

"Cl-o-o-o-ser..." the voice beckoned. "You're almost there."

"This is ridiculous!" Carnegie said as she took a huge step forward and "AAAGH!"—*SPLOOSH!*—sunk up to her shoulders in wet, reedy, dark brown muck.

A red-eared turtle popped his head out of the water, sputtering with laughter. "Oh, I've been dying to do that! Snappy, check this out!"

"Congrats, Morton, you finally got one to fall for it!" said his turtle friend, Snappy, as she swam up and crawled onto Carnegie's back like it was her private island.

"I know!" Morton said, joining Snappy on *Carnegie Island*. "You should have seen her face! Totally didn't see it coming. What a crack up!"

"You're killing me!" Snappy cried. "My shell's gonna split from laughing. What is this long nose thing anyway?"

"I think either a large furry dog or a small furry pony. Hard to say," Morton replied.

"Yeah, that orangey beak thing is throwing me off. Is it like a giant duck?" Snappy said.

"I'm right here," Carnegie interrupted. "I can hear you talking about me. Now that you've had your annoying little turtle laughs, will you kindly get off my back?!"

"Make us!" the turtles yelled in unison.

"I *really* didn't want to do this," Carnegie said, "but if you insist."

She inhaled deeply, submerged herself, and held her breath until Morton and Snappy swam away, which, thankfully, wasn't too long. Surfacing turtle-free but drenched and covered with muck up to her neck, Carnegie dragged herself out of the pond and clawed her way up the rock face to a flat rock. Lying in misery in the moonlight, her mind raced with regret.

Does my family miss me? she wondered. What if they adopt one of those doodle-dogs to replace me? Even worse, a Golden Retriever enemy dog. I can't let that happen to Madison. Maybe if I sneak back into our apartment, everyone will think I escaped from the dognappers...?

Shivering from the cold and anxiety, she curled up in a ball to think. She just needed another perfect plan...but for the first time ever, Carnegie's imagination was as empty as her heart.

At 5:00 p.m., the same time Carnegie was lying on that rock, Madison arrived at Carnegie Hall. The sun had set, but the evening sky was brightened by floodlights for the press conference and by constant camera flashes. When they pulled up to the curb, paparazzi and the press were in a frenzy seeing Madison and stormed their car. The Braxtons were surprised to see "Ten-Foot Cops"—NYPD officers on horses. A black horse touched his nose to the passenger window and Madison tried to sniff him from her side of the glass. The mounted police held back the crowd so that she and the Braxtons could safely walk to the press conference stage that was setup outside the music hall's entrance.

Madison wagged her tail when she saw the giant posters of Carnegie, but then her heart sunk at the reality and pain of her being gone.

After the Braxtons arrived onstage, a group of photographers approached and asked if they could get a picture of Madison by herself. Ana removed her leash and Madison posed like she had learned to do—but without the sparkle in her "irresistibly sweet" eyes.

Photo session over, the press conference commenced. Madison sadly leaned against Ana's leg as they stood listening to the congratulatory speeches about catching the dognappers. But then something grabbed Madison's attention. At first, it was just the faintest whiff. And as she concentrated, it grew stronger. Her ears shot up and swiveled around as her awareness intensified. Could it be? And, suddenly, she knew for sure. *My sister!*

In one swift, surprising move, Madison jumped from Ana's side and dove off of the stage.

"Help!" Ana yelled, with Madison's leash dangling from her wrist.

Moving at blur speed, Madison parted the crowd, ignoring the panicked screams and futile attempts to catch her.

She darted between the TV news trucks that were parked at the curb out into Seventh Avenue, which is two blocks south of Central Park. Taking to the sidewalk, she found it crowded with pedestrians.

Excuse me...sorry...pardon me...Madison silently apologized, as she tried to avoid knocking over the people who blocked her way. She adeptly avoided cars crossing the intersections and quickly reached West 59th Street, where she stopped at the curb. She could see Central Park, but she had to cross six busy lanes of traffic to get there. She took a deep breath and ran into the street, dodging cars, taxis, and tour buses. Miraculously, she reached the other side of the street unharmed and entered Central Park.

Running along the main road, she heard loud hoofbeats. She looked over her shoulder to see a Ten-Foot Cop in pursuit.

Can I outrun a horse? Madison breathlessly wondered. *I will have to! Nothing and no one will keep me from my sister!*

As they drew closer, she realized it was the black horse who put his nose on her car window.

Please! Please! Let me go, she silently pleaded with him as she felt his hot breath on her neck.

Making a sudden sharp turn, Madison leaped from the road into the foliage and scrambled under the nearest bush. Whether the horse sympathized with her plea, or they just didn't see her hiding, the sound of hoofbeats faded and finally disappeared.

Staying concealed in the dark wooded areas, Madison ran her heart out towards her sister's scent. When she reached the Ramble, she stopped to catch her breath.

Carnegie has been here! she realized. And not long ago. Following her sister's trail, she soon found herself looking up in awe at the majestic Belvedere Castle.

Wow! Carnegie's royal palastle! She really found it, Madison said to herself. Her emotions were torn between happiness for Carnegie fulfilling her dream and sadness that her sister was living a different life now, apart from her.

Madison's heart pounded as she opened Carnegie's palastle's front door. She didn't know what to expect, but she didn't imagine finding a dark, empty stone-walled room.

"Woof," she softly barked, "hello." Nothing. She took a few more steps inside and barked louder. "WOOF!" She was only answered by her echo, "WOOF! WOOF! WOOF!"

As she eyes adjusted to the dim light, she spotted something slightly sparkly and familiar laying on the floor. *Is that my royal crown collar?*

As Madison approached it, two pigeons swooped down and landed in front of her.

"EEK!" Madison cried and jumped in alarm.

"Looking for something, mate?" asked Skittles.

"M-m-my s-s-ister," Madison anxiously replied. "I think she had that crown collar with her."

"Sorry, mate. That one's ours," Popcorn said.

Madison leaned over and sniffed the pecked-over collar. "It looks different now, but I'm pretty sure this is the one my sister took. Have you seen her? She looks a lot like me."

"There was a dog here last night. She slept in that corner over there," Skittle said, pointing to the dark, dirty corner.

Madison looked hopeful. "Really?! Was her name Carnegie?"

"Nah," Skittles said. "This dog was called the 'not-something-or-other.'"

"And she couldn't have been your sister, mate. This dog was feral," Popcorn added.

"Feral?" Madison asked.

"Ya know, all alone and wild-like," Popcorn said. "She was gonna try to get adopted by a family."

Madison didn't know what to think. She was sure that was her crown collar, even in its roughed-up condition, but the dog the pigeons described didn't sound anything like her sister.

"Okay, thank you," Madison said sadly. "Is it alright if I look around in case she's somewhere else?"

"If you keep away from our digs up there," Skittles said, pointing up at their ledge, "and our collar down 'ere, have a crack at it, mate."

CHAPTER THIRTY-NINE

Moon Bath

Madison tiptoed into the next room of the palastle, holding her breath, hoping that someone or something else didn't jump out in front of her. It was the gift shop and even in the dark, she could see something horrible had happened there. She walked over and sniffed the toppled metal stands, velvet rope, and strewn paper crowns. Yes, something horrible did happen there and Carnegie's scent was all over it—literally and figuratively—as it matched her style of dramatic crashes.

Madison's heart leapt when she sighted the stairway that led up to the next floor. It would suit Carnegie to be elevated, she thought, as she climbed around and around the dark narrow stairway.

Arriving on the second floor, she unhappily found the room and terrace as empty as the first floor. Without pausing to admire what Carnegie considered the room's majestic design potential, she quickly scampered up the final flight of stairs. Again, nothing!

What must Carnegie have thought? Madison wondered, looking around the small, bare room. She had to be *so* disappointed. And then, the deep tragedy of it struck her. It was much worse than Carnegie being lost to her because she was living a royal life. Carnegie wasn't living anywhere at all. Maybe she really *was* feral now.

Madison went to one of the tall arched windows and looked out over Central Park. The moon was shining down on the black Turtle Pond and creating a satiny white ribbon.

That's pretty, she couldn't help thinking, even in her sorrowful state.

And the moon was shining down on something white on a flat rock above Turtle Pond. *What?!* She focused her eyes in disbelief. The moon was shining down on Carnegie!

At breakneck speed, Madison charged down the circular stairs, around and around without stopping, and out the front door. She ran to the back of the castle and, being careful not to slip, followed the steep embankment down to where Carnegie was lying.

"Carnegie! Is that you?" she breathlessly asked.

"Maddie!!!" Carnegie excitedly greeted her, then stopped herself and casually responded, "Oh yes, 'tis me."

"What are you doing here?" Madison asked.

"Uh…I'm taking a moon bath."

"Is that a thing?"

"Of course. It's like a sunbath but at night. It's quite rejuvenating."

"You're all wet," Madison said.

"That's the therapeutic soaking in moonlit water part. I was enjoying its delightful benefits earlier with a couple of new friends."

"And you're covered in muck."

"If you mean, I'm covered in Mother Nature's soothing minerals, then, yes, I am."

"Is that why your nose is orange?"

Carnegie crossed her eyes and tried to look at her long snout.

"Is it?"

"Uh-huh."

"Must be a lunar tan."

"It looks like cheese puff dust to me," Madison said.

"Moon dust, cheese dust…same, same. The moon is made of cheese. Everyone knows that," Carnegie replied authoritatively.

Madison looked at her doubtfully.

"And now, I'm absorbing moon rays. It's wonderfully relaxing. You know, Maddie, you look uptight. You should try it. By the way, aren't you supposed to be at the theater now?"

Madison looked down at her right front paw. "They closed the show."

Carnegie perked up. "Because of me?"

"Partly."

"Then we better get back. I don't want to disappoint my fans."

"It's more than that, Carnegie. They thought you were dog-napped. The whole city is looking for you. The police are calling it grand theft."

"Grand? Really?" Carnegie asked, flattered. "Did they post a big reward for me?"

"Well, they raised a lot of money to help find you."

"How much? A lot?"

"I don't know, but everyone is upset. The theater even created a whole foundation with your name and picture to rescue missing dogs," Madison said.

"I hope it's a cute photo. Is it on bags of kibble, like missing kids' pictures on milk cartons? Tell me it's not on that cheap stuff that tastes like gravel. I need to see. Let's go!"

"But what about your royal palastle?"

"They're shampooing the carpeting in my royal chamber. A clumsy chambermaid knocked over my bedtime bowl of bone broth. I'll come back when it's dry."

Madison looked up at the dark Belvedere Castle and, with a pain in her heart, thought about the dismal corner where Carnegie had been sleeping.

"Yeah, okay. You don't want damp paws."

"Exactly. How'd you get here on your own, anyway? Did you use my secret magic elevator trick?"

"No. I came from a press conference," Madison said.

"A what?"

"It's where some important persons talk and they put it on TV. I was there with our family and everybody. They were talking about the dognappers getting caught thanks to your missing dog foundation."

"So, I'm kind of a hero," Carnegie said proudly.

"*I* think so," Madison replied.

"They'll definitely want me on that press TV thing. Where's it at?"

"Carnegie Hall."

"You mean *ME* Hall," Carnegie corrected her.

"Uh-huh," Madison replied.

"Lead the way, sister!" Carnegie exclaimed, rising from her rock. She looked even worse standing up with the pine needle fringe hanging from her wet mucky body.

"You don't want to tidy up first?" Madison asked, cringing.

"Are you kidding, Maddie? Think of the made-for-TV drama when I suddenly arrive looking every bit like what I've been through."

"What *have* you been through?" Madison asked sympathetically.

"A *LOT!* I'll tell you about it later. Now, let's go!"

CHAPTER FORTY

MEHall

Madison and Carnegie left Turtle Pond and the royal palastle behind and backtracked to the Ramble on their way to Carnegie Hall. As they passed by the hallucinogenic mushroom patch, Carnegie became nauseous, and saliva started to dribble from her tightly clenched dog lips.

"Are you okay?" Madison asked.

"Of course, I'm okay…unless you think I'm a drooly, droopy, jowly Bloodhound again."

"What are you talking about?" Madison asked.

"Remember the morning of opening night, when I had fur bags all over my face from spending *all* night teaching you your dance steps...and you held up Ana's hand mirror to my face and said to look because I had become a drooly, droopy, jowly Bloodhound? Or was it droopy, jowly, drooly? Either way, that's what you called me."

"*I* never called you that. *You* called you that."

"Funny, I don't remember it that way," Carnegie said. Caught up in being right, she didn't notice that a bat flew down—out of what in a different state of consciousness was a rainbow tree—and landed on her head.

"C-C-Ca-Carnegie…" Madison stammered, terrified by the bat.

"Madison, let me tell it. You know I have a photogenic memory."

"Uh, Carnegie…"

"Listen for once, *please*. I specifically recall that it was the morning of opening night and I was standing on your bed looking down at you, and you said…"

"I th-think there's something on your head!" Madison cried.

"No, what *you* said was…" Carnegie corrected.

Interrupting Carnegie's recollection, the bat leaned over her forehead and came into view, upside down with its mouth open, baring its sharp little teeth and pointy fangs.

"AAAAGH!!!" Carnegie screamed.

"AAAAGH!!!" Madison screamed in a higher pitch.

"AAAAGH!!!" the bat screamed in an ultra-high pitch as it enveloped Carnegie's head with its wings, covering her eyes.

As the cacophony of screaming continued, Carnegie panicked and ran around in frantically fast circles.

Madison instinctively ran in circles to match, both of them going faster and faster until the bat spun off Carnegie's head like a little helicopter blade, its tiny screams fading off into the night.

Their heads still spinning, the sisters wobbled around and then fell into a tall, flowering bush, disappearing completely. Emerging out the other side, Madison appeared with a blossom tucked in her left ear, as if placed there by Laura at the theater.

Carnegie crawled out of the bush with twigs and leaves plastered to her mucky pine-needle-fringed body. Branches now protruded from her head like strange antlers. She staggered to her feet and shook. Madison ducked as a mucky branch flew over her head, leaving Carnegie looking more like a horrific unicorn.

"Lucky for that bat he wasn't a woof," said Carnegie smugly.

"Yeah, lucky for him," Madison agreed.

They started off again and, seeing no one in the park, they felt safe walking on the lit paths. After a while, Madison stopped and spun around in a circle with her nose in the air.

"Don't tell me you're still dizzy, Maddie."

"No, but I'm turned around. I can't tell which way to Carnegie…"

Her sister shot her a corrective look.

"I mean, which way to *YOU* Hall," Madison said.

"I, for one, am not too proud to ask for directions," Carnegie said as the gang of hoodlums she met the first night appeared in their path. "Look! Right on cue."

"Shouldn't we hide?" Madison nervously asked.

"From my fans?"

"They look scary."

"Don't be such a snob. Smile, Maddie, smile!"

The sisters smiled—Madison with a reluctant grin that looked more like a snarl and Carnegie flashing her winningest full-fang version.

"There's two of them now!" the leader yelled. "Let's get out of here before an entire pack shows up!" The hoodlums bumped into each other as they turned and ran off in the opposite direction.

"The public can be so intimidated by fame," Carnegie said.

"Yeah...maybe sometimes," Madison semi-agreed. She spotted a blind man walking with a Seeing Eye dog. "How about if we ask that dog?"

"I think he's blind," Carnegie said.

"The man is, not the dog," Madison said, looking at her sister in disbelief.

"Uh, okay."

As they came closer, the sisters quietly approached and walked alongside the Seeing Eye dog.

"Excuse me, sir," Madison whispered to him. "We need some directions, please."

"Lucky for you that's my biz, angel face. I'm a licensed guide dog," he whispered back. "The name's Marlowe. Ask away."

"How do you get to—"

Carnegie poked her in the ribs.

"Stop it!" she whispered in an aside to her sister. "I'm not going to ask him how to get to *HER* Hall."

"You were saying, hunny bunny?" Marlowe asked.

Madison narrowed her eyes at Carnegie who made a tight-lipped face, then turned back to Marlowe. "How do you get to Carnegie Hall, sir?"

"Practice, practice, practice," Marlowe replied with a wink.

Madison and Carnegie stared at him blankly.

Marlow snickered. "It's an old New Yorker's joke."

"I guess we don't know that one," Madison said.

"Hey, wait! I recognize your voice now, cupcake. You're in that 'Heart' musical. My person, Theodore, has been listening to the early release cast recording. You play Olivia, right?"

"Uh-huh," Madison humbly replied.

"Surely, you recognize me, too," Carnegie said proudly. "I play her sister."

"Sorry, sunshine. Maybe if you recite a few of your lines…"

"Never mind," Carnegie replied. Nobody can *hear* me silently performing my heart out in the background, she thought resentfully.

"We're on our way home," Marlowe said.

"Yeah, it's kinda dark for a walk," Carnegie commented.

"Theodore doesn't really care much about that…but we live near Carnegie Hall if you two dreamboats want to tag along."

"That would be very nice," Madison said.

"Sure, gorgeous. Walk next to me but keep quiet or Theodore will catch on. And, if you don't mind, can the dirty doll walk on the outside? I just got groomed."

The sisters stayed in lockstep with Marlowe, who led them out of Central Park and safely across two intersections to a bank building on the corner of 57th Street and Seventh Avenue, across from Carnegie Hall.

"We part here, lovebugs. Our apartment is down the street. Good luck with your music careers," Marlowe whispered with a wink.

"Thank you, sir…I guess," Madison replied with a confused look, as Carnegie started to dash across the street.

"Wait, Carnegie!"

"What on earth for, Maddie?! ME Hall is right over there!"

"But I think the press conference ended."

"How do you know?"

"The stage is gone," Madison said, nodding toward the front of the music hall. "I was standing right over there with a bunch of people... and...oh no! Carnegie!" she cried. "Our family is gone!!!"

"Don't panic. They're probably just inside the building," Carnegie casually responded.

"There were a lot of news trucks, and they're gone, too."

"You mean the TV stuff is over?" Carnegie asked in a panic. "Oh no!!! What am I going to do, Madison?! I mean, what are *we* going to do?"

Tears welled up in Madison's eyes. "I want to go home, but I'm in trouble, sister."

"What could *you* ever do that wasn't perfect?"

"I ran away. That was bad."

"Yes, *very* bad...the worst," Carnegie agreed.

"I ran away from our family and all the people at the press conference and a policeman and a police horse."

"That's a lot of running away," Carnegie said, thinking she was only guilty of running away from their family—or was she? Dognapping was still on the table.

"You're not in trouble, though," Madison said. "Everyone wants to find *you*."

"And I'm kind of a hero," Carnegie proclaimed.

"Tha-at too-oo," Madison said, suddenly sobbing. She backed up against the bank building and slid down the wall to the sidewalk. Carnegie looked at her sister, lying in the darkness with tears streaming down, frantically licking her right front paw. She wasn't even trying to hide it.

Maddie is falling apart, Carnegie thought with an uncomfortable new feeling of fear. *It's all on me now*. While she anxiously paced back and forth, her dark, muck-covered body disappeared into the night, giving her a beheaded look.

I need the *perfect-est* plan for both of us. *Perfect-est times two*. She continued to pace—thinking, thinking, thinking. And then, it came to her!

Carnegie shook her sister's shoulders. Madison continued licking her paw like she was in a trance. "Maddie!"

No response.

"Madison!"

Madison stopped licking her paw and looked up at Carnegie with dazed eyes.

"Oh hello, Carnegie. I had the strangest dream. You lost your body, and your head was floating in space."

"What?!"

"It was floating back and forth, back and—"

Carnegie bopped her on the head. "Snap out of it, Maddie! We've got a heroic reveal to do."

CHAPTER FORTY-ONE

Heroic Reveal

Carnegie crouched low to the ground and commando-crawled to the curb. "Follow me," she called over her shoulder to Madison who was still lying on the sidewalk. Madison wiped her teary cheeks with her paws and commando-crawled to her sister.

"When I say 'go,' we go," Carnegie said.

"Go where?" Madison asked.

"Go where I go."

"Where are you going?"

"You don't need to know. You're on a need-to-know basis."

"I need to know," Madison said.

"Really?" Carnegie asked, exasperated. "If you *must* know, we're going to covertly crawl across the street, stealthily sneak into the ME Hall stage door, furtively find our way to the main stage, handily hide in the wings and when I say 'go' again, we will dramatically dash onstage and heroically reveal that I have been found...much to the delight of the very relieved audience full of my fans, who will jump to their feet and cheer wildly."

"I don't think I can remember all that," Madison said.

"Precisely. That's why you're on a need-to-...*never mind.* Just follow me."

To even her own surprise, Carnegie's plan was working flawlessly. Within minutes, the sisters found themselves concealed in the wings looking at a massive orchestra performing a symphony onstage.

Carnegie turned to Madison and whispered, "Why are so many

of them playing the same instruments?"

"Maybe some are understudies," Madison whispered back.

"I guess...but aren't they supposed to be down in the orchestra pit like at our theater?"

"Maybe they knew you were coming," Madison said.

"Very funny," Carnegie flatly replied.

"They're taking up the entire stage, Carnegie. How will we dramatically dash onstage to do our heroic reveal like you said?"

"We'll improvise."

"What does that mean?" Madison asked.

"In theatre, actors improvise by making up scenes, dialog, and characters on the spot to create unplanned and unscripted dramatic and comedic performances," Carnegie recited, her eyes crossing slightly.

"Huh?"

"I have no idea how I knew that," Carnegie said. "We'll just wing it. Let's go!"

Carnegie took off dancing—or it would be better described that a scary, mucky porcupine/unicorn hybrid with an orange snout shuffled onto the stage as the audience gasped in horror.

With each step-kick and flailing arm, Carnegie flung wet, mucky twigs, leaves, and pine needles. The pianist was the first to take a hit in the back of the head with a clump of soggy leaves. A wild twig pierced a harp's strings like an archer's arrow. The violin section attempted to continue playing while plucking grubby pine needles from their instruments' strings.

Madison tried to follow along with her "Hearts Over Broadway" dance steps while keeping her distance from Carnegie's flying debris.

When Carnegie reached the terrified conductor at center stage, she did a colossal wet dog shake that flung the rest of her mucky mess and unicorn branch *off* of her and *onto* him—which revealed a "de-monstered" Carnegie to the audience.

She bowed, did a little twirl, thrust her long Borzoi nose in the air and heroically barked, *"Behold! 'Tis me!...Carnegie! I hath found me!"* which was heard as "Woof-woof! Ruff WOOF!...Woof-arf-RUFF! Arf woof ruff WOOF!"

The audience was confused at first, then realized it was Carnegie and began to cheer. And when Madison arrived at center stage, bowed, thrust *her* long nose in the air and barked, "Woof-woof! Ruff ARF!...Woof ruff-arf-woof ruff-ruff, Woof-arf-RUFF!" *("Behold! 'Tis she!...My heroic sister, Carnegie!")* the audience jumped to their feet and cheered wildly, indeed.

Within seconds, "Carnegie Found!" and photos of her and Madison onstage were blowing up the internet—and minutes later, the NYPD and Animal Control pulled up to Carnegie Hall.

The entire City celebrated Carnegie's return but, of course, no one was happier than her own family. How she disappeared from her bed and reappeared on the stage of Carnegie Hall and whether or not she was dognapped is still a mysterious, unsolved case.

And Madison was not in trouble for running away. Quite the opposite, she was met with grateful hugs and kisses.

Carnegie was enthusiastically asked to return to the "Hearts Over Broadway" musical and was given equal star billing with Madison. She finally saw STARRING CARNEGIE in lights on that giant Broadway theater marquee. And her name appeared before Madison's alphabetically, which she considered to be top billing.

A full line of Olivia's sister souvenirs were added to the show merchandise, including plushies which Carnegie found to be adorable but overstuffed in the tummy area.

CHAPTER FORTY-TWO

Re-Opening Night

BROKEN HEARTS (Over Broadway) ARE MENDED AND BETTER THAN EVER!

This reviewer joyfully joins the public in celebrating the dramatic return of sensational sister canine stars, Madison and Carnegie, to the Broadway stage! The musical that seemed doomed to an early demise, has been lifted to new heights by the improvisational charm Carnegie brings to the production. With every show promising to be an unexpected (albeit likely alarming but never boring) performance, this captivating canine's antics will keep audiences coming back night after night. I would be remiss not to add: Thank goodness for orchestra pit nets!

With a generous portion of the show proceeds supporting the now International Carnegie Missing Dog Foundation, hearts will be gratefully reunited worldwide. And that, in this reviewer's opinion, makes Carnegie kind of a hero.

Ding! announced Carnegie's and Madison's return home from their triumphant re-opening night. They blasted out of the penthouse elevator and down the hall to their bedroom, leaped from the door to their beds, and circled three times in unison before dropping into the soft pillows.

"Do you know why we circle around?" Carnegie asked.

"No, I just do it," Madison replied. "Why do we?"

"Something about leaves. I forget now."

"I like being onstage sisters," said Madison sweetly, "but it feels really nice to be home sisters."

"You mean *adorable* onstage sisters and home sisters," Carnegie corrected. With one of us (me) being *more* adorable, she added to herself.

She rolled on her back and stretched her long front legs over her head. She looked up at her paws and admired her new dog booties, custom designed just for her by the House of Pucchi.

"These open-toe booties are so comfy. They're like walking on a marshmallow on a cloud. Lily at the theater was right. Those other Pucchi booties weren't my style. I hate cramped toes."

"They look cute on you," Madison said.

"I know."

"I've been meaning to ask…" Madison said. "Remember when we met at that rock by Turtle Pond?"

"You mean when we rendezvoused on my moon bath deck?"

"I guess."

"What about it?"

"You said you had been through a LOT and were going to tell me about it later."

"I did, didn't I? Well, the royal palastle was luxurious like Mom said it would be. But all the pampering and waiting on me…it was exhausting! And the rich food…how much lobster and filet mignon can I eat? And the constant waving to my subjects wore out my paw. I think I have a carpool tunnel now."

"You mean you have carpal tunnel syndrome?" Madison asked.

"That, too. And don't get me started on the noble attire with those heavy jeweled crowns and itchy fur-trimmed robes. I might be allergic to that weaselly ermine fur. My own fur is lovelier, anyway.

Plus, the endless parades and the majestic ceremonies and the fancy balls and the regal appearances...Really, all that royal stuff was a LOT," Carnegie said with a long sigh.

"Weren't you only there for a day?"

"*And* a night."

"Uh-huh."

"Everyone in the entire palastle begged me to stay but, as you already know, I didn't want to disappoint all my theater fans."

"No, of course not," Madison said, not letting on that she had been to the empty Belvedere Castle.

"I'm really glad you decided to not be royalty, Carnegie."

"Me too. It's overrated. Besides, I don't have to be royal to be the famous-est."

"Famous is as famous does?" Madison asked.

Carnegie turned to her sister and flashed her *winningest* smile. "Don't you mean...?"

"Famous-est is as famous-est does," Madison said with a little grin.

"Exactly, Maddie. It's automatic."

The End

THE AUTHOR BEING "COMPETITIVELY KISSED" BY CARNEGIE (IN BACK) AND MADISON (IN FRONT)

PHOTOGRAPH BY ROGER EASTMAN

About the Author

J. G. EASTMAN loves dogs. Not those snarly, jump-up-and-bite-you-on-the-elbow sort—but most. She adores dog stories—but can't bear the nobody-wants-the-dog scenes that must be endured before the happy ending. She also had captivating stories to tell, so she wrote *Long Nose Legacy* and *Long Nose Legacy II,* fictional novels (without the unbearable scenes) about the good sort of dogs and the people who cherish them.

She is an award-winning author, designer, art director, media and theatre producer, member of the Society of Children's Books Writers and Illustrators, the Dog Writers Association of America, and the Independent Book Publishers Association. She lives on the California coast with her husband and their two show Borzoi, who are related to Madison and Carnegie (pictured below) who inspired her books.

MADISON AND CARNEGIE

PHOTOGRAPH BY JO McGINLEY

The LONG NOSE LEGACY Series

If you enjoyed reading *Long Nose Legacy II*, please consider reading the original novel, *Long Nose Legacy: A Dog's Story of Royalty and Loyalty*. It's the award-winning coming-of-age story of Carnegie and Madison from their puppy days to when Carnegie led Madison on a misguided and perilous journey on her first quest for royalty. If you've already read the first book, thank you!

CRITICS' REVIEWS & AWARDS

"An incredibly fun, tail-wagging romp.
The author brings a uniquely endearing sensibility to the story.
Eastman creates a family of canine characters with fabulously distinctive, sometimes conflicting personalities. A Must Read!"
—BookLife Prize

"A delightful adventure, perfect for dog-loving children.
Highly recommended."
—United Kingdom Wishing Shelf Awards Finalist

"A fanciful and heartwarming adventure of sister show dogs that will delight dog lovers of all ages!"
—Modern Dog Magazine Editor's Choice

Book Readers Appreciation Group Medallion Honoree

IAN Book of the Year Awards Finalist

"A heartfelt and fun story with memorable and charming characters.
Definitely an unforgettable reading experience."
—Readers' Favorite 2 Gold Awards

Dogs Love Cookies

Dogs love cookies.
Writers love reviews.

If you enjoyed reading this book,
kindly leave a review
at your place of purchase.

For an extra treat, check out the award-winning LONG NOSE LEGACY audiobook. Disney and DreamWorks Animation voice talent, Stephen Kearin, brilliantly narrates and performs this extraordinary production.

The books and audiobook are available in the U.S. and internationally though all major online retailers.

For more information, please visit
LongNoseLegacy.com.

Thank you.

www.ingramcontent.com/pod-product-compliance
Lightning Source LLC
Chambersburg PA
CBHW030357310726
48979CB00001B/340

9781732382756